Click.

Bree saw rough angles caught by the flashing lights of the city street. *Click.* Etched cheekbones, straight nose, shadowed eyes, a strong chin darkened by stubble. *Click.* The man looked down and hurried away. Bree knew the impromptu photo session had ended. She began packing up her camera equipment.

Suddenly she felt pressure just under her right shoulder blade. A deep voice muttered near her ear, "We need to talk."

She froze, unable to turn around. "If . . . if you want money," she gasped, "I'll—"

"Just get inside and sit on the floor." He nudged her sharply into the back of a van. The door slid shut with an echoing crack. All she could make out was a hulking shadow of a man less than a foot from her knees.

"I'm not going to hurt you," he said in a rough drawl. "I just need to know what you're up to."

The Novel Bookshop

5116 - 50th Avenue
Innisfree, AB T0B 2G0
Ph: (403) 592-2209

Dear Reader:

Once again, Silhouette Intimate Moments has put together a very special month for you, with the sort of exciting yet always romantic plots you've come to expect from us.

A couple of books this month deserve special mention because their heroes are a bit different from the usual. In *Full Circle*, Paula Detmer Riggs gives us Trevor Markus, a man with a hidden past that threatens to destroy all his hopes for the future. I think your heart will beat a little faster and you may even find tears in your eyes as you discover the secret Trevor has spent years protecting—the secret that may separate him forever from the only woman he's ever loved.

New author Ann Williams brings us another very different hero in her first book, *Devil in Disguise*. "Nick" is a puzzle when he first appears, a mystery man with no memory of his past. Only two things about him are clear: he's the key to the troubles that have begun plaguing tiny Fate, Texas—and he's the most sensuous and appealing man rancher Caitlin Barratt has ever met.

I'd love to hear from you after you've read these books—or any of our other Intimate Moments, including this month's other selections, from Mary Anne Wilson and Sibylle Garrett. Please feel free to write to me with your comments at any time.

Sincerely,

Leslie J. Wainger
Senior Editor
Silhouette Books
300 E. 42nd Street
New York, NY 10017

Mary Anne Wilson
Straight from the Heart

Silhouette Intimate Moments

Published by Silhouette Books New York

America's Publisher of Contemporary Romance

SILHOUETTE BOOKS
300 East 42nd St., New York, N.Y. 10017

ISBN: 0-373-07304-6

First Silhouette Books printing September 1989

Books by Mary Anne Wilson

Silhouette Intimate Moments

Hot-Blooded #230
Home Fires #267
Liar's Moon #292
Straight from the Heart #304

MARY ANNE WILSON

fell in love with reading at ten years of age when she discovered *Pride and Prejudice*. A year later she knew she had to be a writer when she found herself writing a new ending for *A Tale of Two Cities*. A true romantic, she had Sydney Carton rescued, and he lived happily ever after.

Though she's a native of Canada, she now lives in California with her husband, children, a six-toed black cat, who believes he's Hungarian, and five timid Dobermans, who welcome any and all strangers. And she's writing happy endings for her own books.

For Beulah Wilson,
a great mother-in-law
and an even better friend.
Lots of love.

Prologue

San Diego, California
December 18

Good evening. This is *Heart of the Matter*, and I'm your host, James Chapman."

The man on the television screen, lean-faced with collar-length black hair shot with gray, had a full mustache and startlingly clear blue eyes. At the moment, his eyes were filled with endearing concern.

"Do you have a problem you can't work out yourself, a glitch in the system that stymies you?" he asked, looking into the camera. "Do you have a story about someone else in trouble, someone who needs help?" His voice, touched by a drawl and edged with a strangely soothing roughness, reached out to the thousands of Channel Three viewers.

"I've been around forty-one years. I've seen it all. I know how it can be. Instead of hitting brick walls, call me at the number on your screen, or write to me in care of this station. I'll listen, and if I can, I'll help. Trust me."

He paused for a long moment, then continued, "Now, for tonight's story. It all began when the government notified Mrs. Walter Sanderson that, since her husband had died, they would be discontinuing his Social Security checks. Mrs. Sanderson, who desperately needed the two hundred and sixty dollars a month and whose husband was still very much alive, turned to Mr. Sanderson and said, 'We need help, Walter.'"

Murray Landers, owner of the Cracked Cup Café in the old downtown area of San Diego, stared at the small television propped on the butcher-block table by the kitchen's back door. A telephone number ran continuously across the bottom of the screen. He'd tried everything else, and he wasn't getting anywhere.

In his fifty-three years, he'd never felt more helpless. Hannah had been gone for five days, and he was getting scared. He crossed to the wall phone by the back door and dialed the number on the screen. He needed help.

Chapter 1

December 20

James Chapman huddled into the suggestion of warmth in a wedge of space formed by the stucco wall of the bar and a large metal trash Dumpster that jutted onto the street. He muttered, "You, too," when a passerby wished him a merry Christmas, and he wondered if he would ever get over that stab of fear when a stranger talked to him. This wasn't television. It wasn't make-believe, and he wondered for the thousandth time if he'd done the right thing coming here.

He accepted a dollar bill a sailor pressed into his hand and he tried to smile in a duly thankful manner. "Bless you," he said, and the man in dress whites looked pleased to have done his good deed for the Christmas season.

James pushed the money into the left pocket of his dirty gray trench coat, the pocket without the hole in the bottom, and looked up and down the busy street. He hadn't known what else to do to help Murray Landers short of hiring a private investigator. So he'd decided to go looking for Hannah himself.

Garish neon hues from the business signs, mostly bars, mixed uneasily with strings of blinking Christmas lights draped around doors and along roofs of buildings. Strains of "Jingle Bells" droned out of the loudspeaker perched above the door of the Cracked Cup, mingling with the noise of cars and the foot traffic on the narrow side street that led to the highway at North Beach.

James leaned against the wall of the Open 'til Two Bar, wise to the street-people trick of never making eye contact unless you had to. He didn't want trouble. Although he was six feet tall, he was thankful for the illusion of even more size that his bulky clothing gave. Four layers, all well-worn and smelling of age. The boots, a size too big and tied at the ankles with rope, had soles that added about an inch to his height. A ratty navy watch cap covered his thick hair.

Someone touched him on the shoulder, and James stiffened, the sudden contact sending an uncomfortable zing of apprehension up his spine. Cautiously, he glanced up at a slightly built man of medium height with deep ebony skin. Dressed in a dark windbreaker with a faded navy insignia at the shoulder, the middle-aged man teetered slightly on his feet. *Just drunk and getting his balance,* James thought until he made eye contact. Then he felt his insides knot. Blood-shot brown eyes riveted him with their unconcealed anger.

"You the one asking questions?" the man demanded in a slurred, guttural voice.

The odor of stale whiskey drifted on the cool air and made James swallow hard. "Questions?"

"Yeah. Question 'bout Hannah."

James barely nodded, excitement beginning to edge out his uneasiness. "Yes. There's a reward. I know someone..."

"Naw, don't want nothing but for you to leave her alone." The man took a crumpled pack of cigarettes out of his pocket and struck a match to light one. His eyes narrowed in the glare of the flaring match, then the light was gone and he looked at James through the drifting haze of smoke. He tossed the spent match and matchbook onto the ground. "She's an old lady, don't know nothing about nothing, mister. Let her be." The man stared at James hard, then turned and staggered off into the crowds, heading north.

James straightened, about to follow the man, when something struck his right shoulder. He jerked to his left, then let out a sigh of relief when he realized it was just another drunk bumping into him. A sailor. Another man steadied the drunk, muttered an apology and led him off.

James turned to the north, but the black man was gone. With a muttered curse, he sank against the wall of the bar. The closest thing to a lead, and he'd let him get away. A lead? Hell, that guy had been the first to even mention Hannah's name. With disgust, he looked at his feet and spotted the discarded matchbook in the debris, its silver cover reflecting the multicolored lights of the street.

On impulse, James stooped and picked it up, then stared at it. Its gleaming cover held a single initial, F. *Elegant,* he thought. But the man hadn't been elegant at all. James closed his hand around the only link he'd found to Hannah and pushed it into his pocket.

He thought for a minute, then decided to head in the direction the man had disappeared. Maybe he'd get lucky and spot him again. As he straightened to leave, something stopped him dead. Across the street, lights glinted off a camera lens aimed right at him.

Bree McFarland watched the man by the bar from her vantage point in the doorway of the all-night deli across the busy one-way street. Her camera with its heavy telephoto lens hung from a strap around her neck and was hidden in the folds of the navy cape she wore over corduroy slacks and a sweater. It might be southern California, but the temperature near the water had been dropping into the forties at night since Thanksgiving, and she always seemed to be cold.

She pushed her hands into her pockets, still watching the man. Something about him hadn't added up from the first time she'd spotted him in the ring of light from the yellow and red neon sign of the Open 'til Two Bar. He seemed aware of everything going on around him, yet acknowledged no one. Two prostitutes had walked past and looked at him, but he hadn't glanced at them. He seemed intent on studying the sidewalk, yet somehow she sensed that he'd known the instant the two women had wandered off.

Bree wished she understood why she'd used almost a full roll of film with him as the main subject. She flipped her long, curly hair behind her shoulders and away from her face, then lifted her camera again. Narrowing her eyes, she studied him through the lens, but his head stayed down, and his build was hidden beneath layers of ragged clothing.

Click. As Bree froze him in the frame, she confirmed her earlier assessment. In a subtle way, the man didn't fit in.

There wasn't the stoop of defeat in his shoulders or the sense of subservience in the inclination of his head, even when he pocketed money from a passerby. His attitude definitely wasn't the same as that of the people she'd been photographing earlier this evening by the theater.

Click. She took another frame, but she still didn't have a good shot of his face. Even with the telephoto lens, he was little more than interesting shadows, planes and angles. *Click.* She had no desire to get involved on a one-to-one basis, especially not down here, so she wouldn't get any closer. But somehow she wasn't ready to leave—not yet. She kept her camera trained on the man.

She took a deep breath of the cold air and as she studied the impact of the scene in the viewfinder, she swallowed sudden bitterness. The Christmas lights gave the scene texture and irony. Beauty and misery. Christmas. It was only lights and glitter. The poor down here weren't suddenly rich. No magic happened to make everyone happy. No magic at all.

I sound like Scrooge, she thought, and shivered spontaneously. *Forget Christmas. Forget the holidays,* she ordered herself. *They'll be gone soon enough.* She concentrated again on her subject and realized that he'd turned slightly to look at a sailor, finally showing more of his face.

She saw rough angles and planes caught in the flashing multicolored lights. *Click.* Etched cheekbones, a straight nose, shadowed eyes under prominent dark brows, a strong chin darkened by bearded stubble. A mustache flecked with gray. Craggy, sinewy and, strangely, almost attractive—if things had been different.

Click. The play of shadows created patterns and textures that tugged at Bree, lines that appealed to the artist in her, drawing her more deeply into her fascination with her subject. *Click.* Then he looked down, and the moment was gone. Bree felt something in her sag, that peculiar sensation that let her know when a photo session had come to an end. Time to go.

She started to put on the lens cap, but stopped when someone stood in front of the man. Not a sailor this time, but a slender black man wearing a dark jacket, a man unsteady on his feet. He hesitated, then reached out. As soon as he made contact, the stranger pulled back and looked up at him. For a long, awkward moment, the two men stared at each other.

Bree raised her camera again and wondered if there'd be a fight or a mugging. *Click.* She was sure both things happened down here more than she knew. The multimillion-dollar renovation of the North Bay area hadn't touched this street yet.

She watched the men, and her nerves began to bunch painfully. *Click.* She held her breath, but nothing happened. The drunk must have spoken because she could see the man by the Dumpster mouth a single word before the dark man lit up a cigarette. *Click.*

Then the drunk said something else, lurched to the right and wove his way through the people on the sidewalk. Bree flashed to the Dumpster in time to see the man fend off a pair of drunken sailors, then look around. After a second, he glanced down, then stooped to pick up something off the street. He stood, looked at what he had in his hand and pushed it into his pocket. Without warning, he looked up and directly into the camera lens.

For a moment Bree was certain he had caught her intrusion into his world, that he knew she'd been taking his picture. His shadowed eyes narrowed with such intensity that it shocked her. Her finger tightened on the button. *Click.* Then his head dropped until his chin rested on his chest.

Bree lowered her camera slowly, unnerved to find that her hands were shaking. No contact. She didn't want any—not even this sort of eye contact. She wanted subjects that didn't know her, subjects she didn't know. Inanimate objects were best, like the old theater a couple of streets closer to the Bay. She should have stayed there and not come down here.

She knew then that she wouldn't come back to the area again. As she put on her lens cap, all she wanted was to go home and sleep without the dreams. The cap snapped onto the telephoto lens. But she didn't suppose that would happen, not yet. Dreamless nights probably wouldn't come until after the New Year. Then that awful feeling of helplessness would go away for a while, and life would be better. Or at least the cracks in her emotional numbness would heal.

She looked up the street at the café, its steamy windows adorned with Christmas wreaths. An appealingly cheerful building, it stood out from others that simply looked garish and pathetic. It was as if someone had said, "It's Christmas, look festive and happy. It's the season."

She swallowed hard. "It's the season." She'd heard those words enough from well-meaning people—mostly her family. Blinking rapidly, she pushed back her sleeve and glanced at her wristwatch. Ten-thirty. She checked her camera. One frame left. Absentmindedly she clicked off the lens cap, took a picture of the street to the north, then put the cap on as she glanced across the street. The spot by the Dumpster was empty. The man was gone.

She stepped onto the sidewalk, tugged her cape more tightly around her and headed to her Volkswagen van parked near the corner, where the street curved toward Harbor Drive. She felt in her pocket for her keys, arrived at the van, unlocked the side door and slid it back.

She'd taken out the back seats to create a cargo area to carry equipment. An hour earlier, when she'd parked, she'd thrown a blanket over her cases. Now she tugged the blanket up and put her camera into the large sectioned case with the lenses and rolls of fresh and used film.

She adjusted the blanket. As she started to straighten, she felt sudden localized pressure just under her right shoulder blade. At the same moment, a deep voice muttered near her ear, "We need to talk."

She froze, unable even to turn around. "If...if you want money," she gasped, "I..."

"Just get inside and sit on the floor." He nudged her sharply in the back. "Quietly."

She stumbled up the step, almost tripping over her cape in the process, and turned as she sank, trembling, to her knees on the carpeted van floor. The door slid shut with an echoing crack, extinguishing the dome light. There were no streetlights here, none of the gas lamps wired for electricity that lined the streets in the renovated section of the city she'd left an hour ago. The only light now came from the closed store she'd parked in front of.

All she could make out was the hulking shadow of a man, and she felt numb with fear as he hunkered down less than a foot from her knees. Why had she thought she'd be safe around here?

She smelled the odor of old, dirty clothes, and she looked into a face hidden by shadows. But in that instant, she knew him. She'd been watching him for the past hour—the man by the Dumpster outside the bar.

"I'm not going to hurt you," he said in a rough-edged drawl that seemed to vibrate in the confines of the van. "I just need to know what you're up to."

Right then Bree found the ability to move, and she dove to her left, hoping to get between the driver and passenger seats and out one of the front doors. But before she could do more than make a grab at the back of the driver's seat, a large hand closed over her forearm and pulled her back.

"Please don't do that," he said so close to her that she felt the sweep of his breath ruffle her hair. "I swear I'm not going to hurt you. Just tell me what's going on."

Bree twisted sharply and broke free of his grip. But her victory was short-lived when she realized he'd only released her because she was neatly trapped between him, the seats and the side windows. She rubbed her hand where he'd held her and scooted away until she felt the windows at her back. People walked a few feet from the van, yet no one looked inside. "You . . . you tell *me* what's going on," she said in a voice so tight from fear that she barely recognized it as her own.

"Why were you watching me and taking pictures?"

"I . . . I wasn't—" She began the lie, but he stopped her.

"That *was* a camera you had pointed right at me, and—"

"I'm doing research," she gasped.

"What kind of research?"

"About the city at night, all parts of the city. The renovation, the old parts. I swear, that's all I'm doing here."

"Who are you working for?"

"No one. I'm on my own." Wrong thing to say. She knew it as soon as the words were out. "I mean, I'm doing this for myself, but someone knows that I'm here, and he's coming back . . . soon. He's walking down by the harbor."

"I'm sure he is," he murmured.

Why couldn't she be a good liar? "There *is* someone."

"All I need to know is who you're with, the police or the press."

She pointed to the blanket over her equipment box. "That's my equipment. I'm a free-lance photographer."

"Did you take pictures of me?"

"No." She lied without knowing why she was doing it. But right then it seemed important to keep that roll of film secret. "I ran out of film, but even if I had taken your picture, why shouldn't I?"

"That's infringing on my right to privacy, and it could cost me—" He stopped and she heard a deep intake of air, as if he were the one needing to steady himself. "It could cause problems for people I care about." She cursed the lack of light. She couldn't see his eyes in the shadows, yet she knew he was staring right through her. "Now, who are you?" he asked.

She was beginning to shake, and she hated it, but she suddenly realized she had an ace in the hole—if she could get into her purse. "Let me get my purse, and I'll show you some identification."

He hesitated a moment, then allowed, "All right."

She reached to her left and tugged her purse from under the driver's seat. Pushing her hand into it, she felt a quick rush of relief as she found what she wanted. Slowly she closed her fingers around the small handgun and pulled it out. The metal caught a glint of the red, green and yellow lights as she pointed it at the man. For a moment, she felt better as she heard him curse softly under his breath.

She watched him slowly spread his hands palms up and shift back until he was sitting on his heels. "So, the lady's a cop," he muttered.

"No, the lady *is* a photographer," she said. "Now, get out."

He sat very still. "And if I don't?"

Bree fought to keep her voice steady. "I'll put a very small but very deadly hole right between your eyes."

Bree didn't know what she expected, but it wasn't the short, rich burst of deep laughter. "I believe you would."

"I will if I have to," she said with all the firmness she could muster.

"What's your name, lady?"

"None of your business," she said tightly. "Now get out."

The man jerked suddenly as if surprised by something he saw in the window behind Bree, and she automatically twisted around, certain someone was there. It took a split second for her to realize she'd been had, just about as long as it took the man to wrench the gun from her hand. Swallowing hard, she looked into the barrel of her own gun.

James stared at the woman in front of him. A photographer? When he'd first looked up and seen her from across the street, his reaction had been anger. If anyone knew that he was the one asking questions, he'd never find Hannah Vickers. The street people would close ranks. They didn't talk to the police and they certainly wouldn't talk to the media.

"An old street trick," he said, then looked briefly at the gun. "A silly little thing, but effective."

This close, even in the dim lights from the store behind him, he could make out the lovely lines of the woman's face and throat. She was beautiful, he admitted grudgingly. Her long, curly hair, rich sable or possibly deep auburn, spilled around her shoulders.

"I really don't have much money," she said in a voice that sounded more annoyed than afraid.

Maybe she could sense that there wasn't any way he'd hurt her. No, she couldn't know that, not anymore than she could know how much he hated guns. He inhaled, and beyond his own odors, he caught a hint of freshness, a subtle floral scent that tickled his nose. It made him want to breathe in deeply, and that made him feel even more guilty for acting like some two-bit gangster. "I don't want your money," he assured her. "I told you I don't want to hurt you. I just need to know who you are."

"Sabrina . . . Bree McFarland."

"And?"

"I'm a photographer. I told you."

"And?"

She clenched her hands together tightly in front of her. "And what?"

"Why were you watching me?"

He could see her moisten her lips. "I'm doing a project on San Diego, an overall view of the city, the old to the new, and I was over a few streets taking shots of the Fenwick Theater. They . . . they just started keeping the lights on at night—you know, the tiny white ones that frame the roof over the doors and the ticket booth."

"I know the Fenwick," he said.

"Well, I was leaving and came down this street. I thought about the street people who survive around here and I stopped to take some pictures."

When her nervous rush of words stopped, he motioned with the gun to the purse lying at her side. "*Now* you can show me some identification. Slowly."

She reached into the leather pouch again, but this time produced a thick wallet. "Here," she said as she thrust it at him.

"Just take out your license."

While she tried to take the card out of the plastic cover, he almost looked away. Something deep inside him hurt at the unsteadiness in her hands, and he felt awful for acting on impulse and approaching her this way. When she handed the card to him, he took it quickly, but not before his fingers brushed her hand. She jerked as if she expected to be scalded, and her reaction was almost his undoing.

He wanted to toss the gun on the seat and take off, but instead he put more distance between himself and this woman. At the same time, he caught the light from the store outside the van to read the driver's license.

California. The picture that stared at him seemed almost bland compared to the reality. Sabrina Afton McFarland. Height: five feet six inches. Weight: one hundred and eighteen pounds. Eyes: green. Hair: brown. A bland description that gave away none of the rich nuances of the woman herself.

James glanced at her over the card in his hand. "They never do put on licenses what you do for a living."

She touched her lips with the tip of her tongue then fumbled in her wallet and pulled out a small card. She all but threw it at him. "There. Is that good enough for you?"

He laid her license on the carpet by his knee and picked up the stiff piece of paper. A business card, sleek and impressive-looking, like its owner.

Sabrina McFarland, it announced. No address. Just a phone number with a local exchange and, in the corner, simply Photographer. He looked at her. "With a newspaper?"

"No. Free-lance. I do photo essays."

As the lights from a passing car momentarily flooded the van, Bree had a sudden clear view of the intruder's face. No, he wasn't part of the street. The rough stubble of beard and shaggy mustache fit with his ragged layers of clothes, but his eyes did not. In that flashing glimpse, she knew there was too much awareness in them, and none of the inability of so many street people to make direct contact with another human being. Gray, maybe blue, she couldn't tell—but his eyes were on her, and the connection was almost palpable. Intensity crackled in them, and she couldn't look away even after the car lights were gone.

Then the man shifted. The connection was broken. He exhaled a low hiss that seemed to echo through Bree. "God, I'm sorry. I thought…." He started to hand her the gun, but stopped. He stared at it, then with a grating curse, he pushed the gun up to her face. "This is some damned toy, isn't it?" he demanded.

She jerked back, almost as shaken by the sudden anger as she had been by him barging into her van.

"A toy!" he said. "You're lucky I wasn't bent on hurting you. What if I'd had a knife or a gun? What did you plan to do while I was killing you, squirt me with water or frighten me off with caps?" He tossed the useless gun onto the passenger seat and leaned closer to Bree. "Never pretend something's real when it isn't." Then he rocked back, giving Bree much-needed breathing space. "I really am sorry about all of this," he muttered. "I won't bother you any longer."

With that he reached behind him, slid the door open and slowly backed out until he was on the sidewalk. He stooped enough to look into the van, his eyes met hers momentarily, and the shadowy gaze made her shake harder. "Do me a favor, lady. Forget this ever happened. And throw away that damned gun." He jabbed the lock button down, then slid the door shut with a crack and walked down the street.

Bree started after him for only a second before checking to make sure the door was locked. Then she scooped up her wallet and driver's license and awkwardly climbed into the driver's seat. She fumbled in her pocket for the key and needed three tries to get it into the ignition. With a heartfelt sigh of relief, she started the engine, put the van into gear and drove off.

James stepped into the shelter of the first alley he came to and sank against the wall. If word got out that he was down here, this whole thing would be over and done. Thank goodness his disguise had been good enough to keep Bree from recognizing him. He gave a short nervous bark of laughter. His own mother wouldn't recognize him in these rags.

He looked at the business card he still had in his hand. Sabrina McFarland. He started to put it in his pocket with the money and the matchbook, but he stopped. He stood straight and felt in the pocket. There wasn't any matchbook. He pulled out the contents of the pocket—three crumpled dollar bills and some change. Damn it! His only possible lead, and he couldn't find it. He pushed his hand into his left pocket and found nothing except the huge hole.

He tucked the money and card into the good pocket, then hunkered down to look at the littered ground at his feet. Papers and trash, but no silver matchbook. Quickly he stood and looked around the side of the building. Bree was gone.

Without her there, he could retrace his footsteps to try to find the matchbook. If he didn't find it on the street, the only other place it could be would be the yellow Volkswagen van. He didn't have a photographic memory, and he couldn't begin to remember the address on Bree's license. Then his hand closed around the card in his pocket. At least he had her phone number.

Chapter 2

December 21

...And a late-breaking item. Our sources at the San Diego Police Department confirmed that a break in the investigation of the murder of Detective Andrew Dawson seems imminent. Police have an APB out on a Wayne Douglas Concklin, a bartender at the Coach Lantern Bar near North Bay, just two streets from where the officer was found stabbed six days ago.

"The San Diego police department has made no statement about Concklin's connection to the murder, but our sources confirm that he is wanted for questioning in the case.

"That's it for this installment of the Channel Three morning news on December 21, but tune in tonight for our six o'clock newscast and hear *Heart of the Matter*. Tonight James Chapman will be introducing us to a Good Samaritan named George Leone who found out what the term 'raw deal' really means."

"What are you doing in here?"

The question cut rudely into his sleep, and James cringed, pressing his face deeper into the rough tweed of the couch cushions. Peace and quiet were obviously too much to ask for this morning. He hadn't slept well, and now his head ached and his body felt cramped and stiff from being confined to the less than adequate couch since two in the morning.

Reluctantly he shifted, turned on his back and opened his eyes just enough to realize that the harsh fluorescent lights mingling with the crystal clarity of a new day were as offensive as the voice of the man who stood over him demanding, "Come on, James, what are you doing at the station?"

"What in the hell are *you* doing, Bryan?" James moaned and pressed his hands to his eyes. "First you're yelling, then you're trying to blind me with those damned lights."

He dropped his hands and stared at Bryan Lake, a slender blond man whose arms were crossed over his chest and whose clean-shaven face wore a disapproving look. "I'm trying to find out if you're alive, or if that smell comes from something else that crawled into your office during the night and died."

James uttered a rough curse as he slowly sat up. He squinted at the brilliant colors of the posters of sixties rock groups that gave some life to his beige, ten-by-twelve office. With a groan he leaned forward and raked his fingers through his disheveled, gray-streaked hair. "What time is it?"

"Seven-fifteen."

He inhaled and squinted at Bryan. "I'm not very fresh, am I?"

"No. That's how I knew you were in here."

James could see the distaste on Bryan's lean face. "Sorry."

"I thought you were on vacation. But it looks as if you're having your own lost weekend."

Against his will, James chuckled at the statement. He'd always suspected that if Bryan didn't have a sense of humor, he'd be intolerable. An extremely neat man, Bryan was dressed in sharply creased brown slacks worn with a coordinated button-down beige shirt and an off-white V-necked pullover. His polished brown oxfords gleamed. And, James acknowledged, his precise appearance was matched by a perfect memory that was invaluable in the research department at Channel Three.

"I'm deliberately trying to be a bum, Bryan. Not someone you could relate to." He tugged at the worn sweatshirt that might have been green at one time.

"Well, you succeeded. You look the part," Bryan agreed. "Am I supposed to ask why you're wearing a costume when it's Christmas coming and not Halloween?"

"Go ahead and ask." James stood and couldn't help smiling when Bryan backed up to keep a buffer of fresh air between them.

"All right, I'll bite. Why are you dressed like that?"

As James began to undo the twine that held his boots on, he explained. "I was heading out the door for my two week vacation. I had my *Heart of the Matter* spots edited and done—the whole shot. I was finished with this place for a while." He straightened and scratched at his middle. "I was going to go to…" He shrugged. "Never mind. I never made it. The phone rang. A man from a restaurant by the harbor, close to the renovation project, had a problem."

Bryan moved nearer the desk under the window as James kicked off the boots one at a time, sending them through the air to land near the door under a red and black poster of a skeleton holding a single rose. "So you dressed up like a bum?"

"Not then. Not until I went down and talked to the guy. There's an old lady named Hannah Vickers. Did you ever hear that name?"

Bryan shook his head. "Should I have?"

"She claimed to have been a silent movie star. If you get a chance, could you check and see if she was connected to the movie industry?"

"Sure, when I've got some free time. Is that why she's a story for you?"

"It's an intriguing aspect of her background, but I was approached because she disappeared. She's a street person, so no one cares except this guy who hired her to work in his kitchen."

"Why didn't he go to the police?"

James balanced on one foot then the other as he tugged off his socks. "He did, but they don't give a damn about someone like that. They took the report, then promptly forgot all about it. This guy, Murray Landers, is worried. He can't find her, not a trace."

He tossed the socks after the boots, then looked at Bryan. "I called the cops and found out that a detective I met a few months back on another case is working on it. Cal Browsky. But he wasn't encouraging. He said forty percent of the transients are crazy, the other sixty percent are either on alcohol or drugs, or they simply ran away and want to be lost. That's why they're out there. The cops don't have the time or the resources to do much about someone like that disappearing."

"But you care about it, don't you." Bryan didn't ask a question. He made a statement. "And you're going to put it on *Heart of the Matter*."

James stood very still. "Very perceptive." He rubbed his face with both hands, skimming over the bristling beard. He'd been hit hard by the Hannah story right from the first. It took him back a few years to Chicago, to a freezing winter, to a slum-area apartment, to a man who hadn't mattered, who'd lived more than eighty years then hadn't been important enough for anyone to help.

He shut off the memory, only allowing the certain knowledge that he'd had his fill of the idea that some people weren't important or didn't count. The same way he'd finally realized he'd had enough of reporting nothing but problems and horrors. He'd been given carte blanche with this program thanks to Carson Davies, the station manager, and this was a story he wanted to do. He mentally re-phrased it—*needed* to do. "I need to find her, Bryan." And he wouldn't let go until he did—one way or another.

He tugged his sweatshirt over his head. "God only knows what's happened to her. I'm stumped. The people down there won't talk to outsiders, especially someone involved in television. I didn't want to take chances, so I dressed up like one of them. Last night I went down there and did some asking around, hinting that I know someone offering a reward for information. I didn't get anything until I'd been there about three hours."

"You know where she is?" Bryan asked.

James tossed the sweatshirt on the couch and began to undo the pins that fastened the flannel shirt. "No, but think I had a clue of sorts about someone who might know her. A very thin clue."

"Is that why you came in here like that?"

James answered that question with one of his own. "What time does Carson usually get in?"

"Eight or eight-thirty. Why?"

He dropped the pins on the desktop. "That gives me time to use his shower."

"You can't just—"

"I can't get any work done like this."

"And your vacation?"

"Can come later. Right now I need to clean up."

James knew that his behavior offended Bryan from time to time for various reasons. Right now he was offending the blond man's sense of propriety. "But you can't just go into the station manager's private office and use his shower," Bryan repeated.

"You know Carson and I go way back," James assured him. "Long before he coaxed me into working for Channel Three. I've shared more than my bathroom with the man. And I can't walk around like this." He stripped off the flannel shirt. "Carson wants me to project a good image. To be part of the station's image. The station with a heart. The people's news. You care, so we care. You know the slogans Carson came up with. Hell, you probably helped him think them up."

"I'm not in publicity or public relations." Bryan watched as James tossed the shirt over a thick San Diego phone book on the desk. Down to frayed Levi's and a far-from-white undershirt, he crossed to the filing cabinet to the left of the window and pulled out the bottom drawer, marked Stay Out!

"I'll be back in about fifteen minutes, then I need to talk to you." James turned, holding clean Levi's, a folded T-shirt and his well-used Nikes, which he had pulled from the drawer. "By the way, what are *you* doing here so early?"

"Working." Bryan crossed his arms over his chest again. "The *City at Dawn* show needed information about the murder of that undercover cop who was posing as a Santa near the mall. So the producers called me in the middle of the night to ask me to get material. The show might want me for a segment on photographic memories next week." He lifted one pale brow. "You never did explain exactly why you're here."

"I needed information, too. I thought I could find it here, and when I didn't, I lay down to think about it." He deliberately didn't point to the city phone book or tell Bryan about the time he'd spent trying to find a McFarland who had the same number as the one on Bree's business card.

He glanced at the card he'd stuck behind a corner of a Pink Floyd poster above the file cabinet. Why had he finally called the number and waited through eight rings before a husky, sleep-filled voice answered? A flashing image of what the owner of the voice must have looked like touseled from sleep had flooded over him, and he'd hung up so quickly the plastic receiver had almost snapped.

He fingered his rough beard, a good alternative to going over and taking the card in his hands. "I'm out of disposable razors. Do you suppose Carson keeps any in his bathroom?" James asked as he stepped into the corridor.

The deep blue of the carpet that was echoed in a solid stripe at the top of the white walls and the clear red of the doors that opened into the corridor were almost painful to James. He didn't come in at this hour any more than Bryan usually did.

"I wouldn't know," Bryan said as he followed James into the hallway. "I didn't take an inventory of his office when I was in there last time."

James stopped and turned as he realized that Bryan's presence could be a godsend. "Speaking of photographic memories—"

"What now?" Bryan asked, leaning against the door-jamb.

"Ever hear the name Bree McFarland?"

The answer came without the blink of an eye. "No. Bree's an odd name. I'd remember it."

"She's a photographer. Her first name is really Sabrina, her second is Afton." James spelled it.

Bryan stood straight and thought hard for a second. James could almost see the man mentally sorting through the facts so efficiently stored in his mind. Bryan shook his head. "I can't come up with anything."

"Well, there's a Sabrina McFarland somewhere in San Diego." He had a flashing memory of her slender hands as she took out her driver's license. No wedding ring. "I don't know if she's married or not. But I need to find out where she lives." He hesitated, then told Bryan her phone number. "That's all I've got."

Bryan repeated it and nodded. "No problem."

"I'd appreciate anything you can find out about her."

"When do you need the information?"

"When I finish using Carson's shower and razor."

Bree twisted and turned, trying to get away, but knowing she was plunging headlong toward the horror. Dean was there, and she couldn't run. She tried, God knows she tried, but nothing did any good. Snow fell outside and coldness

settled all around her. "You can't leave!" Dean screamed
from the shadows. "You have to stay, you have to!"

A dream, only a dream, yet it seared through Bree, and
she could feel herself losing strength; filled with horror and
helplessness. Then she was heading for the room, toward the
door, and she knew once again that she'd have to face what
happened. She couldn't escape from it or the bone-chilling
cold.

The door came closer, her hand nearing it to push it back,
then she made one last attempt to stop everything. *Wake up!*
She fought the inevitable with all her strength. *Run, stay
alive! It's only a dream. Wake up!*

With a force of will she hadn't possessed the other nights,
she felt as if she burst through a wall, and in one stunning
moment she was fully awake, her only restraint the tangle of
sheets and blankets that had wound around her during the
restless night. But she was awake and thankful for the re-
prieve.

Bree gulped in air. She hated that the dreams had started
again. With her forearm over her eyes, she lay very still on
the king-size brass bed. Would they ever go away for good?
Breathe in, breathe out. Steady. They'd come so suddenly,
and she could almost feel the weakening in her since their
start.

She'd been doing fine, shutting out the past. But now she
couldn't when she slept, and it scared her. Gradually, as the
world began to settle, she realized that the dreams had
changed after the telephone call.

She'd fallen asleep easily last night, then around midnight the phone had rung. But when she'd picked up, no one
had been on the line. When she'd managed to go back to
sleep, the dream had come again, but a new person had appeared through the haze of horror and pain. The man from
yesterday. He hadn't been threatening. In fact, she had almost thought he might have been protecting her in some
way. Maybe holding her against his rough coat before she
could open the door. But she couldn't remember clearly.

She didn't want to remember. That would mean letting the past come into her waking hours, and she would start to fall into a whirlpool of pain and regret about her time with Dean. And she'd remember everything. No. She sat up abruptly, brushed the tumble of curls off her face and supported herself with both hands pressed flat on the bed at her sides.

She stared at the bedroom, bathed in the gray light of dawn. White plaster walls set off black-and-white prints of her photos mounted on special matting boards. Views of San Diego. The reality of the city would be more like it.

"Damned poetic," she muttered as she climbed out of bed. Barefoot and wearing only her oversize Mickey Mouse T-shirt, she padded across the thick ivory carpeting to the bathroom.

Two hours later, in the darkroom she'd made out of the huge windowless pantry just off the kitchen, Bree pulled the proof sheets of the film she'd shot last night out of the finishing rinse. Positioning them on the slanted washboard, she squeegeed them off, then set them on the conveyor belt that moved them through the dryer, a four-by-three-foot metal box.

While the prints went around and around in the dryer, she took off the brown plastic apron that protected her loose white blouse and beige corduroy slacks from chemical spills. As she crossed the floor, the smooth tiles were cool under her bare feet. She snapped off the safety light and switched on the overhead light.

Back at the dryer, she watched the proof sheets fall into the tray on her worktable, which sat along the back wall. A butterfly clip kept her unruly curls out of her eyes as she leaned forward to study the proofs through a hand-held enlarger.

She went over each of the tiny exposures on the eight-by-ten piece of photographic paper. A stab of pleasure came when she realized that the shots were what she had been after—the dramatic light sprays of passing cars, blurred shadows of buildings and ships on the water. The construction sites and the theater.

The bulk of one roll had been of the theater, a grandly imposing building that dated from the early 1920s. Night had made it look fascinating, with its meticulously restored facade, a full-length portico supported by two massive Corinthian pillars and outlined by hundreds of white twinkling lights. More lights ran across the top of eight sets of mahogany entry doors with oval glass insets. Light reflected in shimmering blurs off the sweep of mellow marble stairs and the glass in the octagonal ticket office that stood in front, topped by a Turkish-style dome.

Bree had taken several shots from different angles, then had taken a couple of shots of the sign. Fashioned like a banner, it looked about twenty feet long, set above the line of the portico roof and attached to the bricks behind it. Red and gold lights spelled out Fenwick Theater in script.

The old building had more character than the people she'd photographed on the night streets, who were simply shapes and forms, back-lit and with only a suggestion of humanity, no personalities. Then she looked at the next proof sheet, and she felt a strange clutching in her middle.

Nearly the whole roll was of the man on the street, and she could see plainly how the tone of her photos had changed from impersonal to personal, from nebulous to exact. She couldn't take her eyes from the person who dominated each frame. Angles, shadows, lines, planes, darkness and light. The shot she'd taken when he'd looked up at her caught her eye.

Shadowed eyes held an intensity that hadn't diminished in the transfer to film. It shocked Bree all over again. A trembling began deep within her that she didn't understand. There was no tag for it, no name that fit. So she passed it off as lingering nerves over being accosted in her van—or a remnant of the uneasiness she'd experienced during the night.

Quickly she marked the proofs she wanted to enlarge, including the single shot of the man's face, and got busy.

When she had printed the twenty or so eight-by-ten shots and dried them, she laid them out on her worktable. Quite deliberately she avoided looking at them too closely. Later, after she'd had some coffee, she would go through them and choose the best ones.

James drove his black Bronco slowly up the winding road into the hills above San Diego Bay just after ten o'clock. He drove slowly under the canopy of old eucalyptus and sycamores, up the steeply climbing street with its eclectic collection of older homes, a neighborhood of money without flash. Most of the homes had an impressive view of the distant ocean and were set on large lots, their privacy protected by twists in the road and strategically placed mature trees.

He read the numbers on each rural mailbox as he passed, looking for the address he'd found on the precisely printed note Bryan had left on his desk: *No Hannah Vickers in the silent movies. Here's Sabrina McFarland's address . . .*

James had pushed the note into his pocket. Leaving the station, he'd headed south. By the time he'd turned onto this street, he'd known what he was going to do. If this was the Sabrina McFarland with the yellow VW van and that van wasn't locked or in a garage, he'd try to look in it, find the matchbook and get out without any encounter.

That last thought depressed him just a bit. No encounter. But he didn't have time for diversions, and he certainly didn't want her to know who he was. In the daylight, without his disguise, she'd be sure to recognize him and ask questions. Before he could think too much about it, he was facing a dead end at the top of the hill with the address he was looking for directly ahead.

The white adobe two-story home built on the highest knoll was even more secluded than its neighbors. It had the highest position on the street, with regal sycamores on either side of the drive, with more of the trees showing over the top of the red-tiled roof. The clear morning sun shone through the trees, making crazy patterns on the rough adobe walls. Solid brick fencing that parted only for the driveway entrance looked about six feet tall. The wrought-iron gates were open.

As he drove past the driveway, James could see in enough to know that it curved to the left and around behind the house. He couldn't see the van. He pulled past the house and parked on the downward curve of the street, turned his wheels against the curb and got out. He took a moment to glance around, but nothing stirred; there weren't even any cars moving on the street. Lawn Santas stood at attention, old pines were adorned with decorations, and lights would probably light up the shadows at night. But not a person was in sight.

Then he looked at Sabrina McFarland's house and frowned. It was the only place around that didn't have Christmas decorations on it. No lights, no wreaths and no tree visible in the arched, multipaned windows that faced the street. For several minutes he simply watched the house for signs of life. When he thought it was safe, he pushed his hands into the pockets of the brown tweed sport coat he wore with his T-shirt and Levi's, then walked toward the house. He looked around once more, saw nothing and casually cut to his left, through the open gate and up the driveway. His Nikes made no noise on the cement.

The drive curved around to a detached, two-car garage behind the house. In front of it, backed in to face the street, sat the yellow van.

James glanced quickly at the house, all of its side windows covered with shades or drapes, then hurried toward the van. Cautiously he looked inside. Nothing. Clean. Its back area was completely empty except for a set of back seats and a yellow blanket neatly folded by the door.

He touched the handle, tentatively tried it and exhaled on a sigh when he found it unlocked. Things were working out after all. In about two minutes he would know if the matchbook was here, and he could be on his way. Carefully he began to open the door.

Bree held the telephone so tightly that she could feel her hand tingle and stared at the open door to her darkroom. With great concentration, she forced her fingers to relax, and the same concentration kept her voice even. "No, I won't be coming home for Christmas. I'm busy. I'm working."

Her mother's voice wasn't quite so even, and the slight tremble in it set Bree's nerves on edge. "But, honey, everyone's coming. And you work for yourself. Besides, what kind of Christmas can you have in California? They don't even have snow. I promise, you don't have to—"

"No." Bree interrupted before her mother could get started. She leaned against the cool counter in the kitchen and closed her eyes. "I'm doing fine. I don't need snow, and I'm staying here to work."

"You can give yourself some time off and come home. We want you to."

"But . . ."

"Sabrina."

When her mother used her full name, Bree knew the big guns were going to be brought out. And she didn't want to hear her mother cry or her father get on the line and give her his patented pep talk. She pressed her free hand flat on the cold tile of the counter and rested her forehead on the closed cabinet door in front of her. "Mother, we'll talk later. I've got prints developing," she lied. "I have to go."

Her mother didn't give up easily. "*This* Christmas is going to be wonderful. It can be a time to put the past behind and look to the future. The whole family will be here for a change."

Bree looked at her hand on the tiles as it clenched so tightly the knuckles became bloodless. The numbness of months had faded when the dreams had started. The numbness had become something to treasure, to hold to as tightly as possible. And it was slipping through her fingers. Going home for Christmas would destroy it completely. She couldn't chance that, not now. "I'll call you tonight. We'll talk." And she hung up before her mother could say anything else.

For a moment Bree stayed where she was and closed her eyes. She took several deep breaths. She'd known the time would come when she'd have to deal with feelings, but she'd hoped it wouldn't be this soon. Right now she had to come up with a valid reason for staying here this year. She had to come up with that reason before she called her mother back.

A sound through the stillness caught her attention. She stood straight and turned to look around the square room with its bleached oak cabinets, white appliances and quarry-tile floor. She listened to the continuing sound, a soft sliding. The room's perfect order was unmarred by anything that could be making the sound, and she realized it had to be coming from outside. She crossed to the stainless steel sinks and the double windows over them, lifted one slat of the thin blind that blocked out the world and saw the side door of her van slowly moving.

If she'd left it partially unlatched and it was opening on its own, it was going against all laws of nature by rolling uphill. Then she saw a hand, a man's hand, on the door, pulling it open.

She spun and hurried to the phone but stopped before she lifted the receiver. She couldn't call the police. That was all she needed—the police and some snoopy reporters digging and figuring out who she was. She didn't need more headlines. She couldn't take them and the probing. She had had enough of both for a lifetime.

But she couldn't just let someone break into her van. She couldn't believe how careless she'd been not locking the gate when she'd turned the van around earlier. She remembered that her purse was in the living room. She hurried in, grabbed the gun from her purse on the hearth and ran through the house. She went into the breakfast room, which held a stack of unopened moving crates, stopped at the French doors and held on tightly to the toy gun, small and cold in her hand. It looked so real. And it had worked last night until the man had touched it.

She took a deep breath, then quietly opened the doors that led out to the quarry-stone terrace and the walkway that led to the drive and the van.

Hunkered down by the van, James realized how much of an obsession finding Hannah had become to him. Here he was, trespassing in the hope that the damn matchbook could help find the old woman. He didn't know how it could lead him to Hannah, but he'd discovered a long time ago that in this life, almost anything was possible. The old man who'd dropped the matchbook had tried to threaten him in a way, and he must have cared about Hannah to have bothered. Maybe James could talk to the man again. Maybe the man wouldn't be drunk this time.

The door made a low rumbling sound as it slid back, and James wondered if there'd come a point in life where he'd begin to believe the moon was made of green cheese. That seemed about as likely as a matchbook being the clue to finding an elderly woman. With the door open, James looked inside.

"Don't move," the voice said from behind him.

Taken totally off guard, James lost his grip on the door at the same time he lost his balance on the sloping drive-way. The door slid downhill to shut with a resounding crack, and James ended up sitting on the cold concrete looking up at a gun, then past it into a familiar face.

In the darkness last night, he hadn't been able to take in real details. But he wasn't the least surprised by the beauty of the oval face illuminated by the clear sunlight. A cloud of sable curls was held back to expose a slightly sharp chin, almost haughty bone structure, a perfectly defined nose and finely feathered brows. The richly colored hair fell around slender shoulders, splashing darkness on the pure white of an oversize blouse worn with snug corduroy jeans.

The cape had hidden the slender figure last night, but now, despite the fact that the woman had a figure he would call stunning, it was her eyes, green or brown or maybe a mixture of both, that held his attention. Lush dark lashes framed an expression that riveted him to the spot.

This is definitely an encounter, he thought ruefully. And his whole being seemed to be enjoying it despite the cold cement he was sitting on. He finally gathered his senses and braced himself with his palms on the roughness of the driveway. He cocked one eyebrow at her, flashed his best "the world loves me" smile and waited. She'd recognize him any minute here in the brightness of the winter day. Then everything would have to be explained. He hadn't wanted it to happen, but now it couldn't be helped.

"What do you think you're doing?" she asked, the gun just slightly unsteady.

Did he look so different from his image on television? Sure, he wasn't in his blue blazer, but that shouldn't make much difference. "I can explain—"

"—why you're robbing me?" she finished in a voice tinged with an inviting huskiness.

"I wasn't robbing you." He started to stand, but she stopped him.

"Don't move," she said and backed up half a pace.

He sat with a shrug. "All right." She had incredibly long legs, or maybe they looked that way because he was sitting at her feet. Her hips weren't too full, but contrasted pleasingly with her narrow waist defined by a leather belt. High breasts rose and fell rapidly with each breath she took, the action lifting the soft fabric of the blouse. James quickly shifted his focus from that intriguing sight to the toy gun pointed at him.

Chapter 3

Bree stared at the man sitting on the ground in front of her. Why she thought she knew him was beyond her, but there was something about him. She held tightly to the gun. The clothes—Levi's, Nikes and a tweed sport coat worn over a T-shirt splashed with brilliant reds and blues—might be casual, but they weren't cheap. His hair, almost black and streaked with silver, worn long enough to touch his collar and curl at the ends, looked healthy, thick and professionally styled. He didn't look at all the way she thought a crook should look.

Then she realized who he looked like—the derelict by the Dumpster, the man who'd forced his way into her van last night. But he was clean and shaven, his gray-flecked mustache full but neatly trimmed. It couldn't be. "You?" she breathed.

He stood slowly and brushed at his Levi's before he looked at Bree. "All right, lady, you recognized me. I wondered when you would."

"I don't understand." She backed up to keep a buffer of space between them. Maybe he was only five or six inches taller than she, but he looked wiry and strong. She remembered his hold on her last night. Definitely strong. Not a traditionally handsome man, but there was something about his clear blue eyes under those heavy brows. She nervously moistened her lips. "How did you find me, and what are you doing here?"

He lifted an eyebrow. "That's a long story."

"Why don't you start with last night. Why did you attack me?"

"Attack you?" He actually looked shocked at her choice of words.

"What would you call it? You forced your way into my van. And now you're here, looking like that." She jerked the gun in his direction, then felt her face flood with color.

"I thought we had a talk about toy guns?" He lifted one eyebrow as she slowly lowered the weapon. "It's a crime to do that in California, you know."

She shrugged sharply, annoyed she'd lost any advantage she'd thought she had with him. And she found herself bluffing just as she had the night before when she'd told him she'd shoot him. "I'm calling the police."

That brought an immediate response. He held up both his hands, palms out. "No police."

"Why not? Did you think you could get away with all this?" Her insides contracted, and she wished she could just throw the useless gun into the air and have it disappear. "I'm getting the police."

His hands dropped to his sides. "So are you going to politely ask me to stand here while you go into your house and call the authorities?" An annoying smile twitched under his mustache and danced in the blue depths of his eyes. "I can hold the gun for you, if you like."

He thought this was funny! "No, I..." She looked around. The fence effectively blocked out the other houses, and she didn't know her neighbors anyway. She'd made very sure that she stayed to herself since she'd moved in six months ago. "I don't know. I..." Her words trailed off. She didn't know what else to say.

"Maybe I can save both of us some embarrassment. I don't want the police to come, and you can't go into the house to call them without putting me on my honor not to run as soon as you turn your back." He thrust his hands into the pockets of his Levi's. Slowly, he rocked forward on the balls of his feet. "Can I suggest something, lady?"

She nervously fingered the gun. "What?"

"Let me get what I came for, and I'll leave. That will solve everything." He motioned to the van with a jerk of his head. "I think I dropped something in there last night. Just let me look, and I'll leave quietly."

She looked at him, surprised that she felt inclined to trust him to do exactly what he said. Actually, if he really would leave quietly, she'd agree to just about anything. "Go ahead and look."

"Thank you," he said and reached for the door. He slid it open and climbed in on his knees. Bree watched him search the floor, under the front seats, under the seats at the back, then in the door well. When he got out and stood, he ran his fingers roughly through his thick hair and muttered, "Nothing. It's not there."

"What were you looking for?"

"A matchbook. Silver, with a fancy F on it."

"This was all for a matchbook?"

He nodded.

"Who are you?"

The flash of confusion in his expression came as he asked, "I thought you recognized me?"

"Of course I do. You're the man from last night. I mean, you're all cleaned up, but you're the same man. I just don't know your name or what's going on, or how you got those clothes."

"My name is James Chapman."

"And?"

"James Chapman," he repeated and spread his jacket open farther to expose the red and blue logo on his T-shirt. Now she could see that the red made a stylized heart, and the blue formed a huge number three. Under it was the slogan Channel Three, the Station with a Heart.

An all too familiar dread clutched at her. "A reporter?" she asked in a voice so tight that it was almost unrecognizable.

He let the jacket fall in place. "I'm James Chapman, feature reporter for the station with a heart, Channel Three, San Diego, KHRT, news at five, six and eleven," he quoted glibly.

Oh, God. Her hands began to shake, and she thrust them behind her, gun and all. They'd found her. "A reporter?" she repeated weakly.

He frowned at her, but nodded. "I do specials now and then, but mostly I concentrate on a series of features run during the newscast. *Heart of the Matter*, on the six and eleven o'clock broadcasts." His gaze was intense. "You've never watched it, have you?"

His words blurred around her. He'd tracked her down last night and again today. And she'd given him her card! She felt sick. She clutched the gun in her hand behind her so tightly that it bit into her palm. "I'm sorry. I don't know what you're after, but you came to the wrong place. I'm going inside." She began to inch her way closer to the sidewalk that led to the terrace and the refuge of the breakfast-room doors. "Just go away and leave me alone."

"Listen to me." He took a step toward her. "I *really* need that matchbook."

The matchbook? Hadn't that just been a ploy to get to her? "Why?"

"It's for a story." He glanced at the van and at her. "An important story."

Was it possible he didn't know who she was? Had her luck finally changed? Was this really about a matchbook? She licked her lips nervously and shrugged. "I cleaned out the van a few hours ago. I can't leave my equipment..." She wasn't about to explain any more. "What story?"

"A very important one I'm working on," he said, his gaze never faltering.

She met that gaze and knew that maybe it wasn't logical, but maybe he was telling the truth, and he hadn't tracked her down to dig and pry into her life. "I'm sorry, I don't remember any matchbook."

"Where's your trash?"

"In the house." She wished she could read minds and she wished she understood why she had an instinct to trust this man. She didn't really feel threatened by him, only by what a reporter could do to her.

"This might sound strange, but can I look through it?" He smiled, a heart-stopping expression that crinkled the corners of his eyes. "I promise I can give you a full explanation that will make sense."

James watched Bree hesitate. The fear he'd seen a moment ago had eased, but her confusion seemed almost tangible. Then the ringing of a telephone began inside the house. She darted a glance toward the sound, then at him. "I'll be right back." She ran up a brick walkway toward the house.

He stood on the driveway and watched her, her long hair swinging freely, the curls glinting with gold and red highlights in the clear sunlight. She ran across a stone patio and disappeared into the house through French doors.

James took a deep breath and had an awful thought. What if she decided not to come out, to lock the doors and ignore him? He couldn't take that chance. When he saw the door shut behind her, he hesitated only a moment before following her.

He jogged up to the French doors, stopped, tested one and, when it opened, stepped inside, onto the parquet floor. The room must have been meant as a breakfast room, but all it held were neatly stacked moving boxes along one wall.

"I can't talk right now."

The sound of Bree's voice drew him to the arched doorway through which the kitchen was visible, a cool, clean, sleek room. He caught the fragrance of coffee and saw an automatic brewer on the counter holding a half full pot of steaming brown liquid. Then he looked at Bree.

She stood facing a counter by an open door to the left, her back to him. Her free hand was pressed palm down on the white-tiled counter top, the gun beside it. Her slender shoulders were hunched forward, and her whole stance looked vulnerable. "Why can't you let me be?" she asked in a tense voice. "I already told you, no. Please, I can't."

He frowned at the way her shoulders quivered, a movement that ran along her spine and into the arm that was braced on the counter. She listened without saying a word for a long moment, but her quick breathing echoed in the stillness. Then her trembling increased.

James felt like a Peeping Tom, a real intruder, and the sensation wasn't particularly appealing. It didn't help that he felt the strongest urge to go to her and hold her.

Unreasoning anger at whoever had called and done this to her all but choked him, and he knew that the intensity of his feelings was out of line. He also knew that he either had to get out without being seen or do something. Before he could sort out his motivations, he acted on instinct and closed the space that separated them.

When he touched her shoulder, he expected her to jerk away, to push at him and scream, but she didn't. The receiver hit the cradle with a resounding crack, and Bree turned to him, eyes wide and bright with unshed tears. James took a deep breath and pulled her to him. No fight, no struggle—she seemed simply to collapse against him. Her hands moved up his back and he could feel his jacket being balled tightly in her fists.

The sobs he expected never came. All he could feel was her struggle to breathe evenly, to stop the trembling in her body. And he held her tighter, trying to do his part to ease whatever it was that was tearing her apart.

Then suddenly she did pull back. She blinked rapidly, her eyes startled, as if she just now realized it was him she'd been holding on to. Her expression stiffened as rapidly as her face paled. "What are you doing in here?" she whispered hoarsely, clutching her hands tightly in front of her. The moments she'd held on to him might never have been.

James had his own problems gaining control. He'd never felt an aching this deep at another's pain. He took a step back.

If she wanted to pretend he'd never held her, that he'd never glimpsed that raw edge of vulnerability, he was more than willing to go along with the charade. He didn't need the complication right now anyway. "I came in to look at the trash," he said simply.

"I was going to bring it out to you." She swiped a hand over her face, then moved abruptly toward the open door. Disappearing for only a moment, she reappeared with a plastic trash container and set it on the tiled floor with a crack. "Since you're here, this is it."

Her face was tightly controlled now, but the control didn't quite wipe out the unnatural color that had begun to stain her cheeks or hide the lingering brightness in her eyes.

"Thank you," he murmured and looked away from her to reach for the container.

Bree inhaled deeply, trying to rid herself of the essence of the man that all but overwhelmed her. But the scent of body heat mingled with tangy after-shave and subtle maleness persisted in taunting her. How could she have broken down like that? She swallowed hard, trying to still her thudding heart. Why had her mother called back so soon and brought up Dean? Did she think it would help to say it out loud? That Bree couldn't ignore what had happened last year and had to learn to live with it, not away from it?

With her hips pressed against the counter, she watched him methodically pick through empty film canisters, used chemical containers, candy wrappers, junk mail, last night's newspaper and a tangled roll of film she'd ruined yesterday.

She pressed a hand against her breastbone, hoping that would help her settle down. In that second when she'd turned and found James staring at her, when all she could think of was being held and holding on to someone, she'd felt as if she'd been stripped naked in front of the entire world. He'd seen the erosion in her control, heard her talking, seen her face, caught a glimpse of her at her worst, and he'd held her.

She tried to hate him for his intrusion but couldn't quite manage it. His arms had been her support for that moment, her reason not to drift away into the lurking haze of regret and pain. But how much had he heard? Did he know who she was? She wished she knew how much she'd given away in those moments when she'd come close to breaking down.

He exhaled and stood abruptly. The overhead light revealed tension in his eyes and around his mouth. His disappointment looked very real. "It's not here. Did you empty trash anywhere else?"

She had to concentrate to focus on his question. "I...no, not really."

"What do you mean, not really?"

"I had my purse with me. Sometimes I put things in there to throw away later. But—"

"Where is it?"

She motioned to the double archway at the end of the kitchen. "In the living room, but—"

When he strode abruptly toward the doors, she knew she couldn't stop him any more than she could stop a whirlwind. She stooped to pick up the trash container and set it inside the darkroom. Then she followed him.

As James stepped through the double archway and his Nikes sank into plush off-white carpeting, he stopped. The room in front of him, a large, vaulted-ceilinged space two stories high, was a blur of white on white with only a touch of dark brown in the exposed overhead beams and a splash of deep red in the clay tiles in front of double entry doors that faced an oak staircase. The stairs were a winding sweep of carpet and bleached wood that led to a second level.

It was a beautifully proportioned room, but what had stopped James was the fact it was almost empty except for a loose-cushioned beige couch and two director's chairs that faced a raised adobe fireplace to the right. The only decorations in the room were black-and-white photos in white metallic frames propped on a four-inch-wide shelf that circled the room at eye level.

The kitchen seemed almost homey compared to this space. There was no warmth in here and no hint of the holidays. James glanced at Bree, who had silently passed him and gone to sit on the two-foot-high brick hearth. She looked at him, and his gaze locked with hers for a long moment.

She'd seen his assessment of the room, and she seemed almost to be daring him to make a comment. What could he say? A cold house and a cold room. But as he walked slowly across to the fireplace, he couldn't forget what he'd witnessed in the kitchen before Bree had known he was there. He couldn't forget the woman he'd held so briefly.

She was determinedly contained, almost painfully so, but that control had cracked during the phone call. Was she cold? He didn't think so. But something was wrong if she could live like this and if a phone call could produce so much pain for her that she would blindly turn to a stranger for support.

He stopped within two feet of Bree and fought the urge to ask who had been on the phone. Instead he watched her deliberately lift her leather purse and empty it on the bricks. A small assortment of items tumbled out—her wallet, a pair of sunglasses, wadded up tissues, two candy wrappers. No silver matchbook.

"That's everything," she said as she looked at James. She rested her hands on her knees and nervously scuffed at the thick carpet with her toes. He realized she'd been barefoot all along. "I would have told you it wasn't in there...if you'd given me a chance in the kitchen."

A glance to his right at one of the framed prints stopped any response he would have made. He went close to the nearest one.

A park at dusk, an empty swing, a cloud-heavy sky. He recognized a section of Balboa Park. The picture chilled James. He moved to the next. An old house, its door open, blackness inside, a single chair in the opening, its front leg broken. He glanced along the line of photos, then turned and found Bree standing about two feet from him.

A hint of delicate perfume wafted to him, the same gentle scent he remembered from the night before and when he'd held her moments ago. A beautiful woman, and he could admit she touched something in him, that she stirred him. Yet he couldn't help wondering what kind of soul took pictures like this.

He motioned to the prints and asked a question that merely filled space. "Are these yours?"

She nodded without speaking.

"What were you trying to do with them?"

Her eyes narrowed with a sweep of lush lashes. "What do you mean?"

"Your object in taking them, what was it?"

She shrugged, the action tugging the soft silk of her blouse across breasts that were fuller than James had first guessed. "To capture beauty, form, impressions, ideas," she recited in a husky voice.

He studied her, keeping his gaze on her face. "How about life?"

She blinked, and a touch of color stained her cheeks. "Pardon me?"

"Lady, there's no life in these pictures." He looked around the room. "The way there's hardly any furniture here, and no hint of Christmas."

When he looked at her, higher color dotted her face, the brightness accentuating the delicate line of her cheekbones. "I like it this way."

"Bare?"

"I haven't had time to really furnish it."

"You just moved in?"

"Six months ago, but I've been busy," she said, her tightening tone clearly showing her reluctance to answer any more questions. But James couldn't resist one more.

"Don't you celebrate Christmas?"

"No."

"For religious reasons?"

"No."

The single word hung between them, leaving him at a loss, so he tried to joke. "Are you the Christmas grinch?"

There was no humor in the brown-green depths of her eyes. Just a direct gaze from under the veil of her lashes. "No, I didn't steal Christmas. It's not worth it. I'm just ignoring it."

James knew in that moment that Bree couldn't be ignored, at least not by him. "You're missing all the joy and happiness of the season."

"I'm not missing anything," she said without a hint of hesitation, but a pulse fluttered rapidly in the hollow of her throat where her blouse parted.

"I'm sorry," he said without thinking.

"Why?" she asked, her chin lifting ever so slightly.

Because you're obviously hurting, he wanted to say, but couldn't. He didn't know her well enough to say what he thought—not yet. "Because you're missing the spirit of the season, I guess—caring and sharing, love and joy."

The dazed pain he'd seen when she'd turned to him in the kitchen flashed into her eyes and contorted her face, but only for a brief moment. And this time she didn't reach out. She retreated, ducking her head and going to sit on the hearth. But that glimpse was enough to cut James to the quick. He had never experienced such a need to comfort

another human being in his life. But he knew better than to
act on his instincts again.

So he put distance between the two of them. He crossed
to the couch, sank down on the soft cushions and leaned
forward. Lacing his fingers together as he rested his elbows
on his knees, he swallowed hard. When he spoke, his voice
sounded surprisingly steady. "I promised you an explanation for my apparent craziness."

"I don't need one. Your matchbook isn't here, so you can
go," she said in a breathless rush.

I won't let you get rid of me that easily, he thought. "But
I want you to understand," he persisted.

Bree had no fight left in her, so she took the path of least
resistance. If he explained, maybe he'd leave. Maybe he
didn't know anything about her. And maybe the look he'd
given her in the kitchen wasn't the same look she'd endured
after Dean's death—that look of pity and confusion, of interest yet repulsion. She nodded. "Go ahead."

She saw him take a deep breath, then he began to speak
in that rough yet oddly seductive voice touched with a hint
of a drawl. And after the first few words, she found herself
listening intently, probably because it blocked any more talk
about her house and Christmas. Possibly because the story
really fascinated her.

"I got a call at the station from a man named Murray
Landers. He owns the Cracked Cup Café—"

"I know the place," she said.

"He's had a woman working for him, Hannah Vickers.
She's probably close to eighty, tiny, white-haired. A street
person. She never said where she came from, but she showed
up there a couple of months ago, got a job and came to
work, regular as clockwork. She did odd jobs in the kitchen,
even cooked from time to time. He paid her for six hours a
day, but she'd stay ten or twelve sometimes, sitting out in the
café telling stories about old Hollywood and claiming to be
some long-forgotten silent screen actress. She'd only leave
when he closed the place for the night."

He ran a hand over his face, the intensity in his eyes tangible when he looked at Bree. "He said that a couple of weeks ago, she showed up in a red coat, a Christmas color, she told him, Santa's color. It had been the find of the year for her at one of the missions. She'd been excited about the lights he'd put up in the front windows and about the tiny tree on the end of the counter. Just over a week ago, she disappeared. She was there one day and nowhere to be found the next."

"What did he expect you to do?" Bree asked.

"Find her."

"The police?"

"They took a report, then nothing. They consider her a transient. There are more important things to work on, they think."

He told her about the man last night, about the matchbook and his search for it. When he finished, silence hung between them for several moments, then Bree sat back, not at all certain what to think. If what he said was true, and she felt almost certain it was, he didn't know who she was at all. He wasn't after her in any way. This was all some strange coincidence, and he only wanted the matchbook.

"If you find Hannah..." When his expression tightened, Bree amended her words. "*When* you find Hannah, what then?"

"I haven't thought that far ahead," he said and moved back, tugging one denim-clad leg up to rest his ankle on his other knee. Absentmindedly, he fiddled with the lace on his Nike. "First things first, I guess. I have to find her, then I'll worry about what to do from there."

Could a television reporter, a member of the media, really care about what happened to some old lady? Did it make any difference in his world if she ever showed up or not? James was a gentle man, she knew that much from the way he'd held her in the kitchen. She just wished that she knew how far that gentleness extended.

Bree studied him. His face was apparently open. The eyes under dark brows looked sincere. "This matchbook seems like a real long shot to me."

"It is," he said. "But it's all I have for now."

It didn't matter to her, not really, but Bree found herself wishing he could find that matchbook. Then he'd go on with his search for Hannah, never ask Bree questions again—and never touch her again. Abruptly she stood, that last thought making her feel a sadness that made no sense. "Maybe I should check and make sure it didn't fall out of the trash container."

He stood to face her. "I'll try anything."

She turned quickly and went through the kitchen into the darkroom. She snapped on the overhead light. Quickly, she pulled out the container again, looked behind it, then slid it back and stood. "I'm sorry. That's all there is."

He followed her into the room, the space way too small for both of them, and she quickly moved to one side and toward the door. "You can look again, if you like," she offered.

Without a word, he reached for the container, but this time he upended it and let everything spill onto the tiled floor. Silence hung heavily in the space while he hunkered down and methodically examined every piece of trash again.

After several minutes, he stood. "It was a long shot at best," he admitted.

With the doorjamb at her back, Bree met his gaze, almost feeling his disappointment herself. "You picked the matchbook up after the drunk dropped it and put it in your pocket. That's it?"

"That's the way it went," he said, crossing his arms, his shoulders testing the rough tweed of his jacket. "And I checked every inch of that damned street looking for it. It wasn't there."

"How about your coat?"

"What about it?"

"Did you check it?"

"Of course. I looked in the pocket and even pulled it inside out."

"It didn't have two pockets?"

"Yes, but the left one has a huge hole in it, so I never use it."

She had a sudden thought. "But what if you put it in the torn pocket by mistake?"

"It would have fallen through onto the street."

"Maybe not. When I was little, I was going out to play in the snow, and my mother gave me mittens to wear. I pushed them in my pockets, and when I went to put them on, one was gone. There was a hole in one pocket. The mitten fell into the lining and caught there."

His face lit up. "Damn, I never thought . . ."

"It's worth a look."

James saw the easing in her face, the interest that almost put a sparkle in her eyes. She was younger than he'd first thought. "Thank you for the idea," he said, and looked away, hoping to control whatever it was that she stirred in him. One thing he'd realized was that she was a lot younger than his own forty-one years. Too young.

That's when he saw the pictures on the worktable, and among them, pictures of him. He crossed and lifted one, staring into his own face with its scruffiness and hooded eyes. Way too old. "I thought you said you didn't take any of me."

He turned with the picture in his hand. The light in Bree was fading fast, and he wished he could do something to bring it back.

"I lied," she said softly. "I figured I didn't owe the truth to someone who pushed his way into my van."

James truly regretted that action, even more now than he had last night. "I was afraid you were the press or the police. I thought publicity right then might be dangerous for everyone concerned."

"I guess we're even, then," she said and suddenly smiled. The expression was so unexpected that it took James's breath away. But it fled as quickly as it had materialized, leaving his middle aching from the sudden pleasure it had given him.

He turned quickly to the other pictures on the counter-top. "You took all these of me?"

"You looked interesting. The angles and shadows."

"And I thought you were with the cops." He glanced at her. "You do good work. A lot of real feeling." It was true, he thought, but the feelings were those of emptiness and aloneness, maybe sadness.

She looked surprised. "Feeling?"

"Definitely."

She moved into the room and reached past him to push the prints into a stack. "I was just shooting at random. On impulse."

When she leaned over the worktable, her hair fell forward, parting at the back to expose the vulnerable line of her neck. "How old are you?" he asked, on impulse.

She turned, so close that he could see the way her delicate nostrils flared with each breath she took. "Why?"

"These shots are wisdom on film, but you don't look as if you've lived long enough to have all that wisdom."

"You don't have to be old to know about life," she said softly and continued methodically stacking the prints.

He watched her intently as he muttered, "True."

She turned to look at him. Green—her eyes were green shot with brown, he decided. "I'm twenty-six," she said.

Fifteen years difference. Practically a lifetime, he thought. "That old, eh?"

She flashed another smile, as fleeting as the first, gone before it could be fully enjoyed. Yet again it left its mark. "That old," she echoed.

"Too old for Christmas?" The words came out before he thought, and he regretted them immediately.

She sobered completely, and the life went out of her eyes. *Damn you, James,* he thought to himself. *You couldn't let it be!*

Before he could do or say anything to make things better, Bree stooped and began to put the trash in the container. "Why does everyone think the Christmas spirit can save the world?" she asked, her voice muffled yet infused with very recognizable sarcasm.

"You care, James," Carson had told him when he'd found him in Chicago eight months ago and talked him into going back into television. "That's why you can't be happy unless you're helping people. We want you at Channel Three. Direct your caring in a positive way. Sometimes you care too much, but you care."

James stooped beside Bree and helped her refill the container. Caring. His arm brushed hers, and although only tweed brushed silk, awareness shot through him.

Cautiously, he glanced into eyes as wary as he felt. He wasn't going to examine the whys and wherefores too closely, but he could admit to himself that he wanted to help Bree every bit as much as he wanted to find Hannah. And that meant he couldn't leave her now. He had to figure out how to stay with her. Then he remembered her pictures, and he had his answer.

Chapter 4

Rocked by the appraising intensity in James's expression, Bree stood quickly, out of self-protection. She crossed to the door as he finished picking up the mess and stood very still. Finally he straightened, pushed the wastebasket into the corner, then looked at her. Thankfully he kept the distance between them intact.

"I've got a proposition for you," he said abruptly.

She blinked and felt heat flood her face. "Pardon me?"

"A *business* proposition," he amended hastily.

"I'm not looking for work, Mr. Chapman."

"James, please call me James," he said as he destroyed the buffer of distance with one stride. "Actually, I need your help."

"I don't know where the matchbook is. It could be in the coat lining, but..."

"I'll look there, but this isn't about that. You asked me what I'll do when I find Hannah. I just realized what I'm going to do. It won't be just a segment on *Heart of the Matter*. I want it to be a special after the holidays when everyone's good cheer has waned. It's then that most forget about the poor and the lonely. I can talk Carson Davies, the station manager, into doing it. I'd like part of it to be music and narration combined with your black-and-white stills."

Bree knew she didn't have it in her to cope with any entanglement with other people's lives. She could barely deal with her own. She tried to decline as simply as possible. "I do prints for publication in books or for shows in galleries, not for television. I wouldn't be any good at that."

"Yes, you would," he insisted. "I know you have the ability to catch the soul of the people down there, and Hannah's one of those people."

His statement about catching the soul of the people really stopped her. That was exactly what she hadn't tried to do—not now, not for a year. "I don't think . . ."

"It wouldn't take much time, and if you aren't celebrating the holidays, you'll have more time than most. You could come with me, take the shots, then we can go over them and decide what to use for the special."

She wanted to add the qualifier that there might be no special if the elderly woman wasn't found, or, worse, was found dead. But she didn't because it suddenly struck her that this opportunity might be just what she needed. If she could honestly tell her mother that she had commitments here, a job she couldn't walk away from, she might leave her alone until after the holidays.

While she was thinking, James suddenly asked, "How much would you want to do it?"

Money? She had more than enough for ten people to live on for a hundred years. She didn't want more. All she wanted was to be rescued from having to go home for the holidays. Could this blue-eyed man who had started out as an intruder end up being her rescuer?

"I'll donate my services to help the cause," she blurted, feeling momentarily guilty for sounding so charitable when the project was a means to her own ends.

"We'll have to pay you at least a token amount," James said.

Bree felt relieved as they negotiated for the work, as if a huge burden had fallen off her shoulders. She could put in some time taking pictures and be done with it. "Make it very token," she said.

"Then we have a deal?" He held out his hand to her.

Quickly, before she could back out, she put her hand in his. The physical contact was a mistake, she realized when she felt his touch surround her with seductive warmth and strength. It almost made her want to keep holding him, the way she had clung to him earlier. Almost. Abruptly she pulled back, but not before she saw a smile crinkle his eyes and curl his lips. The expression was every bit as seductive as his touch.

She rubbed her hands together. "A deal," she whispered.

James wondered how he could ever talk Carson into doing this special with the never-ending budget problems at the station, but pushed the thought aside. The station was doing better, and Carson owed him. He wouldn't be above reminding his boss of that very thing. For now he was satisfied that he'd found a way to have continued contact with Bree, even if the special never got on the air. "We need to get going on this. Why don't we go to the station so I can introduce you to Carson? And we need to tear into that old coat."

"Right now?"

"The sooner the better."

Bree's tongue touched her lipstick-free mouth, and for an instant he was certain she'd try to back out. But surprisingly, she didn't. "All right. Let's get this over with," she said. "Wait here while I put on some shoes."

"The sooner the better," he murmured as she turned from him and hurried to the kitchen. When she was gone, he leaned against the counter and ran a hand over his face. He'd jumped into this with both feet, and he had no idea where it was going to lead. This was going to be a very strange Christmas indeed.

He looked again at the prints, then reached for them and shuffled through them. He stopped at one of the shots. So she'd not only taken pictures of him last night, she'd taken a picture of the old drunk who'd dropped the matchbook.

James studied the picture, then frowned at one of him. Bree's explanation for taking the shots had seemed valid, but when he looked at the way he'd appeared last night, he couldn't begin to see what had appealed to her. He looked like a real bum.

He glanced at the ceiling as soft thumping sounds of Bree moving around on the second floor caught his attention. "You're crazy, Chapman," he muttered to himself. "Damn crazy."

He heard Bree walking toward the front of the house, then the sound of her footsteps coming down the stairs. His eyes followed the soft noises until she appeared in the doorway. She had put on a short, white poplin jacket, and hadn't bothered with any makeup. He conceded that she didn't need anything to enhance her beauty.

Bree McFarland might have lied to him last night about taking his pictures, but he had certainly told her the truth moments ago. Her work did touch him. Her work touched him deep in his soul—just as the woman in front of him did.

"Let me get my equipment," she said a bit breathlessly. "Then we can get going."

James picked up the two pictures on the counter, one of him, one of the drunk. "Can I have these?"

She glanced at them, then reached to a shelf over the work area and handed him a large brown envelope to put them in. "Keep them," she said.

"On the news at six, we'll have the latest on the apparent connection of Wayne Concklin to the investigation into the murder of Detective Andrew Dawson.

"Also at six we'll meet George Leone on *Heart of the Matter*. When Mr. Leone played Good Samaritan and called 911 to report a robbery in a downtown office building, he became entangled in a bureaucratic mess that resulted in his own arrest. Find out how Channel Three's people reporter, James Chapman, helped him fight for his rights...and win."

As James turned off the freeway north of the city and headed east, Bree began to realize how impulsive her decision to work with him had been. There should have been another way to get out of going home for the holidays, another excuse her mother would have understood. But she'd chosen involvement, something she didn't want—especially not with this blue-eyed man who was spending his holidays looking for some elderly woman who might or might not be an old silent screen star.

"Why are you putting so much effort into finding one elderly lady?" Bree asked, really wanting to know. "Is it going to be that big a story?"

James raked a hand through his silver-streaked hair, a mannerism Bree was beginning to recognize usually accompanied deep thought or nervousness on his part. Then he lowered his hand to the steering wheel. "Good questions," he said. "As far as the size of the story or its importance, I doubt that it will get much notice. It'll blend with the other stories on the less fortunate. I thought of playing up the angle of her being a silent movie star. Maybe I still will if I find out she really was involved in Hollywood back then.

"I think the real bottom line to this whole thing is I hate it when no one cares. I've seen enough of that in this world."

Bree wondered if he'd ever found out how painful it was to care, to really care about someone, but she closed off that potential path to the past even as it began to open. The dreams were bad enough. Holding tightly to the purse on her lap, she said, "Murray, the owner of the café, seems to care about Hannah."

"That's why he called me. He was watching my segment on the news and decided to see if I could do anything for him. He's trusting me to find her."

As she listened to James, Bree understood why he did well with his *Heart of the Matter* segments. His voice was low and edged with roughness, not the traditional velvety tones at all, but it held something more, something better—a quality that encouraged trust, that could soothe and fascinate at the same time.

She slanted him a look. Much the same way the man himself did. James Chapman had something that demanded closer scrutiny. Charisma? Maybe. Whatever it was, it drew at Bree the woman, and it fascinated Bree the artist. It had lured her into using almost a full role of film on him, and it had convinced her to work for him. She didn't understand either appeal. She pushed the confusion aside as James pointed ahead of them.

"We're almost there," he said.

She hadn't really noticed her surroundings after they'd exited from the freeway. Now she looked around at the broad four-lane street with green Christmas garlands hung with red bells draped overhead, crisscrossing from power pole to power pole above the lanes. Then James turned a corner onto a narrower road and passed a small shopping center.

Even with a scattering of holiday decorations here and there, the street looked bleak. Leafless trees mingled with towering eucalyptus to line a street dominated by cement-block commercial buildings.

"That is where it all happens," he said and pointed to a sprawling building partway down the block on the left.

Bree couldn't have missed it. A huge logo on glaring white walls, visible above a ten-foot-high, ivy-covered security fence, was an eight-foot-tall duplicate of the one on James's T-shirt—a red heart slashed with brilliant blue lettering: KHRT, Channel Three, San Diego's Station with a Heart.

As James drove closer to the three-story building, Bree saw the sparse landscaping of low junipers lining the front walls, a few ancient eucalyptus near the road and two bottle brush at the entry. James drove past the front, where a banner had been draped above glass doors wishing everyone a Merry Christmas from Channel Three.

He turned into a driveway, passed the parking area marked for visitors and stopped at a solid black-metal gate set in the ivy-covered fence. As he rummaged in a pocket on the car door, Bree conceded that any preconceived notions she'd had about the glamour of television stations had been sadly wrong. Everything seemed unrelentingly utilitarian, so much so that it was almost as painful to her artistic eye as the gaudy logo.

James spoke up as if he'd read her mind. "Television stations aren't all that glamorous, and Channel Three isn't any exception." He finally pulled out a plastic card, rolled down his window and reached out to push the card into a slot on a black security box. As the gate slid open, he tucked the card into the door pocket, then drove into a sprawling parking lot half filled with cars.

On the right was a fenced area that held three satellite dishes and, on the left were two panel vans with the garish logo on their gleaming white sides. Obviously Channel Three was determined to let the world know it had a heart, she thought, amused.

"Have you ever been to a television station before?"

The question threatened to bring back the memories. Someone from a New York station had found a way to get her unlisted phone number and had called to offer her a great deal of money to do an interview about Dean. She'd hung up and unplugged the phone from the wall. That night she'd made her decision to move as far away as possible. "No, never," she said flatly.

"We create illusions in this business and don't need much space to do it," James said as he slipped the Bronco into a slot just past the vans, a space labeled Employee of the Week on a cement bumper.

"Most of what we broadcast is network feed or done from our own videotapes," he continued, not waiting for her to comment. "We have three sets, two for news, editorials and specials, that sort of thing. Then one for our morning show, *Dawn in the City*, which we rent out for other uses. The sets sparkle and shimmer for the cameras, but behind the glitz are curtains to create the illusion of space, equipment, more equipment, hard floors and lights that would heat the studio to a hundred and twenty degrees in minutes if we didn't counter it with air-conditioning. It's all for looks and illusions," he said as he turned off the motor. "And it's all hard work."

"I wouldn't have thought you were cynical," she commented.

He looked at her, his head cocked to the side, one dark eyebrow elevated slightly. "I'm not cynical," he said, his voice a shade deeper. "I'm just one of the last genuine realists in this world."

"And you're also the employee of the week?" she asked.

"Never have been. Never will be. That's a reality." He flashed her a grin. "Carson knows me too well. But—" he held up one finger "—I happen to know the employee of the week, and he's so set in his ways I'd bet the farm he parked in his usual assigned spot behind the building." He shrugged. "No use leaving this empty."

With that, James got out into the pale light of the winter sun and pocketed his keys. Bree scrambled out, too, wishing he wouldn't smile like that at her. She wasn't a TV audience he needed to win over. "Do I need my camera?" she asked across the hood of the Bronco as she put her purse strap over her shoulder.

"No, not here. Leave it in the car and I'll lock up." He turned the key in the door. Waiting for her to come around to his side, he casually caught her by the elbow. Short of pulling free and embarrassing herself, Bree didn't know how to end the contact, so she endured his hold as they walked past the vans along a cracked cement walkway and stopped at a door marked Employees Only.

James opened the door, then let go of Bree so she could precede him into the building, into a wide hall decorated with the logo's bright primary colors. Christmas music played softly, and a security guard sat behind a small table by the door.

When he looked up, he dropped the book he'd been reading and scrambled to his feet. Hurriedly he put on a cap that matched his blue uniform and stiffened to attention. "Mr. Chapman," the short, middle-aged man said, tugging at his belt to hitch his pants higher. "Wasn't expecting you, sir."

"Merry Christmas to you, too, Marv," James said with a crooked smile. "How're you doing?"

"Fine, sir." He glanced at Bree. "Does the lady need a pass?"

"No, we won't be here long," James said. "And relax, Marv. You're not guarding national secrets. Besides, there's enough stress in this world without having to stand at attention every time someone comes through that door."

The man colored a bit, but nodded. "You're right about that." He sank onto the chair. "Merry Christmas to both of you."

"Merry Christmas," James echoed and started down the hall to the left.

Bree saw Marv reach for his book again as she turned to follow James. The warm air was scented with hints of coffee and cigarette smoke, and the ever-present Christmas carols continued to play softly. In every movie Bree had seen about television, there had been frantic activity, but there was none here. There wasn't a person in sight, just boxes and packages lining the wall. James had been right. The glitz of television was an illusion.

"Our studios are the other way. Offices are this way. The things in the hall are being stored. I think Carson actually rents the space for so much a square foot." He motioned her ahead of him. "My office is around the corner."

The peace was suddenly shattered by the sound of running feet and loud voices jumbled together. Two men came around the corner. "Get set up," someone called after them. "I'll get Daryl there as soon as I find him."

James pulled Bree to the right near some boxes. "Kyle, George," James said as the two men ran past, each carrying black boxes and wearing bright blue Channel Three windbreakers.

"Short vacation, eh, James?" one called as he disappeared through the door.

"Later, James," the tallest said over his shoulder as he followed the first man. "Got to get downtown. There's a story breaking," he finished, then called to the guard as he started out the door. "Buzz the gate, Marv." And they were gone.

"James?"

Bree turned and saw a tiny woman with ebony hair feathered around a startlingly beautiful face coming from the same direction as the men had. But she walked slowly, and her violet eyes were filled with confusion. "I didn't think I'd be seeing you here until the new year."

"I postponed the vacation. What's going on?" James asked.

She smoothed a clinging jersey dress that matched the shade of her eyes and acknowledged Bree with a flashing smile before looking at James. "I came in to do some editing for the show, and a call came through that the police found someone they've been looking for, something about the murder of that policeman last week. The crew just headed out."

She motioned behind her with a nod of her head. "Carson's yelling because he can't find Daryl, and he's threatening to go down and do the remote himself. Since I have no desire to get mixed up with anyone's temper—" she rolled her lavender eyes upward "—I decided to get out of the way." She fiddled with a delicate gold cross that lay on the pleated front of her dress. "I wouldn't want to be Daryl if he blows this."

"Couldn't they send out John or Stacey?" James asked.

The cross fell from her fingers. "The story's really big. He wants Daryl, and what he wants, as you know, he usually gets." She looked at Bree. "I don't think we've met, have we?"

"Jill . . . Bree McFarland," James said. "She's going to help me on a special I'm working on." He glanced at Bree. "Jillian Segar is the cohost of *Dream Chasers*, our travel show."

Bree knew she looked blank and wished she'd watched some television since getting to San Diego. Especially when she heard James explain quickly. "She doesn't watch television, Jill. She didn't even know who I was."

"I hear ten percent of the population doesn't own a television," the tiny woman said with a smile.

"Oh, I've got one," Bree said quickly, her cheeks warm. "But I never hooked it up."

James stepped in. "What's your considered opinion of Carson's present mood?"

"Lousy," Jill said without hesitating. "On a scale of one to ten, he'd be lucky to get a two." She wrinkled her nose. "He could use some fresh air, or something stronger."

"I need to talk to him, but . . ."

"Use your own discretion. I need to get to work." She tapped James on the shoulder good-naturedly. "Good luck with Carson." She looked at Bree. "Nice meeting you," she added, and walked down the hall.

"I think we should look at the coat first," James said.

Bree agreed. "Sure. Whatever you think." She followed James around the corner into another wide hallway. For a minute she caught a glimpse of what must be the lobby through glass doors, an area that came close to being flamboyant with mirrors, crystal chandeliers and vibrant blue carpet. A ten-foot-tall silver Christmas tree by the entry doors had been decorated with blue and red bulbs and twinkling lights.

Bree followed James down the hall and rounded another corner into a long corridor lined with closed doors, ending thirty feet away with double doors of natural wood. She could hear muffled voices over the Christmas music, but she couldn't make out anything they were saying.

James touched her arm to stop her at the second door on the right. "Mine," he said. One word, done in brilliant blue, was painted on the door: Chapman. He pushed the door open and stood back.

Bree stepped past him into a square room with beige carpeting, a large metal desk under a curtainless window and posters of late sixties and early seventies rock groups papering the walls. A huge poster of the Beatles hung above a brown tweed couch. "A real fan?" she murmured as she went closer to the desk.

James came in after her and the door clicked closed. "A passion of long standing. When I was in 'Nam my favorite song was 'Satisfaction' by—"

"The Rolling Stones," she finished as she turned to look at him.

He seemed impressed. "I didn't think you'd know that."

"I've heard of the Stones," she said with a smile.

"Obviously you're into nostalgia," he muttered and motioned to a ratty coat hanging over the chair and a pile of old clothes at one end of the couch. "Talk about nostalgia."

Bree stared at the faded coat. "Where did you get it?"

"At a used clothing store," he said as he reached for the coat. He turned to her as he held it up by its shoulders. "A coat like this can mean the difference between freezing and just being cold to most people on the street."

Bree wondered what had happened to that coat she'd torn the pocket in as a child. She knew only that it had been gone the next day, a new one in its place.

James walked toward her, shook out the coat and laid it flat on the floor in front of the desk. Then he dropped to his knees and flipped the heavy material back to expose a lining that, amazingly, was completely intact.

Bree dropped down beside James and spotted a bulge at the soiled hemline at the same time James reached out to touch it with one finger.

"I'll be damned," he said under his breath as he traced the rectangular lump.

"A matchbook?" she asked, shocked at the satisfaction she felt at having guessed correctly.

"Only one way to tell," James said and grabbed the old fabric in both hands. He tugged sharply, the lining ripped, and a bright silver matchbook tumbled to the beige carpet. "That's it." James looked at Bree. "You knew what you were talking about," he said softly, and without warning, he smiled and pulled her into the circle of his arms.

Chapter 5

Bree had heard the expression "bear hug," and now she knew what it meant. She felt surrounded and overwhelmed by the sense of being precariously close to losing herself in the essence of this man. A frightening thought that barely had time to materialize before his voice rumbled against her cheek. "Way to go."

Then he was moving back, his touch leaving her, and she felt suddenly adrift, as if a lifeline had been snatched from her grasp. Nervously she dragged her gaze away from James to the matchbook lying between them, and she watched him pick it up. He looked at it, at its only marking, a fancy F on its sleek surface. He opened it. "Nothing," he murmured. "Not even matches."

"Can I have a look?" Bree asked and took the silver object. She sat on her heels and studied it, forcing herself to concentrate on it instead of James inches from her. It had been so long since she'd been held, been able to lean against anyone, and it had happened twice in one day with this man. An emotional reaction, she reasoned as she opened the matchbook, then closed it and turned it over. Graphic Originals was printed in a deeper silver along the bottom edge, an almost invisible insignia. No address or phone number. "Is there anything with an F associated with Hannah?" she asked.

"Not that I know of." She looked at James, unnerved to see him looking as disappointed as she was beginning to feel.

"What was her last name again?"

He stroked his mustache with his forefinger as he stared at the book. "Vickers, and I can't see anyone down there having monogrammed matchbooks. Certainly not the old guy who dropped it. It was a long shot, but I'd hoped..." he stood abruptly and ran both hands over his face. "He must have just picked it up by chance."

"But where?" she asked as she looked at the book again. "This isn't cheap. It's a specialty book."

He towered over her. "A specialty book?"

"When someone has a big party or a coming out or a large—" She stopped, not wanting to finish with "political fund-raiser." "A wedding," she ad-libbed. "Printers make them up specially." She held out the book. "Graphic Originals, in this case."

A knock sounded on the door and immediately it opened. Bree twisted to her left and looked up as a blond man came into the room. "James, I'm glad you're here. I have that information and..." His voice trailed off when he saw Bree getting up.

James stood. "Bree, this is Bryan Lake. He's in research. Bryan, Bree McFarland. She's going to help me with my story on Hannah Vickers."

Slightly built and immaculately dressed in a sweater, shirt and smartly creased slacks, Bryan Lake looked at her in the strangest way. "Nice to meet you," he said finally, then he looked at James. "I guess you don't need what I found, do you?"

"As a matter of fact, I do." He looked at Bree. "I'll be right back." She watched him follow Bryan into the hall and close the door after him.

As she stared at a blue blazer, a white shirt and red and blue striped tie hanging on a wooden peg on the back of the door, she thought about how uncomfortable she felt that a stranger could make her question her decision to be alone. But that didn't change the fact she'd made the decision.

With a shrug, she turned and reached for the telephone book on the desk. It didn't make any difference. She wouldn't be around James long enough to figure out why he could make her so confused.

James moved a good ten feet down the hall away from his office before he stopped and turned to Bryan. "All right. What did you find out?" he asked in a low voice.

Bryan motioned to James's office. "Since you have the real thing in there, what do you need my information for?"

"Humor me," James said.

Bryan leaned against the wall and crossed his arms. "I wasn't sure I had the right Sabrina McFarland until I walked into your office. She's the one, although her pictures don't do her justice. Her name's Sabrina Afton McFarland-Gregory. She's a photographer. She does those huge books that people put on their coffee tables for show. Two years ago she got all sorts of attention back East when she did one on the ages of America—the newborn to the oldest living citizen. She even had a showing of the individual prints at an exclusive New York gallery. I found a copy of the book in our library. Beautiful work. Really beautiful. You should look at it."

"Anything else?" James asked, impatient to know more about the woman in his office.

Bryan studied James, his eyes narrowed. "You don't know any of this, do you?"

James tucked his fingertips into the pockets of his jeans. He exhaled. "I know she's a photographer and she lives alone." *And she's in pain,* he thought, but kept that observation to himself.

"But you don't know who she really is?"

James rocked forward. "Tell me what I *don't* know, Bryan." His nerves were getting raw. "Come on, put me out of my misery."

"All right. A year ago her husband died. He was a potential political whiz kid being groomed for the Senate and who knows what else. Dean Gregory."

James thought he'd heard the name when he'd been in Chicago, but he couldn't focus on any particular story. Politics hadn't interested him in years. "How did he die?"

"A heart attack at their home in Connecticut."

James felt a chill creeping up his spine. "Was Bree with him?"

"No. She found him, and the story went on every news wire. It made every major network in the country, partly because of who Gregory was, and partly because of Bree. Have you ever heard of the Henry McFarlands?"

James nodded as he rocked back. "The manufacturing family that made millions in plastics, isn't it?"

"Yes, and the lady in your office is their youngest daughter. The last of six children, four girls and two boys. The story was big for a while. She made a good marriage to Gregory, who was an old family friend, then he died. Gregory was only thirty-two. He would've entered the Senate race next year. A real tragedy. She hid out at her parents' home for a while, but the last time she was in the news was a small blurb about six months ago. She dropped out of sight completely." He lifted one eyebrow. "Now I know where she dropped to."

James understood the fear in her eyes when she'd found out he was with a television station. She'd no doubt thought he was after a story on her. "How long was she married to Gregory?"

"Three years."

Pain collected behind his breastbone as James faced the fact of how much Bree must have loved her husband. The grief was still there. And the pain. A part of him had been wanting her to be unmarried, but not like this. He swallowed hard. "Bryan, when exactly did Gregory die?"

"A year ago on Christmas Eve."

James felt his discomfort increase. That explained so much. He felt vaguely unsteady for a moment, then reached out to pat Bryan on the shoulder. "Thanks for everything. I appreciate it." He hesitated. "One more thing?"

"Sure."

"Don't mention what you know about her to anyone around here. I think she's been through enough, and I don't want some aggressive reporter thinking he should do a story on her." He pushed his hands into his pockets. "Besides, she'll only be helping me for a few days." That fact stated out loud only made James feel worse.

"I understand."

"Thanks."

"I need to get going. Carson wants me to dig into the background of the suspect in the killing of the cop near the mall. The police are bringing him in now. As soon as I get some free time, I'll try digging around about Hannah Vickers again."

"Whenever you can."

James watched Bryan head down the hall, then he returned to his office. He pushed the door back and looked at Bree sitting on the floor in front of the desk, her legs tucked under her with her jacket and purse by her side on the carpet. The phone book was open on the floor in front of her.

She looked up when he came into the room, and he almost said that he knew who she was, that she didn't have to worry about him digging into her past or trying to do a story on her. But she spoke before he could say anything.

"Can I ask you something?" she said in a soft voice.

He closed the door and crossed the carpet to drop to his haunches in front of her. "Anything at all."

Bree never took her eyes off him, her brown-green gaze direct and unblinking. "Is Bryan the one who found out where I live for you?"

That question rocked James, and he had a hard time keeping eye contact. "Yes," he managed, and heard the flatness in his tone of voice.

An edge of wariness crept into her gaze. "What else did he tell you about me?" she asked, sitting a bit straighter.

He knew right then that she was ready to run if he admitted the truth. So he hedged with a selective truth. "He got your address for me from the DMV." He stood and reached into the pocket of his jacket. "Here," he said and held out the crumpled note from Bryan.

She hesitated, then dropped the matchbook on the open telephone book and took the small piece of paper from him. She smoothed it on her knee, looked at the scrawled writing on the white paper and with a sigh leaned against the desk. "He's good at what he does, isn't he?"

He'd passed a test of sorts, and he felt a knot in his middle easing just a bit. Admitting he knew more about her wouldn't do any good right now. "Very good," he agreed. Pushing the note into his pocket, he motioned to the open telephone book. "What are you looking for?"

"Graphic Originals," she said, pointing to an ad in the yellow pages. She read it to him.

While he listened to her husky voice, he began to feel just a bit foolish. He wasn't about to admit it, but he was coming very close to being jealous of a dead man. When she looked up at him expectantly, he met the full impact of her beauty and it was all he could do to manage a murmured, "Good work."

Color brushed her cheeks before Bree looked away and picked up the matchbook. "What now?" she asked as she got to her feet.

"Work," he said and moved to put some distance between them. His thinking wasn't entirely clear, and her closeness was making it even more foggy.

She bent to pick up the phone book and put it on the desk, then she looked at James. "Maybe you could start by calling Graphic Originals?"

He watched her fingering the matchbook, then nodded and reached for the phone. Taking their number from the book, he dialed. After two rings, a prerecorded message came on. "Thanks for calling Graphic Originals. Our offices are closed for the holidays, but we'll be back at work the day after New Year's. Happy holidays, and remember Graphic Originals for all your custom printing needs."

"They're closed for the holidays," he said, but he'd barely put the receiver in the cradle when the phone rang. He picked it up. "James Chapman."

"Murray Landers, Mr. Chapman. I need to talk to you. Can you come down here today?"

"Sure." He looked at his leather-strapped wristwatch. "I can be there within the hour."

"Great. Come to the kitchen door like you did the first time. We're really full up front with the lunch crowd." He hesitated, then asked, "You haven't found anything, have you?"

James hated to tell him the truth. "No, I'm sorry, but I've got a few ideas."

"I hope you've got lots of ideas." He paused. "I've got another problem."

"What is it?"

"Come on down. I'll tell you everything when you get here." And he hung up.

James slowly lowered the receiver to the cradle, then turned to look at Bree. "That was Murray Landers, the man Hannah worked for. He needs to talk to me."

She had put her jacket on and was doing up the buttons. "About Hannah?"

"I suppose so. We can go there, then start looking for shooting sites around the neighborhood."

She freed her hair from the collar of her jacket with a flip and looked at James from under feathery lashes. "Can you go down there like that?"

"Like what?"

She motioned toward James. "Last night you were afraid someone would know you're with the station. That—" she pointed to his bright T-shirt logo "—is like a neon sign, don't you think?"

He chuckled at her words, but knew exactly what she was saying. "You're right. I may as well put the logo on my forehead." He looked at the old clothes still on the couch. "I'm not getting into those again until I have to. We can drop by my place on the way, and I'll change."

Bree never would have guessed that James lived in an obviously upwardly mobile apartment complex in the hills just south of Balboa Bay about ten miles from the station. While he went inside to change, she stayed in the Bronco at the apex of the street, facing a sweeping panorama of the city to the east and the blue smudge of the Pacific to the west.

She would have expected James to prefer a refurbished house, maybe a Victorian or an older bungalow, not this determinedly Spanish-style complex that stood six stories high. Palms and wrought iron were geared to an upscale image, as were the cars on the sloping street—no cheap transportation in sight.

She shifted in the seat, wondering how she could be so far off the mark in sizing people up. Was she naive? She'd certainly been that in her life. She closed her eyes tightly for a moment. Trusting was more like it. She'd trusted Dean. She'd believed him, and she hadn't admitted a thing was wrong until reality hit her straight in the face. Hugging herself, she took deep, even breaths. Enough of that. The dreams couldn't be controlled, but she could control her waking thoughts.

She opened her eyes as James strode through the building's open gates. He looked at her, their gazes connected, and as he hurried toward the Bronco, he smiled. She was no more prepared for it than she would have been for an electric shock, and by the time she managed an answering smile, he was coming around the car and getting inside.

He settled behind the wheel, then turned to her and pulled open his jacket to show a black, lightweight turtleneck pullover. "Can I pass without being noticed now?"

She doubted that he'd ever go unnoticed, that anyone who had once seen him would be able to forget his face—or his smile—but she nodded. "That's fine."

He glanced at his watch. "It's almost noon. Let's get going." He started the engine and eased out into the street and down the hill to the freeway. As they neared the North Bay area, James drove off the freeway and past industrial buildings into the refurbished older section of San Diego's downtown.

Bree had seen it at night, but it was every bit as fascinating in the clear light of day. The beautiful old buildings had been kindly refurbished, taking nothing from their history, but giving them a new lease on life.

When the traffic on the four-lane street slowed to a crawl, Bree looked ahead and saw crowds on the southern sidewalk half a block ahead. A policeman waved at the cars, urging them to keep moving.

"I wonder what's going on?" she muttered. Two police cars pulled to the curb at a side street, heading the wrong way on the one-way street. And right by one of the patrol cars was a Channel Three van. "Look, your station's here," she said, then spotted two policemen heading for one of the squad cars with a man between them.

The man had his hands behind his back, and his completely bald head was bowed. A uniformed policeman on either side urged him toward the squad car. Flashbulbs and Minicams seemed to be everywhere, and she spotted the two men she'd seen running from the Channel Three building about three feet from the prisoner. A man with red hair was pushing a microphone as close as possible to the police and their prisoner.

James kept going slowly past the street and the commotion. "Daryl got here after all for the big story. That'll make Carson happy, especially if it helps the ratings."

"Ratings are everything, aren't they?" she asked, remembering one appeal a reporter had made to her in the days after Dean's death. "Help me get the ratings points, and I'll say whatever you want on the air," he'd promised her.

"Ratings are money in the bank," James said. "That's the bottom line." He looked ahead. "All these streets are one-way now. We'll have to turn at the next street and double back."

At the next corner, he turned south and went down a hilly street past a multitiered mall with stained-glass windows and heavily ornate cornices at the roofline. A huge pine, at least twenty feet high, stood at the entrance, heavy with gold and silver Christmas decorations.

They passed the mall and Bree looked ahead at the Fenwick Theater on the left, fronted by a series of gas street lamps at the curb. Its obvious age was offset by a sleekly modern, three-tiered parking garage to the south. A crew of men in white coveralls was polishing the brass handles on the doors of the theater, cleaning the glass and running a buffer over the marble stairs. Two more were hanging a banner above the ticket office, but Bree couldn't make out the lettering on it.

"It looks like the theater's about to open," she murmured as they drove past it down the hill.

"New Year's Eve. They want to show off what their twelve-million-dollar rejuvenation budget achieved."

James crossed an intersection and suddenly there were no more gas lamps or beautiful facades. Here the reconstruction was still a plan on paper, not a reality on the streets. Cheap bars, bail bond offices, tattoo shops and liquor stores lined the way, and each had a touch of dreary Christmas decorations.

He turned left, and the second street they came to was where Bree had first spotted James. But he drove past it. Less than half a block beyond, he turned right into an alley that ran behind the businesses, a trash-littered service passage with uneven concrete pavement, graffiti-marred walls and barred rear windows.

"Where are you going?" she asked as they passed a derelict rummaging through a Dumpster.

"To the Cracked Cup. I don't want to go in the front way...just in case. I came this way my first time down here." He pulled to a stop by a chalky brown door with the café's name written on it in faded paint.

James waited for Bree to get out in the chilly air with her camera and close her door. Then he reached over and hit the door lock, got out on his side and walked with her to the restaurant's back door. He rapped twice on the wooden barrier, and it was opened by a reed-thin man with sparse gray hair and wire-framed bifocals.

He squinted at them. "Mr. Chapman."

"I thought we had it settled that you'd call me James," he said. "And this is Bree. She's helping with some photography. Bree...Murray Landers."

The man wiped his right hand on the brown apron he wore over a faded plaid shirt and baggy pants, then offered it to Bree. "Nice to meet you, miss. Merry Christmas."

She shook hands with him, a bit surprised at the sure strength in his grip. "You own the restaurant?" she asked just to say something that didn't have a thing to do with the holiday season.

"Owner, manager, cook, dishwasher," he said with a tight smile as he stood back and motioned them both inside.

Bree stepped past James into a cavernous kitchen where warmth and the fragrance of cooking turkey mingled in the most pleasant way. But as she got a good look at the space in front of her, she felt a bit depressed to see that the aura of the room was more pleasant than the reality.

Everything looked old and worn, from the chipped sinks by a walk-in refrigerator to a massive three-oven stove that looked as if it should use wood for fuel to a blackened grill and a slightly tilted work island in the middle of a floor done in dull brown tiles. A pass-through window by double doors let in the strains of "Jingle Bells," the low drone of conversation and the clink of glasses.

A wooden block table held a small television that was tuned to a news program. On the wall behind the thin-faced newscaster were the station's call letters and the words News at Noon.

"We'll have more on the investigation into the murder of Detective Dawson," the newscaster was saying, "and more about a man who was just picked up for questioning, bartender Wayne Concklin. All of that after this message from our sponsors."

With a disgusted snort, Murray crossed to the television and flicked it off. "Nothing good happening around here anymore," he muttered as he dropped into one of the chairs at the table. He motioned James and Bree to chairs, and as they settled, he rocked onto the back legs of his chair and called over his shoulder, "Nate! Where'd you get to?"

A heavyset man with a wild mop of black hair and a long gray beard that hid most of his face looked into the kitchen. He did a double take when he saw James and Bree, but didn't ask any questions. "Something wrong, boss?"

"Take care of the front until I get up there, and if you get any more orders, send Frank back here to make them."

"Sure thing, boss," he said and drew out of sight.

Murray's chair hit the floor with a thud as he sat forward. "Thanks for coming so fast." But instead of saying why he'd asked James down, he stood abruptly. "You two hungry?" he asked.

Her last food had been a candy bar last night, and with her appetite having been almost nonexistent for so long,

Bree was surprised at her sudden hunger. "I'm starved," she admitted.

Before she could say another thing, Murray was halfway across the kitchen. "We've got homemade vegetable soup or sandwiches or both. Or I could make you a burger. What would you like?"

"Soup sounds wonderful," Bree said.

James agreed. "Soup."

Murray took two bowls out of a drainer by the sink, then crossed to the stove. "Made just yesterday. After Christmas, we'll have turkey soup as the special for a month."

"What's the problem you spoke about on the phone?" James asked as Murray set bowls filled with steaming soup in front of them.

"This place is going crazy." He took spoons and napkins from one of the pockets in his apron. "A cop's murdered just blocks away and people disappear into thin air. It's crazy. Pure and simple. You want something to drink?"

"Milk's fine," James said and looked at Bree.

By the time she nodded agreement, Murray was in the walk-in refrigerator. "What happened, Murray?" James called after him.

"Old William didn't show up last night for work." His voice came out the open door. "Then he didn't show for work today." He appeared with two cartons of milk. Stopping to take glasses from a tray by the sink, he came back to the table and gave them to Bree and James. Finally he sat, leaned forward and pressed both his hands flat on the tabletop. "Gone, into thin air, just like Hannah."

Bree stirred the soup slowly. "Who's William?" she asked before she took a taste.

"An old guy who works here in the kitchen. He helped Hannah out a lot. Nice old guy."

"Was he here when I talked to you before?" James asked.

"No, I don't think so." Murray exhaled and ran one hand across the scarred surface of the table. "He's gone, just disappeared."

Bree tasted the soup, a wonderful concoction of vegetables and rich broth. When she looked at Murray, she didn't know what to say except the logical. "Don't you think that's the nature of the people around here? I mean, they sort of drift in and out, and maybe they go off to some other place?"

Murray shook his head sharply and frowned. "Sometimes, but I can tell the type. Neither Hannah nor William is that way. They want to belong, to have a place, to have people. They were getting to be good friends with each other."

The soup was spreading a welcome warmth in her middle. "Then William must have been worried about Hannah."

"He took to drinking again, that's for sure. That's why I figured he didn't show up last night. But he'd never stay away today. We're doing the Christmas cooking. Twenty turkeys have to be finished before Christmas Day."

Bree realized James had been eating without saying a thing, and she glanced at him. He was sitting back, brushing at his mustache with a napkin. From nowhere came a sudden memory of a date she'd had, a man with a mustache. When she'd kissed him, it had felt prickly. She brought herself up short and looked away from James. Silly thoughts, she chided herself, and she opened a carton of milk. "Twenty turkeys?"

"We serve a turkey dinner on Christmas Day. It's a tradition around here. And William was really excited about helping. We've got lots more birds to cook and lots more pies to make. He wouldn't let me down. Not now. I know he wouldn't."

And you're a trusting man, Bree thought, touched that a real optimist still existed in the world. They were few and far between and destroyed so easily by harsh reality.

"Don't you think William probably went off to look for Hannah?" James asked as he tore open his carton of milk.

Murray began to smooth the tabletop again, making circles on circles over the wood. "Could have, but he would have said. He got really upset when I told him I went to the police. Police scare him—they do most of the people down here. I don't even think I should go to them about William, not after the way they acted about Hannah."

"They took a report," James said.

"Sure, but that's it."

"You don't know—"

"I do." Murray stared at his hand as it stilled on the tabletop. "I went over to the place where Hannah lived. I thought William might be there, maybe waiting, maybe drunk, thinking she'd come back. Liquor can make the mind crazy. I found out he'd been there, but almost a week ago."

James drank from the carton, put it down and asked, "Did the police let you look at her place?"

At the question Murray's face tightened, his eyes narrowing behind his spectacles. "What police?" he muttered. "They haven't even been there."

"Not at all?"

"No. The guy who runs the boardinghouse looked at me like I was crazy asking what the police had said. They never even stopped by. I asked him a few questions and found out he last saw Hannah on the thirteenth, in the afternoon. She was wearing the hat and coat, like always. Said she was coming here." He looked at Bree and the tight smile came again. "I wish I had a picture of Hannah for you, you being a photographer and all. She's real tiny with snow-white hair, and she wears a big black hat with a brim that's sort of limp. She's got this coat that's red, and it's way too big for her, goes almost to her ankles, but she likes it. Said it was Santa's color."

He sat back with an unsteady sigh. "When she came in looking for work, I thought she was a real character. Maybe a touch childlike, but pretty smart in some ways."

While Murray talked, James drained the last of his milk, crushed the carton, then stared at it. "I've had someone looking into her past, but he couldn't find any Hannah Vickers who'd ever been in the movies, silent or talkies."

Murray swept away that bit of information with a wave of his hand. "It could be one of her stories, for all I know. It doesn't matter. Hannah matters, and I'm scared for her." He clasped his hands together tightly on the tabletop. "She'd sit up front in the booth by the window and tell stories. Maybe they're real or maybe they're what she wanted them to be. She'd tell things like when she was thrown off a cliff and landed on a horse." He shrugged sharply. "Probably just stories."

Nate stuck his head into the kitchen again. "Hey, boss, you'd better get up here. Some guy I never seen before is asking a lot of questions about Hannah."

Chapter 6

Both Murray and James were on their feet immediately. "I'll be right there," Murray said as he hurried toward the doors.

When the swinging doors stilled, James crossed to them and Bree was right behind him. She looked over his shoulder as he opened one side of the doors a crack to look into the restaurant. Bree moved closer, but to see into the other room, she had to press lightly against James's arm and shoulder. She concentrated on what she could see through the doors and not on the solid heat of James's body.

The front section of the Cracked Cup Café was long and narrow with a Formica counter along the right wall and booths along the other. Wagon-wheel lights hung from the high ceiling, and a huge banner, draped over mirrors behind the counter, wished everyone a very merry Christmas. An instrumental of "The First Noel" started over the speakers, a tinny sound on the warm air.

"Too bad they can't shut off that horrible music," she muttered.

James glanced at her, his face within inches of hers, and although she could see his frown, he didn't say anything. He turned to the door, and Bree bit her lip hard. Then she looked at Murray as he said hello to a woman in the first booth before he glanced at Nate behind the counter.

The bushy-haired man nodded to a customer sitting three stools from the kitchen end of the counter cradling a cup of coffee. Murray went closer and his voice carried to the kitchen when he spoke. "Are you the one who's been asking about Hannah?"

The man set down his mug and turned to Murray. He looked about fifty, with a narrow, heavily lined face, and he wore a wool plaid jacket with faded jeans. "Yeah, I'm the one."

Murray took the empty stool next to him, sitting with his back to the kitchen. "Have I seen you in here before?"

"Not here, but I've been in the neighborhood a while."

Murray held out his hand to him. "Murray Landers."

The man shook hands. "Roy Lester." He took his time lighting a cigarette before he spoke again. "I was looking for that old lady that works here, but this guy—" smoke trickled out of his mouth and nose as he motioned to Nate busily wiping the counter nearby "—says she isn't here anymore."

"That's right. What did you want with her?"

James shifted, and the rough tweed of his jacket brushed Bree's chin. It was then that she realized how close she was, almost surrounded by the scent of after-shave and maleness. She moved a bit to her left, giving herself a cushion of space, and tried to concentrate on the conversation.

"I heard she was some sort of movie star," Roy was saying. "I just wanted to see her for myself. Any idea where I could find her?"

"No."

"Maybe I could catch her where she lives."

"She's got a room two blocks over at Dreeson's boardinghouse, but she hasn't been there for a while. I checked."

Ray took a drag on his cigarette, then shook his head. "Oh, well. I just thought I'd try." He smiled through a haze of smoke, a tight expression that didn't touch his eyes. "Not every day you see a real live movie star, eh?"

"Yeah, that doesn't happen every day," Murray murmured.

Roy stood and laid some change on the counter by his coffee mug. "Maybe I'll check back later to see if she's shown up."

"Sure, any time," Murray said as he watched the man go step outside. Then he turned and came toward the kitchen.

Bree stepped back and James moved to let Murray through the doors. Disappointment was clear in Murray's eyes. "You heard?" he asked.

James nodded. "Yes."

"This is scary for people to just disappear," Murray said softly. "First Hannah, now William."

Bree was touched by the genuine care in Murray for people most would overlook or want to ignore. Caring *should* be able to really make a difference, she thought with a stab of pain. Too bad it couldn't most of the time. Quickly, she crossed and picked up the camera case resting by her half-finished bowl of soup. She wanted to be out of here into the fresh air so she could control her reactions. "Maybe I'll wander around outside and take some shots," she said to James.

"Pictures, I forgot completely," he said as he hurried past her and out the door. In a few seconds he was back with the brown envelope she'd given him that morning. He took out one of the glossies as he crossed to Murray, who was still standing near the swinging doors. "Do you recognize this guy?"

Murray glanced at it, then did a double take and came closer. His eyes widened behind his glasses. "William," he breathed. "That's William." He looked intently at the print. "And you, that's you. Isn't it? Where?"

"Yes, that's me. I figured if I came down here as one of the street people I'd be more apt to get answers. This man approached me last night when I was across the street by the bar." James watched Murray carefully. "Are you sure it's William?"

"Positive."

While James slid the picture into the envelope, he said, "He told me to leave Hannah alone. He said not to be bothering her, or something like that."

Murray took off his glasses and pulled a hanky out of his apron pocket. With nervous movements, he cleaned each lens thoroughly. "I don't understand," he muttered. "Not at all." He slipped his glasses on, pushing them high on his nose with the tip of one finger. "He must have thought you were with the police or something. He's terrified of them. They've given him a pretty rough time in the past."

James reached into his pocket, took out the matchbook and held it out to Murray. "Have you ever seen one of these?"

"No, never. Where did you get it?"

"William dropped it."

As James pushed the matchbook into his pocket, Murray asked, "Why's that so important?"

"It probably isn't. It was a thread to who the man was, that's all. A pretty flimsy thread. But since you recognize him, and now he's disappeared—"

Bree felt uncomfortable. She didn't belong here. She was supposed to be taking pictures, not getting caught up in the mystery of Hannah and William. "I'm going outside. I'll take some shots of the alley."

James looked at her. "I'll be right out."

Bree hurried into the cool afternoon air, stopped as the door shut firmly behind her and took several deep breaths. Photos. That was why she was here. She exhaled one last time, then looked around. After a minute of sizing up the lighting and random patterns of the shadows cast by the noontime sun, she began to take shots.

By the time she got to the street, she'd used half a roll of film. She stopped at the street and watched two police cars cruise past, then she looked toward the mixed atmosphere of newness in the direction of the harbor and the closer run-down old area. At the alley entrance a bar stood on one side and a boarded-up building on the other.

"Bree?" She turned at the sound of her name and saw James locking the door to the Bronco. She headed toward him.

"Are you up to walking a bit?" he asked.

She nodded. "I guess so."

He motioned down the alley. "This area is crisscrossed with service alleys. That way, across into the next alley, then east a block and a half is the way Murray said Hannah used to come to work. I think we should retrace her steps and take a look at where she lived."

Bree agreed, and when James started off, she fell in step beside him. "I can't believe the police haven't even been to her place," James said.

"I've been wondering where William lives. You'd think he would have told Murray."

"The old man never said exactly, only that it was safe and out of the way. Murray remembers him mentioning something about being low. Murray got the impression he was talking about being underground, but that doesn't figure around here."

"No one at the café ever found out?"

"No, he'd just vanish after work, then show up the next time he was scheduled to work . . . until last night."

"Is William as expendable as Hannah?" she asked as she hunched her shoulders a bit in the chilly air.

"More or less," he muttered.

She smoothed a loose curl off her face, then pushed her hands in her pockets. "How can people write off others just because they happen to be old or they aren't important enough, or they drink—" She bit off her words, a sudden choking sensation flooding over her. It would have been so much easier to write Dean off, but she'd never been able to figure out how to stop caring.

She stumbled on a crack in the concrete, but James steadied her and kept going, his hand still on her upper arm. His hold felt sure and safe, and she didn't back away from it. "I've wondered that myself," he murmured softly.

"Everyone deserves to have someone who cares no matter what," she said flatly and resisted the urge to kick at a loose can on the ground.

"Yes, they do," he said softly.

As they approached the street, she considered James and realized that he cared about an elderly lady and about an old drunk. What she wanted to know was who cared about him. Before she could stop it, she spoke her thoughts aloud. "Who cares about you?"

When James stopped by the curb, pedestrians walked around them, jostling them a bit, and Christmas music came out of speakers from the nearby stores. His hand let Bree go, and he faced her. In the stark brightness of the winter sunlight, his eyes still seemed shadowed. "I've got family."

"A wife and children?" she asked before she really knew she was going to say the words.

"No. That's part of the reason I was willing to leave Chicago." He pushed his hands into the pockets of his jacket. "To make this brief, I've been married and regretted it. And that's old news. No children. I regret that more than I can say, maybe more than the marriage failing. But I have good friends in Chicago, and my parents and two brothers in Texas along with assorted nieces and nephews. I have a few very good friends here."

She narrowed her eyes as she looked at him, his features incredibly clear at that moment. Everything about him—the tugging at one corner of his mouth under the mustache when he spoke, the flash of even white teeth, the fanning of lines at his eyes, the way the sun caught the silver glint in his wind-ruffled dark hair—seemed to be imprinted in her mind. She killed the urge to raise her camera and snap a picture.

"Who cares about you?" he countered, and she felt foolish that she hadn't expected the question.

If she pried into his life, he had the right to do that with hers. But she wanted to stop more questions before they came. She stiffened a bit, but kept her voice level. "Do you want a thumbnail sketch of my past?" she asked.

"If that's what you want to give," he said in a low voice.

"I'm a widow. I have been for a year. And I have a family that's always there for me." She tried to think of the right words to say without saying too much. "And I have my career."

Instead of the follow-up questions she expected, James said softly, "You look awfully young to be a widow."

Anyone is too young, she wanted to say, but instead answered, "It doesn't happen to someone who's at a particular age. It just happens." She cut off anymore talk about her with another question. "Were you raised in Texas?"

The smile came, and with it an inward sigh of relief for Bree. "How did you guess?"

She shrugged. "Just a touch of a drawl in your voice, and you mentioned family there."

"You're one smart lady," he said.

She wasn't about to argue with him right now. There was no reason for him to ever know how stupid she'd been in her life. And all because she'd cared too much. It could have made a difference, but it hadn't. She'd never been enough for Dean, no matter how much she'd tried to be. She deliberately tried to shake off the strange mood that seemed to surround her, and she stared at the busy street, not daring to look at James. "It's getting cold, isn't it?" she asked.

"Good old sunny California," he murmured. "Palm trees, sunshine, perpetual summer."

When he spoke, even though the words were almost those of a travel agent, his voice held a gentleness Bree wanted to run and hide from before she was tempted to get lost in it.

She'd experienced the same impulse earlier today when he'd held her in her kitchen, then at the station. She couldn't let that happen, not again, not ever. She trembled and hid it under a fabricated shiver. "Where to now?" she asked.

"Across there." He motioned to the alley opening across the street. "Come on."

She darted across the busy street with him, then into the next alley. From time to time she took a shot of the buildings they passed, mostly stores that were closed at the back, barred or boarded over. The unpleasant mixture of trash and garbage, along with pungent fumes from passing cars, filled the cool air.

"Where are *you* from?" James asked as they approached the next street.

She kept walking, looking straight ahead. "From the East. Where it gets very cold." She slanted him a quick look, glad to find him looking straight ahead. "You should understand cold if you've lived in Chicago."

"That's another reason I'm living out here," he said.

They crossed the street and went into an alley that angled east. Bree stopped to take a shot of a building whose walls were covered with graffiti. James touched her arm. She lowered the camera and looked at him, then followed his gaze.

A uniformed policeman stood about thirty feet down the alley near the delivery area for the Coach Lantern Bar. The officer was watching them intently. Slowly, Bree put her camera in its case and let it hang from the strap around her neck. Then she took her lead from James and stayed by his side as he started walking ahead again.

They came to the policeman and passed him by. When the man was well behind them, James spoke up but kept walking. "Nate said William did some drinking in that bar." He glanced over his shoulder at the policeman before looking ahead. "Wonder what a cop's doing there? Maybe it's got something to do with that guy being picked up earlier."

"Maybe," she murmured, and she could almost feel the policeman still watching them. When they came to the end of the alley, they crossed another street, still heading east, and walked into an easement that went behind old houses and took them out of sight of the policeman.

She saw sagging chain-link fences, weed-filled backyards and old California bungalows that had seen better days. James stopped near the middle of the block, then pointed to a house, a three-story wood structure painted chalky gray. "From Murray's description, I think that's where Hannah lived."

He led the way along a narrow walkway that went up the side of the yard and out to the street. As they walked along the cracked sidewalk past a narrow lawn, brown and un-tended, and up three steps onto the wraparound porch, Bree stayed with James. He stopped by the front door and knocked twice on wood that framed a deep oval window.

Nothing happened for a moment, then the curtain on the window moved and dark eyes peered out from the shadows.

"Is this Dreeson's boardinghouse?" James called through the glass.

"Yeah, who's asking?" a raspy voice demanded.

"I'm looking for Hannah Vickers."

The curtain fell in place, then the door swung open. An obese man in saggy pants and a dirty T-shirt that couldn't begin to cover his protruding stomach looked out at them. "Whadda ya want with the old lady?" he muttered.

"I need to talk to her."

"Too bad. She ain't here," he said.

"Would you know where she is?" James asked.

He shook his head. "Naw, I don't have no idea."

The man moved back and probably would have closed the door in their faces if James hadn't put one foot forward to block it. He looked right at the man. "How much do you want?"

The man studied James. "For what?"

"To let me in her room."

"Why'd you want to do that?"

"I'm her nephew, and I'd like to leave her a note."

The man didn't believe James, he didn't even pretend to. He just got to the point. "What's it worth to you?"

"Ten?"

The man scratched his beard-stubbled jowls. "That's all it's worth to leave something for your dear old aunt?"

James slipped his wallet out of his back pocket and took out a twenty. "How about this? Would it make me a good nephew?"

"The world's best," the man said without a smile as he took the money. With a grunt, he opened the door to let them in.

Bree followed James into a dimly lit foyer that gave the general impression of dark, warm mustiness. Stairs to the right of the door were covered with threadbare carpeting, and a single fixture overhead gave just enough light to show a hallway through an arched doorway directly ahead.

The man fumbled in his pocket and brought out a pass-key. "Top floor, at the end, number three," he said, and added glumly, "And you'd better not steal nothing."

James took the key without another word and motioned to Bree to follow him up the stairs. They went up into another dimly lit hallway with four doors opening onto it, each with a hand-painted number.

"Bring that key back when you leave," the manager called up to them. "I'm in number two down here."

James didn't answer as he kept going to the end of the hallway. He stopped in front of number three and put the key in the old lock. With a click, the door swung back, and he stepped inside.

Bree hesitated in the hallway. She felt like just what she was—an intruder. And it bothered her a great deal that anybody with twenty dollars could invade Hannah Vickers's world.

A light flashed on overhead, and through the open door Bree saw the yellow glow exposing a room with a double bed, a dresser and an overstuffed tweed chair by a draped window. The room was dreary but immaculate. Even though Bree had never met Hannah Vickers, she could sense the elderly woman's presence in the room with lace doilies on the dresser, needlepoint squares on the chair, an ivory lace spread on the bed and a hint of lavender in the air.

"Come on in and close the door," James said.

Bree hesitated, then stepped inside and swung the door shut. "What are we looking for?" she asked in a hushed voice.

"Why the whisper?" James asked, but even his voice was lower than usual.

"I feel like an intruder," Bree admitted. "Don't you?"

He nodded as he glanced around the sparsely furnished room. "Yes, I guess I do."

Bree shifted from foot to foot and nervously fingered her camera case. "Don't you think we should just leave?

"Not until I see if there's anything here that can help me figure out what happened to Hannah." He scanned the room. "I thought she would have put up something for Christmas, from what Murray said about her."

Bree remembered Murray talking about the lady's coat being the same color as Santa's. "She might not have had a chance to do anything before she left," she said in a whisper. "Or she might not have had the money to do it."

"Maybe." James crossed to a door and opened it, exposing a tiny closet where three dresses hung neatly on wooden hangers. Bree looked away from the meager display of Hannah's belongings, proof that she hadn't packed and left.

She crossed to the dresser and knew James had been wrong. There was a touch of Christmas here. Not a Christmas tree or any garish decorations, but on one end of the dresser sat a miniature nativity scene, each piece no taller than two inches. The five pieces looked very old, but lovingly preserved.

Bree almost reached out to touch them, then spotted a picture about three inches high in a wooden oval frame behind the figurines. She picked up and looked closely at a sepia-toned photo.

A little girl with pale hair done in ringlets sat on a dark horse in front of a backdrop painted to simulate a Western town. Very tiny and delicate, with round cheeks and a huge smile, the child looked about five years old.

A slender man dressed all in white cowboy clothes, with slick black hair parted in the middle and a pencil-line mustache, waved a huge Stetson hat above his head. The spidery inscription in the lower right corner was faded, but Bree could make it out. *For Sweet Little Hannah, the best costar I ever had. Bill. February, 1915.*

"James," Bree whispered. "Look at this." She turned and held it out to him as he crossed the room to her.

He took the picture and looked at it. "So they weren't wild stories," James said, surprise and a touch of awe in his voice. "Hannah really was a movie star."

Bree took a deep breath and the fragrance of lavender seemed to be everywhere. "But you said your friend Bryan checked."

James set the picture on the dresser and shrugged. "Maybe she used another name. She could have been married five times and Vickers was her last husband's name. After all, this was taken over seventy years ago." He looked at Bree. "Life can change so quickly, even in a few days or weeks. God knows where she's been or what she's done since that picture was taken."

Bree knew firsthand about life's ability to alter in moments. She looked at the nativity scene. "But she had to come from somewhere, and someone has to know about her, be wondering what happened to her." She pointed to the nativity. "She must have had that with her since she was a child."

James touched one of the tiny pieces, then lifted it and looked at it closely. "Hand carved," he said as it rested in the center of his palm. "It's as light as air, as if it doesn't exist. But it does, and so does Hannah. There has to be some way to find her."

Bree looked at the tiny lamb cradled in his palm. "How?"

"I'm going back on the streets tonight. There's a chance William might spot me again, or that someone else will approach me about her."

Bree felt a niggling uneasiness about him exposing himself to that danger again. "That seems like a long shot."

"It's the best I can do right now."

She looked away and at the room while she tried to come to terms with the fact that she didn't even have a right to tell him to be careful. "I hope you find something." She looked at him when a sudden idea came to her. "Did you ever consider going on television and appealing to the city?"

"I thought about doing that, but Murray said it would scare people off, that the ones who would know anything wouldn't want anything to do with the media. The idea of television exposure really upsets some people."

She understood that all too well. "It was just an idea."

He looked at Bree intently. "You care about this, too, don't you?"

Bree didn't want to be involved to the point where she cared. It hurt too much. But she would concede that she was interested and more than curious. "I'd like to see her found."

James touched her cheek, the contact feathery light. "Isn't it strange to feel this focused on someone we've never met?"

She looked at James, stunned when the thought materialized that it wasn't any more strange than it was to feel so connected to a man she'd met less than twenty-four hours ago. "Yes, it's strange," she whispered.

"Life's incredible the way it takes strange twists and turns. I thought I'd be in Texas now getting ready for a huge Christmas with my family. I didn't know I'd be here, trying to find an elderly woman I only heard about last week." He studied her from under lowered lashes. "I certainly didn't know you existed yesterday at this time."

Incredible was a word she'd use for the man inches from her. She nervously touched her tongue to her lips and reminded herself that she was doing a job. A way to stay far from her parents . . . a means to an end. With that thought firmly rooted, she said, "Crazy is a better word."

"That, too," he said, and the crooked grin appeared. Thankfully, he turned then to glance around the room once more, and Bree was spared the full impact of his smile. "I'm glad you're helping me with this."

"I'm not," she said quickly. "I mean, you hired me to take pictures for your show."

He didn't speak for a moment, then he shrugged. "I did. What I meant was just being able to talk to someone who knows what's going on helps."

Of course that's what he meant, and Bree felt foolish for overreacting. "Sure, of course." She fingered the strap of her camera case. "I want to take some pictures of the room."

He nodded and moved off, slowly looking around the room. She busied herself getting her camera out and focusing. "The light might not be good enough," she said. "But I'll chance it."

He was by the dresser again. "Get what you can. I wonder why Hannah left the picture and the nativity behind?"

Bree hated to say it, but it seemed to just underline the idea that Hannah hadn't planned on disappearing. "She obviously intended to come back, otherwise she would have never left them—or her clothes." She kept taking pictures because she didn't want to see if her words pained James. She knew they probably would, that he wanted to believe Hannah would walk into this room someday, whole and well. And she knew how painful it was to have hope taken away from you.

Bree studied Hannah's room through the camera view-finder and pressed the shutter release over and over again until the film was gone.

When she lowered the camera, James was by the door. "Can we stop by the station before I run you back to your place?"

"I've got an important call to make, but..."

"I promise I'll have you back to your house by..." He looked at his watch, then at her. "It's three-thirty now. I can easily have you home by six."

If she didn't get there until six, she could call her mother then and spend the rest of the evening developing the film. The time would be filled until she went to bed. She was getting very good at filling up the empty spaces of evenings, and she was thankful to have enough work to keep her occupied. "All right. Six."

"Good. Let's go," he said.

Bree took one last look at Hannah's room before James closed the door on it. Then she put her camera in its case and looped the strap around her neck. Silently, she and James headed down the stairs.

When they got to the bottom, the manager was standing waiting for them, a can of beer in his hand.

"Took you long enough to leave a note, didn't it?" he said to James.

James held out the key. "Thanks."

The fat man took the key, but didn't move to let them pass. "Hey. You been here before?" he asked with a lifted eyebrow.

"No." James took Bree by the arm to lead her around the man to the door. "I'd remember if I had."

"Well, you look sort of familiar," the man called after them as they went out the door.

Chapter 7

When they walked up the alley to the Cracked Cup's back door, Bree saw Murray by the Dumpsters. He turned as they walked up to him. "Anything interesting at Hannah's?" he asked.

"No, not a thing," James said.

"What're we going to do now?"

"I'm coming down here tonight. I'll go back to the bar where William met me last night. Maybe we'll get lucky and he'll come back."

Murray raked his fingers through his thinning hair. "What can I do?"

"Be here in case either William or Hannah tries to contact you. Maybe you could check with the police again, too. Talk to a detective there, Calvin Browsky. He can find out if there's anything new. Tell him I told you to contact him."

"All right," Murray agreed. "I'll go down there in a bit and try to see him."

* * *

While they drove to the station, Bree silently stared at the passing city, but she couldn't forget the picture in Hannah's room. She wondered about the little girl with the huge smile. How had she ended up being an elderly lady with a red coat and no one to miss her but a kind-hearted man who really hadn't known her long at all? There had to be someone for her.

She closed her eyes for a moment and thought about calling her mother. She'd keep it brief, just let her know about the job. She had her excuse not to go home. She had a job. Her mother would understand that. She didn't have to know about James or the television station. Bree opened her eyes. A photography job; that was enough of a description.

"I didn't expect this traffic," James said.

His voice pulled her out of her thoughts, and she looked ahead at the four lanes of the freeway clogged with cars. James fingered the steering wheel as he slowed to about ten miles an hour. "I'm not looking forward to this evening. It's a crazy world down there." He slanted a look at Bree. "What ever possessed *you* to go down there alone at night?"

She shrugged. "I hadn't meant to. I'd been up and down the street earlier in the week and noticed that the workers were putting in the lights at the Fenwick, the ones that line the overhang and the ticket booth. So I went back to see it lit at night. I got involved, lost track of time, and before I knew it, it was past nine. When I was driving to the freeway, I took a wrong turn and ended up on that street. It fascinated me in some way, so I stopped."

"Don't they have streets like that back East?"

She thought about the streets in the cities she'd driven through with Dean when he had been on the way to his never-ending political gatherings. "Of course they do. But the lighting and the people down here . . ." Her voice trailed off. She shifted in her seat, finding it hard to describe her impulsive behavior.

When Bree moved, James could feel the stirring of air and caught the subtle hint of her fragrance. Clean and gentle. "The impulsive behavior of an artist?"

"Exactly."

"What about the pictures you took today? Do you know what they'll be like before they're developed?"

"Sometimes I do, and sometimes I'm shocked when I see them printed." She shifted again, and this time he could sense her looking at him. "It all depends if I've taken chances with them or not."

He kept silent for a moment, then decided to take a chance of his own and ask a question about her marriage. "Was your husband a photographer or an artist?"

Total silence filled the car, then he heard Bree take a deep breath. "No."

He'd hoped she'd open up a bit, that she'd share a glimpse of her past with him the way she'd begun to earlier while they walked. So he didn't respond, hoping it was true that sometimes silence was the best way to draw people out. When she took another breath and spoke softly, James knew he'd done the right thing.

"My husband was an attorney, not an artist of any sort. He didn't even know how to focus an instant camera."

A lot of political hopefuls started out as attorneys, he reasoned. "That sounds like me."

"Was your wife in television?" she countered unexpectedly.

James felt relieved that she seemed to be taking the conversation in stride. "My ex-wife was...is still, as far as I know, a perpetual student." He had to stop the car completely when the traffic came to a standstill. "She took any and all classes she could find on any subject that came up. I sometimes thought she started in the college catalogue with the As and worked her way through the alphabet."

"She doesn't have a career?"

"No, but she's working on finding one." He was just a bit shocked that there wasn't any bitterness in him at the thought. And it was easy to say, "Her new husband has enough money to indulge her whims. She must be to the Ls by now." He pointed to the tangle of traffic ahead. "And by the time we get off of here, she could be to the Rs."

Bree laughed softly, a gentle sound that ran lightly across every nerve ending in his body. "Now that does sound cynical," she said.

"I told you, I'm one of the last realists."

"So you did," she murmured.

He looked at her, and her delicate beauty, enhanced by the soft curving of her lips with humor, almost took his breath away. She'd come into his life in the strangest way, but he'd long since stopped questioning fate's role in his destiny. Things happened for a purpose. He accepted that. Now Bree was in his life, and he knew right then that he hoped the situation was more than temporary. He'd told her that life was incredible. Now, looking at her, feeling the awareness of her fill him, he realized just how incredible it could be.

When Bree walked into the Channel Three building with James for the second time that day it was after a two-hour freeway tangle. They'd finally taken an off-ramp and driven through the city. Around five-thirty, they stepped into the station.

The guard at the desk had changed. This one looked young enough to be a teenager, and he smiled as they passed but didn't get up. As they went down the hall, the station seemed to explode with people. Most of them were heading toward the studio area, and they all seemed to be in a tremendous hurry. A few called out greetings to James but didn't stop. James kept Bree near the wall where they wouldn't be jostled.

"The six o'clock news is coming up," James explained. "They're getting ready." As they rounded the corner, Bree caught a flash of movement just as a man ran directly into

James. Both men lurched backward, and Bree instinctively reached for James, closing her hand on his arm, but only gripping the tweed of his jacket. She heard a ripping sound as the sleeve and shoulder of his jacket separated, but he didn't fall. As he righted himself, Bree looked at the man who had run into him.

He had steadied himself by grabbing a doorknob. Taller than James by a few inches, lean, blond, with gray-blue eyes, he looked to be about forty-something and very harried and impatient.

"Damn it, James," he muttered as he tugged at the cuffs of his blue pin-striped shirt. "You could have killed me."

"I wasn't trying to," James countered and frowned at his torn shoulder. "My favorite jacket," he moaned.

Bree finally released her hold on the fabric and would have apologized, but the other man cut in. "Your jacket?" His eyes narrowed in a frown. "What the hell are you doing here, anyway, and with a beautiful woman?"

James exhaled. "Hello to you, too, Carson. Merry Christmas. And this beautiful woman is a photographer working with me. Her name is Sabrina McFarland. I call her Bree. You can call her Ms. McFarland."

So this is Carson Davies, Bree thought. She could almost feel his tension. "I question your judgment in men," he said to Bree. "But since you're working with him, I'll keep quiet." Then he looked at James. "I thought we were rid of you until after the New Year."

"You've heard about bad pennies, haven't you?" James drawled. "Would you believe I stayed in San Diego just to run into you?"

"Sure, and it's going to snow any minute in southern California," Carson muttered, then spoke to a man passing by at a slow jog. "Is editing through with the tape?"

"I'm on my way to pick it up now," the man called as he rounded the corner.

Carson leaned one shoulder against the wall and let out a heavy sigh. "What, James?"

"That's it? 'What, James?'"

"I know you wouldn't stay in San Diego even if it was my birthday, and I can sense that you're ready to start a long persuasive story in an attempt to convince me of something. I'm making it easy on both of us. Cut to the bottom line and tell me what you want in ten words or less. I'm on a deadline."

Bree watched the two men as they interacted, one intense and nervous, the other at ease. But she could tell there was a connection between these two vastly different men, some invisible bond that she couldn't begin to fathom.

"To prove Channel Three is a station with a heart." James ticked off the words on his fingers as he said them one by one. "And that's exactly ten words, Carson."

"So, you *can* count," he said.

"And *you're* in a lousy mood," James countered, his tone like that of no employee Bree had ever heard talking to an employer. "And I'm the one with a ruined jacket."

But it didn't anger Carson. In fact, he suddenly smiled, an expression of wry humor. "Sorry." He crossed his arms. "You're right on the mark. The only excuse I can offer is this crazy business and the fact that I've just had a run-in with Jillian."

"Another one?"

"I've lost count. This time she wants to go off to some godforsaken South American country to show the viewers of *Dream Chasers* places to go cheaply out of season. But the budget she says she needs isn't cheap, and heaven only knows who would want to go to that place anyway. But she's insisting."

"And?"

"I was in there arguing with her, trying to convince her that she really isn't starring on a program dedicated to fluff, when the remote crew came back with fantastic tape of a suspect in the police killing being picked up for questioning. It'll be tight to get it on at six, but I think we'll have some exclusive footage. The news director's gone for the holidays, and his assistant—" He stopped. "You get the picture. Anyway, all Jill wants to do is argue about her trip. And she just got back from Mexico."

The man who had passed by came back holding what looked like a VCR tape. "It's ready to run," he told Carson.

"Put it into the machine in my office. I'll be right there," Carson said, then looked at James. "Can this hold for—" he checked his watch "—ten minutes?"

James nodded. "Ten minutes would be fine."

"I'm not going to ask what they'd be fine for," Carson said. "Nice meeting you, Bree, and I'm sorry about the collision. James never looks where he's going." He headed for the corner. "Ten minutes, in my office, James." And he was gone.

"Carson Davies," James said as he looked at Bree. "The lord and master around here."

"But he's not yours, is he?" Bree asked, amused at the relationship between the two men.

James glanced at her, that crooked smile of his firmly in place. "Lady, I said you were smart," he murmured, then looked at her camera. "Did you get anything good today?"

"Maybe. I won't know until I develop them."

"I don't know how you would feel about it, but could someone here do the developing?"

She didn't want that at all. The developing was her time filler, and she needed that desperately. "I'd like to do it myself. I can have them done for you by tomorrow." She looked at his torn jacket. "And if you give me your jacket, I'll have it fixed, too."

"No, you don't have to."

"I tore it."

"But I owe you. You saved me from an ignominious fall on my—" he grinned "—my pride." He took her arm and led her down the hall to his office. He let go when they arrived and he saw that the door was ajar. "What's going on?" he asked as he stepped inside.

When Bree followed him, she saw Bryan sitting behind James's desk. He was on the phone, and he held up one finger as he kept talking into the receiver. "Thanks, I appreciate that. Any time. No problem." And he hung up.

He rested his elbows on the desk and looked at James and Bree. "I came in here because the rest of this place is like a madhouse. Even trying to go into the news department is taking your life in your hands."

"Anything new?" James asked as he went to the desk.

"No." Bryan stood and stretched his arms over his head. "I finally got in touch with the Hollywood Museum of Silent Picture History. They found out that they have never had a listing for an actress called Hannah Vickers. Sorry." He looked at James's jacket. "Trying to be a bum without the beard and old clothes?"

"I ran into Carson," James muttered as he shrugged out of his jacket and tossed it over the arm of the couch. "We found something today, a picture of Hannah when she was a child. Its inscription was, 'To Sweet Little Hannah, the best costar,' and signed by Bill. The date's 1915. She's on a horse, with a guy in cowboy clothes standing next to her."

"'Sweet Little Hannah.' I wonder if that could be a nickname like Baby LeRoy or Little Gloria Jean?" Bryan straightened the collar of his shirt. "She wasn't just spinning stories, was she?"

"No, she wasn't." James reached into his pants pocket and took out the matchbook. "This was produced by a place called Graphic Originals. They're closed for the holidays, but do you think you could get the owner's home phone number for me?"

Bryan came around the desk, took the matchbook from James and studied it. "I don't see why not. It might take a while, but I'll try."

James motioned for him to keep the book. "Do what you can."

"I'll get back to you," Bryan said and left.

James looked at Bree. "I think Carson has had his ten minutes. Let's go and get this over with."

She went with him to the double doors at the end of the hallway. He knocked once, but didn't wait to be invited in before he opened the door and stood aside to let Bree pass. She was a bit surprised to step into a large room that didn't have a bit of blue, red or white in it. The space was paneled in oak that matched the tone of a huge desk in the middle of a floor covered by an off-white, plush carpet. Oak shelves were filled with books on the left wall and three television monitors hung on the right wall. A large window behind the desk was covered with a thin-slat blind that closed out the world.

Carson sat behind the desk, his chair tipped back, his leather loafers resting on the desktop. He glanced at Bree and James and nodded toward the middle screen.

Bree looked at the monitor and saw the flash of the Channel Three logo. Then the screen went black. In less than a second, it exploded with a shower of small square pictures that come out of a central point. The shots looked as if they came from travelogues, with brilliant color everywhere. The music behind the shots was dreamy, almost gentle. Then words formed from a shimmering silver that blazed from infinity to splash across the screen: *Dream Chasers!*

Then the woman Bree had met came on the screen standing in front of what looked like a grassy pyramid.

"Welcome to *Dream Chasers*," she said into the camera. "I'm Jillian Segar, and I want you to meet my new cohost, Sam Rollins." A strikingly handsome man towered over Jill, his tanned face bright with a wide smile. The phrase "Greek Adonis" came to Bree's mind. "Sam comes to us from our sister station in Philadelphia." She looked at the man. "Welcome to Channel Three, Sam, and we hope this is just the beginning of a very long and happy relationship."

"Thank you, Jillian, and hello, San Diego," Sam Rollins said in a deep, rich voice. "I'm glad to be working in one of the best cities in the country and excited that tonight on *Dream Chasers* we are taking you with us to the Yucatán Peninsula."

Carson hit one of several buttons on a panel on his desk and cut off the sound while the picture kept going. Then he sat up, his chair hitting the floor with a muffled thud. He looked at James and Bree. "Getting Sam Rollins cost us a small fortune, but he's going to be worth it. A good addition and glad to have been in on the Mexico trip. You'd think that would be enough for Jillian, wouldn't you? But she's got this crazy idea—" He cut off his words. "Never mind. What's your crazy idea, James?"

James dropped into one of two leather chairs that faced Carson's desk. He motioned Bree to the other one, and when she was settled, he sat back and crossed one leg over the other, his ankle resting on his knee.

"I'm staying in town for the holidays because I came across an interesting story a few days ago."

Carson checked his wristwatch, then nodded to James. "What story?"

While James explained his idea for the Hannah special to Carson, Bree watched as he started to fiddle with the lace of his Nikes. It struck her that it was the same mannerism he'd displayed at her house that morning when he'd been telling her the story of Hannah Vickers.

The thought shocked Bree. Had it really only been this morning when he'd come to her house and she'd held the toy gun on him? It seemed as if a lifetime had been packed into the past nine hours.

Bree looked at Carson who leaned toward James with his elbows resting on the desk, occasionally glancing at the silent monitor. James stayed back in the chair and spoke in his drawl, letting the words make the impact instead of any actions. When he finished, he simply sat and waited.

Carson clasped his hands behind his head and tipped back in his chair. "You want to do a special?"

"Yes."

"When?"

"After the New Year."

He shrugged. "I can go to programming for you, but what happens if you don't find the old woman?"

James sat forward on that question, and Bree could see the gathering tension in the way his jaw worked. "I'll find her even if I have to go to a private detective."

Carson looked right at him. "But if she isn't found, or if she's found dead—"

That brought James to his feet. "You'll have your special one way or another. Trust me."

"I do. You know I do." He narrowed his eyes. "I'm just wondering if this could end like the last time?"

James was so still for a moment that Bree could barely see him breathe. Then he threw his hands up abruptly. "Is that it, the low blow of the month?" His anger crackled in the air.

Yet Carson didn't seem particularly affected by it. "I had to ask," he said evenly.

"I'll give you a good program. That's my answer."

"All right. I'll see about getting a slot in mid-January." He motioned to Bree. "Put her on the payroll, if you want."

"She *is* on the payroll," James said, visibly relaxing.

Bree had no idea what had just happened, but she didn't want to hang around for more. She stood, more than ready to leave. "If you need to talk some more, I can take a cab to my place," she said.

"No," James said. "I'm done in here, unless Carson has any more questions."

The men looked at each other for a long moment, then Carson shook his head. "No more questions."

James turned and headed for the door without another word. But when the door was closed, James stopped and turned to Bree. "Can you wait a few more minutes? It'll save me a lot of time if I get changed into the old clothes while I'm here, then I can head downtown from your place.''

"Sure, I guess so."

He didn't bother knocking before opening Carson's door again and leaning in. "Can I use your bathroom in a few minutes to change clothes?"

Carson was still at the desk, his attention on the screen on the wall. The sound was back up. Without looking at James, he asked, "Since when did you ask?"

"Since I decided to be respectable," James countered.

Carson shrugged. "All right, but bring your own razor."

Bree waited in James's office while he changed. Sitting behind his desk, she stared out the window, watching the colors of twilight spread in the sky beyond the ivy-covered fence. She heard people running in the hallways, shouts that she couldn't quite make out, and she turned to look at the closed door.

Nervously, she began to stack papers on the desk, then she turned in the chair and looked at a Pink Floyd poster on the wall. Slowly, she got up and crossed to the poster. With a frown, she reached out and tugged her business card free from the corner of the stiff paper. Her business card?

She stared at the slightly rumpled card, then turned as the door opened. James walked in, transformed by the old clothes into a semblance of the man who'd caught her attention the night before. But the hooded, dark look wasn't there anymore, nor was the scruffy unshaven touch.

"Where did you get this?" she asked and held out her card.

He crossed and looked at it. "You gave it to me last night, and I used it to get your address."

She hadn't remembered giving him the card. "Oh," she managed, feeling a bit foolish, and she changed the subject. "Are you ready to go?"

He grinned at her and turned slowly to let her get a good look at the costume. "What do you think?"

She thought he could get hurt going down there, and that worried her. But she pushed it aside. It wasn't any of her business. "You'll fit right in."

"I'll take that as a compliment," he said, a dimple to one side of his mustache deepening. "Come on. I'll drive you home."

As James drove onto the freeway and headed south, the night outside darkened, and the heater filled the interior of the Bronco with delicious warmth. Bree settled in the seat and rested her head against the window. "Tell me how you started *Heart of the Matter*," she said.

"It was Carson's idea, actually. He wanted a people reporter, but not like the other stations had. He didn't want someone who was a consumer advocate. He wanted someone to go one-on-one with the public, someone to really care about what happened to the little guy." He laughed softly. "He said that I care too much, but that's all right. I'd rather do that than not care at all."

"Sometimes it's better not to care at all," she heard herself say, and she pressed her lips tightly closed.

"Now who's being cynical?" he asked softly.

She didn't know what to say after letting that slip. "Practical," she finally said. "There's a difference."

"And what happens if you make yourself not care?" he prodded.

She exhaled softly. "You don't have regrets or pain."

"Isn't that what makes our lives unique? What we go through, and what we survive?"

"Pain forms character? Is that it?"

"No, pain lets you enjoy the happiness that much more," he murmured.

"But maybe it's not worth it. What if the happiness doesn't come?"

He slanted her a quick glance, and she kept her eyes straight ahead. "That's a chance we have to take, isn't it?"

"No," she said. "We don't."

James kept quiet, and Bree silently thanked him for it. She didn't want to talk about caring or taking chances or about pain and happiness with him. He'd never understand, just as she couldn't understand where he was coming from, not when he seemed intent on putting himself on the line all the time for complete strangers. If he wanted to take chances, he could. She wasn't about to.

Bree felt weariness engulf her. The steady rhythm of the motor, the hum of tires on pavement and the warmth combined, and she closed her eyes as she felt herself slipping farther from reality. She welcomed the comfort and peace until the images came.

They had only come in dreams this past week, but never when she was awake. She opened her eyes quickly, seeing car lights coming out of the darkness ahead, and she almost couldn't breathe. She felt the terror of the past rushing at her from secret places, and she only stopped it by sitting up abruptly and taking a deep breath.

"Pardon me?" James asked from the shadows to her left.

"What?"

"I thought you said something."

"No, I didn't." She felt her muscles tightening, as if she could physically ward off the past.

"I've had only a few Christmases when it snowed," he said softly.

Snow. She remembered strange warmth even though the storm had raged all that day. "Snow..." She licked her lips and stared ahead into the night. "It's overrated."

He chuckled softly. "It's cold, that's for sure."

And isolating, she thought. That's why she'd run out of the lodge into the storm that night. That's why she'd taken her car and driven down the mountain away from Dean. "Yes, it is."

Images nudged and prodded, coming at her from all angles. Dean, edgy and irritable, giving his stock answer for not being there for her. "I'm not feeling well. I've got pressures." After three years, she'd known the translation for those words. "I'm coming down. Don't bother me."

"Do you ski?" James asked, his voice a strange echo in her head, mingling with the memories.

"I used to," she said, but heard Dean's voice inside her. "We'll go skiing during Christmas. I don't need help, just a vacation. I'm not an addict. It's a social thing, a release from the tensions. It keeps me going. But I'll prove I'm no addict. I'll stop."

"Bree?"

James was talking to her, asking questions, and she had no idea what he'd said. All she knew was that Dean had left and come back less than an hour later. One look told her where he'd been. "Just this once, then no more," he'd told her. She clutched her hands tightly on her purse in her lap. "I'm sorry," she murmured to James, her voice sounding as if it was coming from a great distance. "What did you say?"

"I just asked where you'd skied before."

The lodge, her family's. "I don't remember," she lied.

Two days had been all she'd had with Dean before he started again. She didn't even know where he got it. She just remembered knowing. Looking in his eyes and knowing. It was then she'd admitted total defeat and left.

There'd been no man in her life except Dean from the time they'd met. She was ten and he was sixteen. Dark and intense even then, he'd seemed so exciting to her. And after she'd found out about his problems, she'd only tried to close in around him, to protect him, to help him.

Until she'd reached the end. She'd felt sick, tired, totally drained. There had been nothing more in her to give, to cope with Dean or his addiction. So she'd left.

She'd gone out into the snowy night, gotten in her car and driven off to leave the pain behind. After three hours of driving aimlessly, she turned around and headed to the lodge to try again.

Not because of love. No. She thought she probably hated Dean that last time, but she had to try. She'd gone into the lodge, up to their bedroom . . . the open door . . . looking in.

She clutched her hands so tightly her nails dug into her palms. Desperately she wanted the memories to stop, to disappear into the dark shadows. But they didn't. She tried to say something, anything to James, but her throat closed and ached. And the memories ate at her, pinning her in the past.

Dean on the bed . . . still, so still . . . the mirror on the floor . . . white powder clinging to it.

A scream exploded inside her.

Chapter 8

Bree?"

In that split second she realized the scream had never escaped. It was trapped inside her, echoing through her being but not leaving her.

"Yes." Her voice sounded breathless and tight from the vibrations of shock and horror still dissipating in her.

"We're almost to your house."

The sound of his voice made her recall another memory. She now knew what she'd been trying to remember about her dream last night. James had been there; he'd been the one to pull her, to turn her from the door and shut it. Fantasy, she realized. Wishful thinking. Maybe desperation for delivery from the past. And she knew no one could do that for her.

She tried to ease her hands open, spreading them on her purse. She took a deep breath and looked to her left. James was a shadow to her, the old clothes making him seem bulky and foreign. "I didn't realize how close we were."

"I thought you'd dozed off," he said as he turned onto her street.

She looked away from him to the night outside. "No, just thinking."

James drove up the street and swung the Bronco into the driveway. He stopped by the back walkway but didn't get out. "I don't know if I should be seen around here dressed like this. Your neighbors might get a little upset."

Bree hesitated to get out, knowing all she faced was emptiness in the house. But she couldn't think of one reason to stay with James, and she knew she couldn't anyway. "I'll develop the film tonight." She picked up her purse and camera and got out, but looked into the Bronco. The dim interior light etched James with shadows.

A sudden rush of uneasiness hit her, a more defined version of the emotion she had felt at the station when he'd said he'd be going out on the streets. "Let me know how it goes tonight," she said.

"I will."

She hesitated. "When do you want to see the prints?"

Words killed time, putting off that moment when his car would drive off into the night. "Tomorrow. Why don't I give you a call in the morning, and we can set up a time to see the prints and go down to take more?"

"Good," she said and made herself swing the door shut. But she didn't move. She stood in the driveway and watched until James had pulled onto the street and the car lights had faded in the distance.

Only then did she turn. She wished she'd left some lights on, she thought while she put her key in the lock. As the door clicked open, the telephone began to ring. By the time she was inside and closing the door behind her, it was on its fifth ring. She went through the darkness and reached for the switch on the wall in the kitchen. She blinked at the brightness, then crossed to the phone by the darkroom door.

"Hello?" she said into the receiver.

"Finally. I've been trying to get you for hours," her mother said.

"Mom. I was going to call you in a bit."

"Well, it's almost ten o'clock here and I need to get to bed."

"I'm sorry." She put her purse and camera case on the counter and touched the cool tiles with the tips of her fingers. "I keep forgetting about the time difference."

"I was getting worried."

"You know I'm fine," she said.

"I worry about you. You sounded so upset today. Then something happened here."

Her fingers stilled on the smooth tile when she heard the tone of her mother's voice. "What?"

"Well, I'm not sure, honey. Maybe it's nothing, but a man came here this afternoon. He wanted to know how to reach you. He said it was about insurance, but I've met enough reporters to recognize one when I meet one. I was afraid he might find you."

She bit her lip hard before she responded. "I thought they would have given up by now." That wasn't entirely true, she realized. She'd thought James had been one of those reporters just this morning. "I guess I hoped they would, at least."

"Dear, even if the worst happened and the truth came out sometime—"

"No!" Her hand curled into a tight fist. "That can't happen. Dean's dead, and he deserves some respect. He tried, he really did, but . . ."

"So did you, Sabrina. Sometimes I think you tried harder than he ever did to make things right."

She forced her hand open and pressed it flat on the tiles. "I wasn't a success, was I?"

"You did all you could. Listen, dear, I've been talking to your father, and we've decided it might not be a good idea for you to come home after all."

Hardly believing what she was hearing, she asked, "You what?"

"You shouldn't be here. I don't want you being hounded by the press. Not again, dear. But I hate for you to be alone. Your father and I want to fly out there and—"

"No. That's not necessary, I promise. I've got a job, an outside job for a private party, and I'll be busy right through the holidays."

Her mother hesitated. "But you'll be alone."

"I'm fine alone," she countered and closed her eyes.

"Sabrina, I hope you aren't just saying that. I know you must be lonely. Your father and I could be there tomorrow."

"No. You enjoy Christmas there—and everyone's coming." Impulsively she offered, "After the holidays I'll come home for a visit."

That got her mother's attention and the two of them talked for a few more minutes. When Bree hung up, she turned and leaned against the counter. She'd accepted her aloneness a long time before Dean died. He hadn't been there for her. But she hated this sudden sense of loneliness that seemed to be engulfing her. She even knew when it had started. When James had driven off.

"Get busy," she told herself, and she did just that. She grabbed her camera from the counter, opened the door to the darkroom and turned on the overhead lights.

In a little over an hour, she had the roll of film developed and drying in the revolving tub. She watched as it tumbled over and over. Finally the prints slid out the slot. Quickly she went through them, sorting the bad from the good, then the better from the good, then the best from the better, and finally the exceptional from the best.

She put three of the thirty-six prints aside. The first showed the alley behind the restaurant, forlorn and abused with its stark shadows emphasizing the decay of the structures and making a geometric pattern of the cracks in the concrete. The other two were of Hannah's room. The way the shots had been framed and the lack of bright light made the space seem shadowed and deserted and very sad.

Bree turned from them when they began to make her feel more isolated, and she started to clean up. By the time she had everything put away, it was close to eleven, and as she stepped into the kitchen, she realized that the silence was oppressive.

She went through the house, shutting off lights, then went upstairs. But instead of running a hot bath as she'd planned, she found herself looking in the sealed boxes in the extra bedrooms. Her small portable television had been packed, but she couldn't remember where the movers had left it. After ten minutes of looking, she found it in the closet in a back room she'd intended to use as an office. She carried it up to her bedroom, put it on the nightstand by the telephone and plugged it in.

She switched it on, but no matter what station she tried, she got nothing but streaks and static. She fiddled with the antenna but couldn't focus the picture and ended up turning it off in disgust. So much for television, she thought, then settled for a long, hot bath.

She intentionally stayed in the sunken tub until she felt ready to fall asleep, then got out and wrapped a towel around her. As she walked into the bedroom, the telephone rang. Her mother again? She debated answering it, but after three rings, she crossed and picked it up.

"Hello?"

"Bree?"

James. She sank on the bed, only then realizing how she'd deliberately tried not to think about him on the streets while she worked and soaked in the tub. "Hello. Did you find anything?"

"No. I just called to ask how the prints turned out."

She tugged the towel more tightly around her, then scooted back on the bed until she was sitting against the coolness of the brass headboard with her legs crossed. "Good. I found three that I really didn't expect." As she talked to him, she felt the loneliness dissipating. Just knowing he was on the other end of the line made things seem better.

"That's the best kind of good, isn't it? Something turning up when you least expect it and where you least expect it."

Just like you, she thought. But she said, "Yes. It's exciting. About tomorrow. When do you want to get started?"

"Why don't I come by around noon? I'm not sure when I'll be finished here tonight."

"You're still downtown?"

"No, thank goodness. I'm at a friend's place, and I'm not sure how late it'll be before I get home."

Bree closed her eyes. A friend's place. She felt foolish that she'd never even thought of him having a girlfriend. He might not be married, but he was certainly an attractive man. The idea of him being alone didn't seem very logical. But that logic had escaped her until now. "I can meet you down at Murray's," she offered, shutting her mind to images of James with a woman. "It might make it easier for you."

"No, I'll come by for you." She heard a murmur in the background, then James spoke again. "I have to get going. See you at noon. And Bree?"

She held tightly to the receiver. "Yes?"

"Have a good night." And the line went dead.

Bree didn't understand her sense of loss after James hung up, not any more than she understood why all remnants of sleepiness she'd carefully nurtured in the tub had fled. She got off the bed and carefully did everything the doctor had suggested to help her sleep. She went through her routine— brushing her hair, cleaning her teeth, turning back her bed— then she set the radio to soft music and got into bed.

She turned out the light, pulled the blankets over her, rested her arms at her sides and stayed very still. "Even if you don't sleep, you're resting," the doctor had told her.

She lay there with her eyes closed, wanting sleep, yet more and more afraid to embrace it in case she had the dream. Finally she felt herself drifting off, but as soon as she began to let herself go, the dream came. But not gradually this time. One second she was resting in her room, the next she was flung into the lodge, into the bedroom...Dean...the doctor...the ambulance...the reporters at the hospital. She wasn't absorbing details, just a blur of emotions and pain.

As suddenly as it began, it stopped. She was being held, free from the horror, cradled in strong arms and the most remarkable rough-gentle voice crooned in her ear. "I'm here. I'm here." And James had come to her rescue again.

And it seemed right, so right. Bree snuggled closer to him, into silken heat and strength, and she relished the intimacy that held no fear for her. For the first time in a very long time, she experienced a sense of peace that she hadn't thought would ever come to her again. And she slept without any more dreams.

Hannah didn't like the dark. She never had. Not when she was little and not now. But she didn't dare move in case *he* heard her. William had promised he wasn't close by, but she thought he must be. The man wouldn't give up that easily. Not him. Not after what he'd done.

She closed her eyes, pulled the wool blanket up higher over her coat and played her game to fight off the fear. Remember. Remember. And she slipped back to when times were so good, a long time before the Home. So wonderful. Mamma was there, and she told stories to make the dark less frightening.

A thud made her bolt to a sitting position. She listened intently, her heart pounding, then when silence followed, she huddled closer to the brick wall. William hadn't come back for so long, and she'd heard people moving overhead and in the alley. She was terrified one of them would be the bad man.

She closed her eyes. At least she had food, four chocolate bars, some nuts and some doughnuts. And the water William kept. Even a tiny bathroom. She knew why William had kept this place secret, why he had hoarded it all for himself and never told anyone about it.

She just hoped that he'd be back soon. She scrunched her eyes more tightly shut and trembled. Remember. Remember. And she did. The movie with Bill. He'd bring her candy, and he'd let her sit on his horse. He was such a lovely man. She'd been surrounded by Indians, and he'd come to rescue her on his huge horse. She let herself slip farther back until she could hear the sound of horse's hooves and almost smell the paint that made the backdrops. And Bill had rescued her. Just like William had. Dear William.

"William, where are you?" she whispered into the darkness.

James sank into the well-worn leather couch in the small living room of the apartment and cradled his brandy. It had been two hours since he'd talked to Bree, but he hadn't been able to get her out of his mind. Not any more than he'd been able to since leaving her at her house. She'd invaded his world and seemed to be staying in his mind.

"James?"

He looked up as Bryan offered him more brandy. "No, thanks. I've got to drive." He looked at his wristwatch. "In fact, I need to head out now."

He stood. "Thanks for the drinks, for asking me over." He looked at Bryan's girlfriend, Penny Something-or-other, a name he could never remember, talking to one of the other people they'd invited over for Christmas drinks. James wouldn't have come if he hadn't run into Bryan at the studio when he went to pick up his clothes. "Thank Penny for me, will you?"

"Sure," Bryan said and walked with him to the door. When they were away from the others, Bryan said softly, "I found out something else you might be interested in about your friend."

James looked at him. "Bree?"

"Yes. I got in touch with a friend who works for a sister station near her parents' house. He called me back just before I came home."

James tossed the last of his brandy to the back of his throat, then handed Bryan his glass. "What did he say?"

"Dean Gregory died at Bree's parents' vacation home. He and Bree had gone there for the holidays. By the time a doctor got there and they got Gregory to the hospital, it was too late. It made the late news that night. My friend went by her parents' home, and her mother practically denied having a daughter called Sabrina."

"They're protective," James guessed and liked her mother even though he didn't know her. "She's their child." He slipped on his tweed jacket with the shoulder still looking ragged. "Thanks, Bryan."

Even though Bree could have sworn she'd just gone to sleep, when she woke sunlight filled the room. She looked at the clock by the bed and was shocked to see it was almost ten o'clock. Filled with a strange lethargy, almost as if she'd had more sleep than she could use, she had to force herself to move. She slowly got up and dressed in a hunter-green, loose-knit sweater with full sleeves and black linen slacks pleated at the front. Barefoot, she went downstairs. She looked at the coffee maker. The pot was empty. She'd forgotten to set it the night before.

She opted for a glass of milk, then went into the darkroom and looked through the prints again. The three she'd singled out the night before still impressed her, but she put them in the stack with the other thirty-three prints. James could choose the ones he felt were right.

When she heard the doorbell, she glanced at the clock. Eleven o'clock. James had said noon. As she approached the front door, she remembered the visitor her mother had had and she hesitated. "Who's there?" she called out.

"James."

With a sigh of relief, she fumbled with the bolt, then pulled the door open. The image of James in front of her with the grayness of a cloudy day at his back brought her a surge of pleasure that she tried unsuccessfully to kill. It bordered on the fleeting memory she had of the end of the dream last night.

The collar of his tan chambray jacket had been flipped up against the chill in the air, his hands were pushed in the pockets of well-worn jeans that clung to his strong legs, and his silver-streaked hair had been ruffled by the wind. His Nikes squeaked slightly as he rocked forward on the balls of his feet and smiled at her. "Good morning."

She wondered now how she could have felt he was a threat to her. If ever a man was safe, it was James. "You're early," she said and didn't mean to. The phrases, "It's nice to see you," or, "I've been waiting all morning for you to come," seemed more natural, yet she'd said the one thing that didn't matter.

"I was finished earlier than I thought I would be, and since it's not a particularly lovely day, I figured we should get going as soon as possible."

She stood back to let him inside, and as he brushed past her, she caught his essence—fresh air, soap and maleness. And her whole being seemed to become charged with awareness, a dangerous thing that demanded all her will to ignore. "I'll get my things," she murmured and turned to go upstairs, but she stopped on the second stair and looked at him.

He was just closing the door, then he turned and she found herself not looking directly at him. A spot somewhere near his left ear seemed safe enough. "The photos from last night are in the darkroom." She motioned in the direction of the kitchen. "You know the way. I'll be right down," and she ran up the stairs two at a time.

When she came down with her purse and wearing her jacket, she found James in the darkroom bending over the workbench studying the prints. Without saying anything, she moved close enough to look over his shoulder, but she made very sure she didn't make contact with him.

She was surprised and a bit pleased that he'd set the same three prints aside that she'd chosen the night before.

"These," James said without turning to her. "They're good." He tapped one of Hannah's room. "Good, hell, they're terrific." He turned to look at Bree from under lowered lashes. "What do you think?"

She took two steps backward. "I thought they were the best, too."

James looked at the prints. "Lady, these are emotional pictures. I can feel the desolation, the surrender of those who exist there. Damn, they're powerful."

That was exactly why she didn't want to look at them now. "Maybe they're too depressing to use?"

"No." He stacked them, then reached for one of the protective envelopes on the shelf and slipped the pictures into it. He turned and leaned against the workbench. "They'll touch anyone who's not totally without feelings. You're a very gifted artist."

She felt her cheeks warm, wishing that James's words didn't overlap with other words from well-meaning people. "Take your pictures and keep yourself busy. You need something to focus on right now. Something to fill your time, to give you an interest." Actually that had happened. Her work had become a time filler, but now she was beginning to feel that old excitement, the nudging of desire to do the work because she liked doing it. It surprised her pleasantly. Maybe the cracks in her numbness weren't all bad after all.

She hooked her purse strap over her arm and reached for her camera. Quickly, with fingers that weren't quite as coordinated as they should be, she loaded it and put two extra rolls of film in her camera case. When she turned to

James, she found him staring at her, and it made her heart lurch vaguely. "Is something wrong?" she asked as she put the strap over her shoulder.

"I was just thinking about how stupid I was to think the matchbook could lead me to Hannah, but how lucky I was it brought me here." He tapped the envelope. "I would never have been able to find someone who could do this for me."

"Blind luck?" she ventured.

"More like dumb luck," he murmured and smiled suddenly. "Sort of like the guy who wins the lottery because he bought one ticket and used his dog's birthdate and weight for the numbers."

She found she could answer that smile easily, and it felt good. "Or his girlfriend's social security number?"

"You've got it," he said and touched her shoulder.

Her smile faltered at the contact simply because every nerve in her body seemed to shift and focus on the spot where his hand rested. There didn't seem to be room in her for more than one intense emotion at a time now. "Are you ready to go?" she managed as she moved away from his touch.

"Yes."

Quickly she went out of the room, yet even though the closeness had been destroyed as they walked through the house, she could still feel the light pressure of his hand on her shoulder. She had to touch the spot surreptitiously as she walked toward the door, to make sure James wasn't still touching her.

The ride to the restaurant passed in companionable conversation with James indicating points of interest to Bree. She might have been in the city six months, but she'd never really noticed Montgomery Field, San Diego State University, the zoo or the airplane museum. Although the day was gray and the clouds heavy in the sky, Bree found herself enjoying the ride.

When they pulled up to the back door of the Cracked Cup Café, she got out and went with James to the door. He knocked once, and Murray opened it almost immediately and invited them inside.

The warm air in the kitchen was heavy with the aroma of cooking turkey, and two men who hadn't been there before were stuffing several large birds in the central work area. They glanced up long enough for Murray to introduce them as Charles and Delmore, but kept working.

Murray sat opposite James and Bree at the table and flipped off the television that was tuned to a talk show. "Anything?" he asked James.

"No. I stood out there for three hours last night, but all I got was four dollars and almost arrested for loitering."

Bree looked at him. "You were almost arrested?"

"They didn't like my looks," he said with a smile. "So I moved on, and they left."

"No William?" Murray asked.

"I'm afraid not. How about you? What happened with the police?"

"About as much. I asked for Detective Browsky, but he wasn't there, and no one else seemed to have any idea what I was talking about." Murray took off his glasses and began to clean them with a napkin. "I didn't expect much, but—"

The sudden wail of sirens close by tore through Bree and made her flinch. Then the swinging doors burst open, and Nate ran into the kitchen. "They found something at the construction site at the far corner. Someone said it's a dead body."

"Oh, God," Murray gasped as he put on his glasses. "Who?"

"The guy didn't say." Nate's face twisted. "You don't think it could be Hannah, do you, boss?"

Murray didn't answer. Instead, he got up and ran past Nate into the restaurant. He yelled over his shoulder for

Nate to stay with the restaurant, then the front doorbell rang and the door shut.

James looked at Bree, and she was on her feet and headed for the door before he even said, "Come on." She hurried after him into the chilly air of the alley, and as naturally as if they had a relationship that could be counted by years instead of hours, James grasped her hand and took off at a jog up the alley toward the scream of the sirens.

"It . . . it could be something to do with all this construction, couldn't it? A worker or someone who slipped?" she gasped as they got to the street.

James hesitated. "Could be." Then he pointed west, toward flashing lights from police cars in front of a three-story structure near the corner. "There," he said and pulled Bree along with him toward the commotion and gathering crowd.

Scaffolding ran up the front of a stone-block building Bree vaguely remembered passing on their way to Murray's the day before. As they got closer she could see pale beige paint on the upper part of the wall and a darker brown outlining high-arched windows covered with metal grills. A plywood barrier separated the work area from the street.

Bree looked at the end of the street toward the refurbished section. Scaffolding and construction sites dotted the street. A wind that skittered in off the ocean, cold and damp, made Bree tremble and she held more tightly to James as they hurried along the sidewalk.

When they stopped near the back of the crowd and next to the curb, an ambulance roared past so close that Bree could feel the rush of air and the heat from its exhaust. Then it squealed to a stop by the curb ten feet from them, as near as it could get to a section of the construction fence that had a gaping hole in it. Police cleared a path through the gathering crowd for two paramedics who jumped out and headed for the opening.

Bree thought she caught a glimpse of Murray near the opening where the two paramedics disappeared with a rolling stretcher. But the crowd surged closer and she lost sight of him. James waited with her at the edge of the crowd, flipping his collar up with his free hand, still holding her hand with the other. One of the paramedics ran out to the ambulance, leaned into the cab and spoke quickly into the radio, then raced to the barrier with a large black box in his hand.

The crowd moved closer, only stopped by a few policemen who were trying to keep the opening clear. Bree spotted Murray near the opening again. Then she spotted another man about ten feet behind Murray—Roy Lester. He stared intently at the opening in the fence.

"Clear the way," a policeman yelled at the crowd, and as the paramedics reemerged, Bree's attention was claimed by the stretcher between them. A still form had been strapped to it and partially covered with a gray blanket. One of the attendants held an IV bag in the air, the plastic pouch whipped by the wind.

Murray broke from the spectators and bent over the stretcher, then a policeman spoke to him and urged him back so the paramedics could get to the ambulance. As they neared the ambulance, Bree got a fleeting glimpse of the person strapped to the stretcher. The man's face was bruised and swollen, the skin ashen, and an ugly gash, matted with dried blood, ran from his temple to his jaw. An oxygen mask had been strapped over his nose and mouth, but Bree knew who he was. William.

Chapter 9

Bree felt a surge as the past flashed to life, just as it had in the car last night. A wintry night...paramedics...the stretcher... She wished she could wake up and find everything had been a nightmare. But she hadn't been that lucky. She'd stood and watched the paramedics take Dean to the ambulance. His form had been completely covered.

She pressed a hand to her mouth, struggling to free herself from the horror that invaded her mind and body. Then she realized Murray was in front of her, saying something to James, hugging his reed-thin body tightly against the cold wind.

Finally she understood what he was saying. "He isn't dead, but he's only hanging on by a thread." He closed his eyes for a brief moment before speaking in a rush. "I'm going with him. They're taking him to Mercy. Could you two go back and ask Nate to keep things going until I know what's going to happen?"

"Sure," James said.

He had no sooner agreed than Murray turned and called, "I'm coming with him," to the paramedics. He climbed into the back of the ambulance, then the doors were fastened and the driver ran around to the front.

Bree tried to breathe, to ease the knots inside and make the images of the past less real. But she didn't know how. So she kept holding on to James. He'd become her anchor to the present, and she knew she couldn't let go—not yet.

As the ambulance took off in a squeal of tires and blaring sirens, then disappeared from view around the corner, the sound of the sirens dying away, Bree realized how much she hated that sound.

She jumped, startled, when James touched her cold cheek. "Are you all right?" he was asking from what seemed a great distance, and his face was vaguely blurred.

She didn't know. But she couldn't explain, so she nodded, and she felt the jerkiness of the motion. "Yes, it's just . . . so terrible," she managed and blinked to clear her vision.

"It sure is," James said softly. "Stay here, and I'll go see what I can find out from the police."

She nodded, unable to say anything else.

"One more thing. I need my hand," he said softly. The smile that lifted the corners of his lips was filled with bone-melting gentleness as he held up his hand with hers almost fused to it.

"Oh, I'm sorry," Bree gasped and jerked back, but she only succeeded in pulling both their hands against her chest with a soft thud. Then their fingers were untangled and she was free, her hand staying to press hard against her breastbone. Cold air chilled her skin where a moment before James's heat had been. "I didn't realize—"

His smile deepened, but it didn't compensate for the lost contact. "Hey, any time you need it, it's here," he said in that deep, rough-edged voice and touched her softly on the chin with the tip of one finger. "Stay here. I'll be right back." Then he turned and headed toward one of the police by the construction barrier. Most of the spectators had wandered off, their interest gone with the departure of the ambulance.

Bree stared after James as he moved away from her. An anchor. Foolish. She couldn't let him become that to her. That could only happen in dreams. She couldn't ask anybody to be strong enough to keep back the past. She certainly wasn't.

James walked slowly to the nearest policeman, more than a bit shaken by Bree's reaction to what had happened to William. But he understood. It must have reminded her of her husband's death in some way. It had certainly brought back memories to him, but the man in those memories hadn't been anyone he'd even met before.

The cop looked up as James got within a few feet and folded his arms on his chest as if taking up a post at the broken wall to the site.

"Excuse me," James said. "Can you tell me what's been going on here?"

The uniformed man shrugged. "Some old drunk fell off the construction scaffolding. Although how he could get up there with all the liquor he must have drunk is beyond me."

"He's pretty bad off?"

"As bad as he can be and still be alive. A guy from the building department found him way out of sight along the side of the building. Real lucky. They weren't even supposed to be working on this place until after the holiday, but the inspector came past to check. The old guy would have died for sure if he'd lain there much longer."

James pushed his hands in the pockets of his jacket and hunched his shoulders a bit. "He looked like he'd gone ten rounds with a heavyweight champion."

The cop frowned. "Yeah, he looked pretty bad. If I was laying a bet, I wouldn't put it on him to pull through." The cop shrugged off the old man's fate. "Maybe he jumped.

Who knows? Drunk as he was, he probably doesn't know himself."

The uniformed man stopped talking suddenly and stared at James, then his eyes widened. James had seen the look before, that split second when recognition nudged at the person studying him. "Hey, aren't you that guy on Channel Three, the guy who does stories on people?"

James shook his head and hunched his shoulders a bit more. "Sorry, pal, that's not me. He's a lot younger and a lot better looking," he said and walked away.

He started to walk back to where he'd left Bree, but she wasn't there. He looked up and spotted her down the street near the entrance to the alley. She was leaning against the wall of an empty office, and there was no doubt in James's mind why she was hugging herself or why her eyes were tightly closed. *Damn the way life treats people,* he thought and went to her.

When he got within a few feet, he began speaking, wanting her to know he was there before he startled her. "I was looking for you back there."

Bree had been trying to practice the deep breathing exercise that the doctor had given her to help ease her tension. But it hadn't helped any more than it had before. When she heard James speak, she realized that the sound of his voice was potentially more soothing than deep breathing could ever be.

She stood straight and looked at James, touched when he held out a hand to her. "Do you need it?" he asked softly.

She was tempted, so tempted, but she shook her head and put her hands in her pockets. "No, but thanks. Sirens upset me." That was a monumental understatement. "I'm sorry."

He touched her cheek fleetingly, leaving a path of heat where his finger trailed to her jawline before he pulled away. "No apologies. Sirens aren't my favorite sound, either."

"What did the policeman say?" she asked.

He zipped his jacket. "They think William was drinking, and he must have—"

A car pulled off the street and into the alley, screeching to a stop right by James and Bree. The front window rolled down, and the fat man from Hannah's boardinghouse leaned out and motioned to James. "Hey, mister. Thought that was you."

James moved closer to the car. "You were looking for me?"

"Naw." He motioned to the driver of the car, a man Bree couldn't quite see, and looked at James. "My friend and me came down to check out the excitement when I saw you standing here. I figured you should know your aunt's room was broken into."

"What happened?" James asked.

The fat man shrugged, tugging at the buttons of his soiled work shirt. "I heard something going on early this morning and went up. But whoever did it took off before I got up the stairs. They went out the window. I can't tell if anything's gone. It's pretty messed up, though."

"What did the police say?" James asked.

"Didn't bother calling. They'd just make more of a mess." He shrugged. "Nothing they could do, anyhow."

"Are you going there now?" James asked.

"Yeah, soon as we pick up a few things at the store."

"I'll meet you there in fifteen minutes. Okay?"

The fat man shrugged. "Suit yourself." Then his friend backed the car onto the street and drove off.

James watched the car as it disappeared down the street. "Why would someone break into Hannah's room? There wasn't a thing there worth more than a few dollars."

Bree didn't have any more idea why that had happened than she did why the past never let go of her. She balled her hands into fists in her pockets and asked, "Why do you want to go back there, James?"

"I don't know. But I should." Then he turned to the alley. "Lets go talk to Nate first."

She followed him down the alley, staying by his side as they walked in silence. Finally she spoke up. "You never said what the policeman told you."

"They think William fell from the scaffolding, and he'd apparently been lying there for a long time before they found him."

"Why would he climb on one of those things?"

"A good question," James murmured. "I didn't want to talk to the cop much longer. He suddenly put two and two together and recognized me."

"What did you say?" she asked, feeling stray tendrils of hair that the wind caught brush her cheeks.

"That James Chapman is much younger and much better looking than I am."

"And he bought that?" she asked.

"Probably, but I didn't hang around long enough to find out," he said.

Bree realized she'd never seen him on television to compare the image with the reality. Slanting him a quick glance, she wished that she'd been able to get her set to work last night.

James looked at her and their gazes locked for a moment before he asked, "What are you thinking?"

"That I've never seen you on television," she replied honestly.

"Maybe you're better off for it."

"No, I bet you're good." She was almost positive he would be. "You were probably born to do what you're doing."

He unexpectedly put an arm around her shoulders and held her to his side. Her camera case caught between the two of them, but it wasn't uncomfortable on her hip. "Wait until you see me, then give your considered opinion, all right?"

"It's a deal."

"On the other hand, I *have* seen your work, and I'd say you certainly were born to be a photographer."

"I love it," she admitted. "I always have." She jumped at the chance to talk about something that would take her mind off what had happened at the construction site. "When I was very small we had a summer home at Martha's Vineyard. That's—"

"I know where it is," he said without breaking stride or his hold on her.

"Well, I was given a little pocket camera. I suspect my mother gave it to me to keep me busy during summer vacation."

"Did it?" he asked, their pace slower and easier now.

"For every waking moment, and when I wasn't taking pictures, I was begging my mother for a darkroom."

"The beginning of greatness?" he asked.

She laughed softly at that. "No, more like the beginning of another part of my life."

"Did you have a happy childhood?" he asked unexpectedly.

"I think so. It seems wonderful when I look back at it, no problems, no responsibilities, no pressures, no..." She bit off her words and took a deep breath. "Golden days of youth, I think that time's called."

"I suppose it is."

"How about you? Were you a terror when you were a kid?"

"How did you know?" he drawled and cast her a slanting look from under dark eyebrows. "Hell on wheels, lady. That was me."

"And did you always know you wanted to be a television reporter?"

"No, not at all. I lucked into a gofer job at a local station in Texas, and one day I realized I liked it. I wanted to do news, to reach people. The rest, as they say, is history."

They neared the back door of the Cracked Cup. "You couldn't disappear without anyone noticing, could you?" she found herself asking.

"No, I couldn't." His hand tightened on her shoulder. "Could you?"

That brought her up short, and as they stopped by the door, she moved away from him, using the excuse of straightening her hair to break the contact. She *had* disappeared, but only because she hadn't known what else to do. "No, I guess not."

James didn't even have a chance to knock on the door before Nate opened it. "Was it Hannah?" he asked before Bree or James could say anything.

"No, not Hannah," James said, but before the bearded man's relief could get too great, he finished with, "it's William."

Nate blanched and backed into the kitchen. "Oh, God, is he—"

James and Bree stepped into the kitchen. "No, they took him to Mercy Hospital. He was still alive, but he looked bad."

"What happened?"

"They said he fell off construction scaffolding at a place up on the corner—a three-story place that's being painted."

"Yeah, yeah," Nate said and sank onto one of the chairs by the table. He wiped a shaky hand over his face and beard as he muttered, "Damn."

"Murray went with him in the ambulance, and he wants you to take over here until he gets back."

"Sure, of course." He looked at James. "When did it happen?"

"They didn't know, but he'd been lying there for a while."

Even before Nate spoke, Bree knew what he was going to say. "Hannah could be lying somewhere, you know. And who gives a damn, man, who gives a damn?" As he stood and began to pace, he unleashed a string of epithets that shocked Bree. Then he stopped suddenly and Bree understood that if the man had been different, he would be crying.

"I'm sorry, ma'am. Real sorry, but when I think of that little lady..."

Bree brushed aside his words. "It's all right." She turned from the sight of the stricken man and glanced around the kitchen. More turkeys were in the oven, and the makings for coleslaw sat in tubs on the table.

"We can't give up," James said softly.

"No, you're right. Damn right. Things'll be all right. Hell, they didn't think we could do the food, just Murray and me and a couple of others, but we're doing it." He crossed to the table and picked up a knife. Cutting methodically through a head of cabbage, he muttered, "We'll find her. Damn right, we'll do it."

"Nate?" Bree said.

He looked at her. "Yeah?"

"Who's paying for this meal?"

"Murray. Always has. It's his thing, doing this at Christmas."

"What about his family?"

"Doesn't have none I ever heard about. He lives upstairs and he's here all the time." He motioned with the knife to the huge ovens. "Some of the birds were donated from people around here, but most of it's right out of Murray's pocket. Murray never tells anyone." He shrugged and began to chop the cabbage again. "Never."

"We need to get going over to—" James stopped in midsentence, and Bree understood that he didn't want Murray to know about Hannah's room being broken into. "We'll stop by the hospital to check on William. Anything you want me to tell Murray?"

The man shook his head. "Just tell him I'll be here until I see him come through the door."

Five minutes later, they parked the Bronco in front of the boardinghouse, and as they stepped onto the porch, the front door opened. "Wondered if you were going to come or not," the fat man said as he pulled the door open to let them in.

Bree stayed close to James as they went inside.

"You didn't give me no name, so I couldn't call you or anything, mister. Lucky to see you like that."

"Yes, it was lucky," James murmured. He glanced up the staircase. "Can we go up?"

When James reached into his hip pocket for his wallet, the man shook his head. "Naw, you don't need that. Just go and see what happened. It's open. No charge."

James took the stairs two at a time and Bree followed as quickly as she could. A bit breathless from the fast climb, she stepped into Hannah's room and froze in her tracks.

Nothing was the way it had been the day before. The dresser's contents were spilled on the floor, drawers and all. The chair was overturned and the bed was torn apart. James was at the closet door, looking inside. And from where she stood, Bree could see the clothes ripped from the hangers.

It made her ache to see what little Hannah had ripped apart. She felt precariously close to tears. Today had been devastating for her. Now this. She closed her eyes, then looked at the bare dresser top and felt her heart lurch. The nativity and picture were gone.

Hurrying across to the dresser, she knelt by the piles of things that had been dumped on the floor. She pushed clothes aside, then heard something softly hit the floor. She pulled back a thin navy sweater and saw a nativity piece—the lamb. Quickly, she began to search through the pile, and when James knelt by her, she didn't stop. Silently he began to help, and one by one they found the pieces of the set.

When Bree found the last piece, the donkey, and saw a small nick in its ear, she muttered, "Damn the person who did this. Why? Why would anyone want to hurt Hannah? Why would they break in here? God, couldn't they tell she doesn't have anything?"

Without saying a thing, James picked up a simple wooden box lying in the clothes. It wasn't more than four inches by five. When he turned it over, Bree could see a scrolled H carved in the dark lid. He undid the simple clasp, opened the box, and Bree knew what it was for.

There were five indentations, perfect receptacles for the pieces of the nativity. He carefully put the pieces he had in their places, then he held out his hand to Bree. She dropped her pieces in his palm and watched him put them in their spots. Then she sank on her heels and bit her lip hard. She felt very close to tears. "We have to find her, James."

"Yes, we do," he whispered.

She rocked back and caught a glimpse of wood half hidden behind the front leg of the dresser. She reached for it and pulled out the picture, intact except for a single crack in the glass from top to bottom.

She stared at the little girl smiling up at her from the old print. "Who would do this?" she breathed as the picture blurred in front of her.

"I don't know." He stood and set the nativity box on the dresser. "I've been thinking about getting a private investigator to try to find her."

Bree got to her feet and put the picture by the nativity box. "You said you thought about going on television about Hannah before. I think you should, but don't wait until you do a special." She blinked and felt the dampness clinging to her lashes. "Do it now. You've done all you can without going public. Let the city help."

He frowned. "I'm worried about the street people here. They avoid the media like the plague."

"It's not them you're after now. It's others, someone who might have seen her on the street, on the bus, or a businessman who sold her something. Anything." She talked in a nervous rush, feeling such an urgency to find the woman she could barely contain herself. "Run some sort of announcement over and over again, the way the police do sometimes when they're looking for someone. Like a bulletin. But whatever you're going to do, do it now. I don't think you can wait any longer."

"No, you're right. We don't have any more time to lose."
He shook his head. "We need to get right on it."

She looked at James, stunned when she realized that an
elderly lady she'd never met had connected her in some way
to a man she'd met less than forty-eight hours ago. "Yes,
you do," she whispered. She didn't want to be involved to
the point where she cared. It hurt too much. Tears filled her
eyes as the truth came. "I can't stand the thought of Hannah having this done to her, or of her being hurt like William and lying somewhere alone."

James touched her cheek with the tips of his fingers.
"Tears?"

She didn't realize the tears had begun to fall. "I'm scared
for her, James." And she was scared at the way she was exposing herself emotionally.

"So am I," he whispered and reached out to her.

James held her tightly for a long moment, almost the way
it had been in the dream. Then he tipped her face with one
finger under her chin and his lips tasted the saltiness of tears
on her cheeks. Gently he kissed her eyes, first one, then the
other, his mustache grazing softly over her skin. Slowly, he
trailed his mouth to her lips and captured them with his
heat.

As she absorbed the feeling of his lips on hers, the taste
of her own tears there, she felt mesmerized. But without
warning, everything began to shift. The comforting gentleness blurred and receded, melting into a passion that seemed
to come from nowhere. It came slowly, tentatively at first,
then suddenly it was there, white-hot and explosive. It ric-
ocheted so violently through Bree that she was literally unable to move.

She knew she should run, that she should keep it from
finding life, yet another part of her wanted to feel it and
make it last forever. She felt swamped by feelings, and the
subtle scent of lavender mingled with the essence of the man
holding her.

When James drew back, Bree knew she hadn't moved, that her hands had never spread on his chest or felt his heartbeat under her palms. Yet she felt as if she had tried to absorb the man in some strange way, and that she'd almost lost herself for a split second.

Foolish, stupid idea, she told herself, yet incredibly, she regretted that it was only a fantasy. And her regret frightened her.

Nothing made sense to her, and she had a hard time looking at James. It didn't help to see the same shock she felt echoed in his gaze. "Why..." She had to try again to get the words past a tightness in her throat. "Why did you do that?" she managed.

The question echoed through James, and he had a simple answer. He'd wanted to. He'd wanted to comfort her, to ease her pain, and it had seemed as natural as it had been to put his arm around her on the way to the restaurant. Then he'd been literally lost in the taste of her. He'd felt his arousal, a fire in his loins, but when she hadn't responded, he'd forced himself to stop. To keep very still and hope she didn't have any idea how much he had wanted her right then.

Why had he kidded himself thinking of Bree as a cause, or as a hurt child so much younger than himself? What he felt went well past that. She set fires in him and fascinated him. She tugged at him in the most elemental way. He only wished she needed him the way he was beginning to need her.

Now, when he looked into her eyes wide with shock, he felt stupid. The last thing he wanted to do was to scare her or make her not trust him. "I'm sorry," he said, knowing the magnitude of the lie. He was only sorry that his impulsive action might make her bolt and run. "I'm afraid I'm that sort of person—spontaneous. And your idea's terrific." Awkwardly, he patted her shoulder. "I'll try to do better, I promise."

"All right," she breathed, but he didn't miss the way she clutched her closed hands to her middle.

"All right," he echoed. "Your idea's great." He turned from her and looked at the room. "We've got an artist at the station who does sketches when cameras aren't allowed in the courtroom. I'll get him with Murray so he can do a sketch." He closed his eyes for a brief moment, thankful that he could feel his body settling down again. "I'll do that as soon as we leave here."

Bree nervously touched her tongue to her lips again and felt her heart skip when she found his taste still there. He hadn't meant the kiss. And she was doing a job. That's what she was doing here with him. That thought helped her heart return to a more normal rhythm.

"All right, we have to come up with a plan to find Hannah." He hesitated as he looked at her. "You *will* help, won't you?"

That was too much, especially after the kiss. "It's your story. I'm just along to take pictures."

"And not to get involved?"

He'd hit dead center with the question, and she felt heat rising in her face. "It's a job," she murmured, facing the fact that this man could elicit stronger emotions from her than anyone had for a very long time. And she wasn't comfortable with that fact at all.

"Lady, are you trying to tell me that all that anger and those tears mean you aren't involved?" he asked in a low voice.

No, she couldn't risk it. So she withdrew as quickly as she could. "I'll do what you asked me to do at the start—take pictures for you to use any way you want to."

He didn't speak for a moment, then shrugged. "Have it your way. I can do spots on *Heart of the Matter*, and I'll want some of your photos to go with it. But first I need to get the artist to Murray as soon as possible."

"What about this?" she asked about the room, grateful to have the conversation rerouted.

"We can't do anything about this mess." He reached for the box that held the nativity. "But we can do something about this. It's the only thing she has of any value, and I'm not going to leave it here to be stolen or ruined."

She felt strange about what he was doing, yet she understood. "But what if the police come and—"

"Who's going to call them?"

"Hannah could come back and find it gone."

"I'll give it to Murray to keep. I'll bet he's the first one she'll contact anyway." He held out the small box to her. "Would this fit in your purse so we can get past the manager? I don't want to have to explain things to him."

"I...I guess so," she said as she took the tiny box. It felt silky smooth and didn't weigh more than a few ounces. Just holding it made her start to worry again about the lady who owned it, and she tried to steel herself against that.

James picked up the framed picture. "And I can use this on the air, proof of who Hannah once was." He opened his jacket, tucked it into the waistband of his jeans, then tugged his jacket closed and zipped it. "I'll give it to her when she comes back."

Bree saw the determination in his expression, that need to believe this would all end happily ever after, so she slid the box into her purse. It wasn't her business if he believed in rainbows and happy endings. She took out her camera and snapped the case open. "I should take some shots of this."

"It wouldn't hurt, for reference if nothing else."

Bree took off the lens cap and raised the camera to look through the viewfinder at a very different room from the one she'd photographed the day before. Looking at the composition of the shots and not at the devastation of a life, she set the shutter speed, focused and clicked the shutter.

When she lowered the camera minutes later, she found James watching her intently from the door. "Did you get enough?" he asked.

She nodded and snapped the lens cap back on. "More than enough," she muttered.

"Then let's go," he said. "I need to see Murray, to get the artist down here and figure out what kind of spots to do about Hannah."

Bree followed, thankful to put the destruction behind her as the door closed. At the bottom of the stairs, James hesitated, then led the way through the arched doorway into a back hall. At the second door on the left with a two on the faded wood, he stopped and knocked once.

The manager opened the door, a can of beer in one hand. "Can you tell what's missing?"

"No. But I wanted to thank you for telling me about what happened."

He shrugged. "Hate that sort of thing going on around here. I suppose you can get in touch with her grandson and tell him what happened, can't you?"

Bree felt James tense as he asked, "Her grandson?"

Chapter 10

Yeah, her grandson," the fat man said. "But he didn't look no more like her than you do."

"What *did* he look like?" James asked, feeling his whole being tense.

The man took a long drink of his beer, then wiped the back of his hand across his mouth. "Shorter than you, darker, not too fancy, maybe fifty and wearing a plaid work shirt. I figured it was strange, you being her nephew and all and being younger than that guy who says he's her grandson."

Roy Lester? "When was he here?"

"Yesterday after you'd been by. Near evening."

"Did he tell you his name?"

The manager shook his head. "No. But you both had the same password—Andrew Jackson."

Twenty dollars seemed to be the going rate to invade an elderly woman's world, James thought as he swallowed bitterness at the back of his throat. "What did he want?"

"To leave his old grandmother a little something."

James hesitated, then committed himself irrevocably to going public about Hannah. He reached in his pocket and took out a business card to hand to the man. "If he comes back, would you call me at this number?"

The man took the card, read it and sucked in a breath as he looked at James. "I knew I'd seen you. Is old Lady Vickers really your aunt?"

"No, just someone I'm worried about," James hedged.

The man held his beer in his left hand and held out his other hand to James. "Oscar Berkeley. Nice to meet you, Mr. Chapman."

James shook hands with the man, a cool, clammy grasp, then drew back. "Call me." He started toward the front door with Bree silently walking by his side.

"I'll be sure to do just that," the man yelled down the hall after them.

James stepped outside and went down the stairs toward the Bronco. He took a deep breath of the cool, late-afternoon air. The sky had become more heavy and dark while they'd been inside and, once in the car, James turned on the heater. He turned to Bree, the first time he'd looked directly at her since the kiss. "Does the description of Hannah's grandson sound familiar?"

"Roy Lester," she said, her tone flat.

He undid his jacket and took out the picture, then put it in the console between the two seats. "But that doesn't mean he was the one who broke into her room," James said as he put the car in gear. "If he paid twenty dollars to go up there, why would he turn around and break in?"

"A movie star fanatic?" Bree offered, resting her purse and camera on her lap.

James drove slowly down the street, trying to concentrate on Roy Lester and the break-in, but all he could concentrate on was the way Bree had been withdrawing, pulling away from him and the situation. And he didn't know how to stop it.

Then he saw a sign pointing east toward police head-quarters, and he decided to try to prolong his time with Bree any way he could. "Would you object to a short detour?"

"What detour?" she asked, and he glanced at her as she took the nativity out of her purse and set it by the picture.

"Police headquarters is just a few blocks away, near the freeway. I want to stop there and talk to a detective I know, then head for the hospital to talk to Murray."

He sensed, rather than saw her shrug. "Sure," she said.

He turned right, went up a few streets to Broadway, then headed east on the busy road. He stole a quick look at Bree and felt a rushing renewal of the fear he'd experienced in the room after he'd kissed her. He'd been terrified Bree would break away from his world permanently. He could sense that point was very close.

He stared straight ahead as he absorbed the haunting sensation of desire that, with this woman, went well be-yond the physical. Bree touched him in a way he couldn't begin to comprehend. And maybe he'd better not try. He didn't know if she could give anything to a man—yet. And he had an idea that if he once had her, he wouldn't be able to ever let her go.

His hands tightened on the steering wheel as police head-quarters came into sight, a new blue and gray mirrored building that rose ten stories, shiny and new, out of a ragged neighborhood that bordered the freeway. He slowed at the entrance to the visitors' parking lot.

Bree tensed. Along with rows of squad cars and visitors' cars, a whole platoon of news vans and trucks clustered around two metal gates that protected the entry to the underground parking garages. One of the vans from Channel Three was right near the gate, and a crowd milled around the woven metal barriers.

James rounded another corner, drove to the back side of the building and parked at the curb. He got out, walked to the parking meter and pushed coins in the slot on top.

Bree didn't move. She never should have agreed to come here. The milling press made nerves bunch in her stomach. The press and the police. The last time she'd talked to a policeman had been the day after Dean's death—a uniformed man had come to the lodge, his dark eyes filled with pity.

"I'm sorry to have to ask these questions, but we need to make out a report. You weren't there when your husband died, were you?"

"No." *I was running away from everything.*

"How long were you gone?"

"Two or three hours." *Long enough to know I couldn't keep going, that I had to come back.*

"Was your husband complaining about feeling ill?"

"No." *Just about life, and about me.*

"This is just routine in cases of sudden death," he had assured her. "Did he have a history of heart problems?"

"No." *Just a history of not being able to cope with life without help, of taking and taking from me until I didn't have any more to give.*

"Are you coming in with me?" James asked as he pulled her door open. "We can go through the back and avoid all the traffic."

It was too easy for her to slip back into the past, to feel it all again. Right now it seemed more important not to be alone with her thoughts than to stay out of the station, so she said, "Yes, I'll come."

They got out and Bree fell into step with James as he headed for an entrance about a hundred feet from the confusion in the parking lot.

Detective Calvin Browsky wasn't like any policeman Bree had seen before—rather, he had the look of a dedicated surfer, complete with Hawaiian shirt and jeans. And he didn't act like any of the policemen Bree had had contact with. He was easy in his manner, with dark eyes that seemed genuinely friendly, shaggy blond hair around a tanned face

and a high-school class ring on one finger. But he did have
a gun tucked into a leather shoulder holster.

Bree stood in front of his desk in an office on the second
floor, a glass-walled area done in greens and browns and
smelling of new paint and carpeting. "I can't tell you anything new about the investigation, James. I'm only in here
today because I'm clearing up some other business. This is
supposed to be my vacation."

James stood so close to Bree that his arm touched hers
when he moved. "Your men haven't even been to her
boardinghouse, Cal," he said.

The man leaned back in his chair and began to turn the
class ring around and around on his finger. "I don't know
if they have or not. I told you, technically I'm on vacation.
But I promise to try to get some men over there as soon as I
can."

"It's been ransacked," James said.

Cal sat forward. "What?"

"Someone broke in there last night or early this morning
and went through it."

"When was it reported?"

"It wasn't. The guy who owns the place isn't the sort to
look to the city's finest for anything except harassment."

"I'll send someone over."

"When?" James persisted.

"When we have time. There's something going on right
now that has top priority. But I promise we'll do all we can
to find the lady."

James leaned forward, resting his hands flat on the desktop. "She's been gone too long, Cal."

"Maybe she wants to be gone," the policeman said, but
not in a mean way. "That happens all the time in that area.
People move on. They get restless."

"The lady's close to eighty, for heaven's sake. She left
everything she had in this world. Where would she go?"

"Maybe she got confused and headed to the place she
lived before she landed in San Diego." His logic wasn't easy

to push aside. "I don't know. But I do know we don't have the manpower to put a full team on—"

A sudden commotion on the other side of a glass wall drew the attention of all three people in the office. There was yelling, banging and the sound of running feet. As James turned, Bree twisted around to look through the glass. The first things she saw were bright lights, and she knew all too well that meant the press with their cameras and floodlights.

"We're transferring a guest," the detective said. "And we didn't send out announcements. It beats me how everyone knows what we're going to do before we do it."

Bree went closer to the barrier and watched a man being hurried down a central aisle between desks that held computers. The bald man she'd seen being picked up the day before was being escorted toward doors on the far side of the squad room. An officer was on one side, a short man in a dark suit on the other. A phalanx of uniformed men opened a path for them through a crush of newspeople.

The sight of the press going after someone like a school of sharks made Bree vaguely sick. They never stopped if they thought they had a story. Never.

"Your priority case?" James murmured.

Bree turned her back on the scene and looked at Cal, who was staring past her into the other room. "Yes, actually he is. *Top* priority."

"He's the one you picked up for the murder of the cop a bit back?"

His face tightened. "He's the one who *might* have killed Andy Dawson. Andy was my partner when I worked vice. Concklin's being held for questioning."

"Did he do it?" James asked bluntly.

"Friend to friend?" Cal responded.

"Yes."

"On a gut level, yes. I'm sure he did it. And if we get lucky, we'll be able to build a case to justify an indictment."

"You don't think you have enough on him?"

Cal stared into the other room until the doors swung shut and peace returned. Then he leaned back and looked at James. "I'm not sure, not yet. We've got a knife that's his, but it's wiped clean. The blade might match the wound pattern, but so could a hundred others. His clothes had traces of blood on them, but it's type O, and half the world has that type—along with Andy. And Concklin might have a motive. He was getting close to being nailed for drug dealings, and Andy was the one getting the evidence. It might stick. It was enough to bring him in and hold him for seventy-two hours. What we need is a witness, but you know how the people downtown are. No one saw anything. Cops are the enemy."

"A real image problem."

Cal studied James for a moment from under pale lashes. "I'll make you a deal, James."

"What's that?"

"If you try to help our image with the good citizens of San Diego, I'll look into the Vickers case myself—even though I'm on vacation."

James hesitated, then reached his hand across the desk. "You've got a deal."

It wasn't until James was driving the Bronco toward the hospital that Bree thought of something. "Does William have insurance?" She felt heat in her face as soon as the words were out. Of course he wouldn't. "That was a stupid question. What I meant to ask is, do you think he'll get good care?"

"He's probably in on charity, and I hope that doesn't affect the quality of his care." James drove toward a massive complex of older Spanish-style buildings, then turned at the entry that was marked by a starkly modern tower of mirrors and parked on the street.

Bree might not want to get any more involved than she had up to now, but she did have money. She admitted it was probably a token to ease her conscience. But she made an offer. "I've got enough money to help him."

James shut off the engine and turned to her. "Enough money?"

She wouldn't tell him she could probably buy the hospital if she wanted to. "My husband left me very well off." She could deal with that sort of involvement, writing a check and making things easier for someone. "William is going to need a lot of medical attention."

"But you don't want to get involved in looking for Hannah?"

His direct question took her aback. "I didn't say that. I'm concerned about Hannah and mad about what's happened to her, but it's your job. I—" She bit her lip. "I just wanted to help William in some way."

"And I'm sure William will be grateful." She couldn't read his tone, and before she could say anything else, he had the door open. "Let's go in and find out what's going on."

"No."

He stopped and turned to her. "What?"

"I don't want to go in. Just go and talk to Murray about the artist seeing him and see what William needs. I'll wait here."

He didn't argue with her. "I'll be back as soon as I can," he murmured. He got out and took off at a jog for the entry.

It wasn't until James was going through the glass doors that Bree realized the small case with the nativity was still sitting on the console between the seats, along with the picture.

Going after James wasn't even an option. She wouldn't go into a hospital, with its deadly silence and odors of medication and death. Sinking back in the seat, she took a deep breath and closed her eyes.

Hannah heard sirens outside, muffled but clearly distinguishable. If only she had a watch. She didn't know what time it was, or how long William had been gone. She had another candy bar left. But she didn't want to stay here. She didn't feel safe anymore. The people were getting closer all the time, and *he* was one of them. She could feel it.

She slid down on the bed, tugging the covers up until they were over her head. Curling into a ball, she closed her eyes. She'd wait. William had told her not to leave, not to show herself. She wouldn't, not yet. But if he wasn't back when the last candy bar was gone, she would have to go look for him.

"It's all set," James said as he got back into the Bronco fifteen minutes later. "The artist is coming right down, and he'll get a sketch back to the station as soon as he can."

She sat up as he closed the door. "How's William?"

"Hanging on, but barely. Murray's going to stay until he's out of surgery, which could be a few more hours."

"The bills?"

"Murray's putting up what's needed now, but I told him you wanted to help. He was touched. His very words were, 'The Christmas magic always works.' Then he said to tell you, 'Bless you.'"

She swallowed hard. "It's only money," she muttered. "Not magic."

"That's where you're wrong. Magic is in the eye of the beholder. That's a Chapman saying from way back." James reached for her hands, clenched together in her lap. "Trust me. It's true."

She straightened, breaking the contact immediately by reaching for the nativity box. "You forgot this."

"Completely." Then he glanced at the hospital. "I think we'll hold on to it until Murray's back at his place. He doesn't have anywhere to keep it in there."

As Bree put it back on the console, James started the engine, but hesitated and looked at her. "Now we have to figure out what to put on the segment about Hannah. I'd like your input on how it can be done most effectively."

"I told you," she said quickly. "This is all yours. I wouldn't know where to begin, doing something for television." She fingered her camera case on her lap. "Speaking of pictures, I need to get some soon or the light will be gone."

"I could take you now, but I need to get back to the station right away. Could you hold off on the shots until tomorrow?"

She reached for the handle. "I can take a cab."

"No. I don't want you down there by yourself." Quickly he added, "It'll be dark soon, and it's not safe. Come with me to the station, then I'll take you home and we can get some shots tomorrow." James held his breath, not wanting to argue with her but desperately wanting her to stay with him a while longer.

"I can get a taxi from the station," she said, and she let go of the handle.

A minor concession, but he accepted it immediately. "Sure. Or I can drive you home if I get done there quickly." Without waiting for her to respond, he headed for the freeway. He kept himself from looking at Bree, but with the intent of getting her involved in the program in some way, he began to talk. "I get the most done in my work by thinking out loud. I've had long conversations with thin air getting my thoughts straight, so bear with me."

When she didn't say a thing, he continued, "If I get the sketch in time for the taping, I think it should be on the screen as long as possible. Maybe for the full segment. It needs to be imprinted in people's minds."

Bree sat very still, but he could sense her looking out the window at the late afternoon traffic on the freeway.

"But it has to make an impact, as much of an impact as if we ran film of Hannah." He took a breath. "The spots the police put on television, the bulletins you were talking about, were they like wanted posters?"

"Yes," she said.

"Black and white?"

"Uh-huh."

"Head and shoulders?"

"Uh-huh."

He gripped the steering wheel tightly but didn't give up. "Is the moon made of green cheese?"

"Uh—" That brought her up, and he sensed her turning to him. "What?"

"Just seeing if you were paying attention."

"You said you were talking to yourself," she murmured.

"But I like to hear someone talk back to me. I'm not doing very well on points today, am I?"

"I wasn't aware we were keeping score," she muttered.

"We aren't." He took a chance and reached out to touch Bree's hand, thankful when he felt her tense, yet she didn't jerk away. "Can I be honest with you, Bree?"

"Please."

Here goes, he thought. "I like you. No, strike that, I am fascinated with you." Boy, he was putting his cards on the table. A calculated risk. "And I wish we could just talk or ride or walk and get to know each other." He finally looked at her, but she wasn't looking at him. Her head was turned to the window, her forehead resting against the glass. "Bree?"

"I heard you," she breathed.

"And?"

"And what?"

"Can we start all over and get to know each other?"

"Why?"

Her hands felt so tiny under his, and so cold. "Lady, I don't usually have to beg someone to be my friend. I don't want to start now."

"Friends?" she asked softly, and he sensed her turning to him.

"Please," he said, coming closer to begging than he ever had with any woman.

Bree felt the tension in his hand on hers, and she knew there was no point in lying. She could tell him the truth, at least a part of it. But she couldn't do that if he was touching her, so she drew away, pushing closer to the door. "Do *you* want the truth?"

"Yes," he said without hesitating.

"I'm not good at being friends. It's not one of my strong suits. My...my husband and I were friends for years before we married. He was my older brother's friend, around the house all the time, and when I was grown, we realized we were in love." It sounded so neat, so simple, and it had been anything but that. "To make this short, he's gone, and I've decided that I'm better off alone." That sounded neurotic, and she wondered why it hadn't before. "I mean, I think I'd rather just do what I want to do and—"

"Survive?" James asked.

"Is it wrong to want to survive?" she asked, her voice getting tighter.

"No, it's just damned lonely," he muttered.

"But it's my choice," she countered, wishing her voice would stay steady instead of beginning to quiver.

"That's right. It's your choice."

"And it's none of your business, is it?" she asked.

He didn't say anything for a long time, then as he turned toward the station, he finally spoke up. "I apologize. I told you I act on impulse. I also speak on impulse. I'm sorry."

Bree sank back in the seat, unaware until then that she was having trouble breathing. "I'm sorry, too. I overreact."

"We're even," he murmured and patted her hand, but his touch didn't linger. "Back to the Hannah spots. I can make them like a police bulletin, I suppose. The picture on the screen with a voice-over, 'Do you know this person,' and a description."

He paused, and she knew he was waiting to see if she was going to respond. Feeling foolish, she forced words past the tightness in her throat and was surprised that she sounded normal. "That would work for the announcements, but what about your spot on the news?"

"That's another matter," he responded evenly. "It has to be longer and more provocative."

James heard Bree take a deep breath, and he was relieved when she spoke again. "You could start by telling about Hannah, then use the old picture. I don't know what you can do with your equipment, but what if you start with the old picture, then fade into the sketch of Hannah now?"

"They can do wonders with computers in editing. I can tell about Hannah the child star, then Hannah the elderly lady working at the restaurant." He could feel excitement, that peculiar sensation he experienced when he knew he was on the right track with a story. "I've got three minutes tonight on the broadcast. The inserts will have to be fifteen seconds and run as public service announcements."

"Will Carson go for that?" Bree asked, her voice soft in the gathering shadows of early evening.

"Sure." James knew he sounded a lot more assured than he felt. It would take some talking, but if he pointed out that it would promote the station's image, it might get through. "He's given me full control over my segments for *Heart of the Matter*. I'll work on the rest."

Rain began to fall in large drops, spotting the windshield and blotting out the daylight. James snapped on the headlights and turned up the heater. Things were going better than he'd hoped with Bree, now that she was finally talking to him again.

Bree looked away from James, in the leather chair by hers, and across to Carson, tilting back in his chair behind the desk. The office became ominously quiet after James finished his pitch for the Hannah segments. Only the sound of blowing rain on the window broke the silence.

When James looked as if he couldn't stand the silence any longer, he said quickly, "And what a time to do it, Carson. Christmas. The season of giving, of caring. Families. Little children. Christmas trees. Love of fellow man."

"Enough," Carson said, at the moment Bree thought the same thing. Carson sat forward and held up one hand, palm out. "Stop before you bring up motherhood and apple pie, James."

James shrugged. "Well?"

Bree swallowed hard, trying to get past James's words and concentrate on the interaction between the two men as Carson asked, "Well what?"

"Will you give me the time during the day for fifteen-second public service spots?"

"As far as *Heart of the Matter* goes, you know you can do what you want. The viewers will probably love it, but I've got a commitment to a set list of charities that come under the public service heading. And the programming for them is already decided."

"So? You're the boss around here." James sat forward. "What's a few fifteen-second blurbs? You can't fill them with anything better."

"They have to be filled by recognized charities. Otherwise we don't fulfill our community commitment. You know that."

James stood, pressed his hands flat on the desk and leaned closer to Carson. "Recognized charities? What about people? What about a poor old lady who happened to be a child movie star? Do we relegate her to the status of a statistic?" He stopped long enough to take a deep breath. "What about *you* having a heart, forgetting business for once, and doing it out of simple caring?"

Carson studied him intently before saying anything. "I asked you this once, and I'll ask again. Is this a repeat of Chicago?"

James jerked back from the desk as if he'd been burned, and Bree saw that his hands were unsteady as he pushed them into his jacket pockets. She spoke up quickly. "James, the spots on the news will be good. They'll—"

"They aren't enough, Bree." He spoke without taking his gaze off Carson. "Not nearly. I won't chance doing that again."

"You didn't do anything," Carson said.

A knock was followed by the door being opened and someone asking, "Is James in there?"

Bree turned and saw a man coming into the office carrying a huge drawing pad. When he spotted James, he crossed to him. "Here're your sketches," he said. "I did three. I hope they're what you want." He handed the pad to James.

"Thanks, Al," James said.

Al nodded and said, "Sure, anytime." Then he left.

As James opened the pad, Bree stood and went to look over his shoulder at a head-and-shoulders charcoal portrait of a fragile, tiny-featured woman. Wispy hair feathered back from a wide-eyed, gently lined face, and the smile, joyful and filled with the wonder of life, was instantly recognizable—the same expression the small girl on the horse had possessed.

"Hannah," James said softly, and in that single word he irrevocably made the woman real for Bree.

He reached for the framed picture of the child he'd set on Carson's desk and held the sepia photo by the sketch. The same person seventy years younger.

"Yes, it's her," Bree said softly.

Carson had come around the desk. He stared at the two pictures for a long time before he spoke softly. "Do the spots, but keep them to fifteen seconds and tie them in with the station."

"I'll have the logo branded on my forehead," James muttered.

"When do you want to start?"

"If I can have studio two tonight for the *Heart* spot to put on the eleven o'clock broadcast, then have a studio again around nine in the morning, I'll have the other spots ready to start tomorrow after eleven."

"Tonight's no problem," Carson said. "I'll have to let you know in the morning when you can have a studio tomorrow."

"Can you run the spots between the soaps when a lot of people are watching?"

"I'll try," Carson said, and sat in his chair.

James looked at him. "Thanks." Then he headed for the door, and Bree followed him to his office.

In the office, James put the pad and picture on the desk, then picked up his phone. Bree watched from the open door as he pushed three numbers, then spoke into the receiver. "Carson said I can have studio two to shoot a spot. When will it be clear? . . . Good, get a crew ready and tell makeup I'll be there in fifteen minutes."

When he came toward her, Bree moved to the desk. James closed the door. "Now, to get ready to project my image," he said as she turned to him.

It took her a minute to realize he was taking off his clothes, first his jacket, then his shirt. He laid them on a nearby chair, then reached for the blue blazer with a station logo on the breast pocket, the off-white shirt and the tie hanging on the back of the door.

Bree felt her mouth go dry as she was faced with his naked chest with its dusting of dark hair on a ripple of solid muscles. Then he turned and she saw his back, smooth and strong, and it made her heart flop crazily against her ribs.

It took her a full heartbeat before she could manage to look at the sketch on the desk. But she only saw blurred lines. Compared to how she felt now, it had been easy for her to deal with the emotions she'd experienced during the kiss. But now, she was stunned by the strength of her desire for this man. She'd never faced anything like this in her life, not even for Dean at the start of their marriage.

Protectively, she closed her eyes, as much to regain her composure as to make sure she didn't look at James again. If he knew what she was feeling right now, if he had any idea . . . Desire shouldn't have been born so quickly and so easily, taking her breath away like this. It had to be the timing, the intensity of what had happened today with William, then Hannah's room and finally seeing the sketch.

When she heard James near the door, she moved past the desk to the window. With an unsteady hand she parted the blinds and stared at the rain driven by a wind that bent trees with its force. The intensity of the storm outside seemed to echo the unsettling emotions inside her, emotions she'd never experienced until she met James.

Chapter 11

I wrote some text for the special last night, but it'll work perfectly for this,'' James said from behind her.

Scrunching her eyes shut tightly for a fleeting moment, Bree tried to pull away emotionally from the things that had happened in the past two days. But it was a struggle. For a fleeting moment, the stunning image of being held by James, feeling his chest against her breasts, his heat pressed to hers, flitted through her mind. And she tried to kill it by letting go of the blind and speaking as she turned.

"How long will this take?" Steeling herself, she looked at James, inordinately thankful to see him fully dressed and tying his tie.

With a tug, he squared it with the collar of the shirt, then straightened his jacket. "Not too long," he said. He was still wearing his jeans and sneakers.

"Good," Bree managed, unable to take her eyes off his hands tugging at the lapels of his jacket, strong hands but gentle hands. When they'd touched her...

James picked up the sketch and the old photo. "Let's go. I still need to get into makeup."

Bree nervously hurried after him down a wide hallway with thirty-foot ceilings. They turned the corner and passed a set of twenty-foot-high metal doors with a huge numeral one painted in blue, then stopped at the next, emblazoned with a two.

But he didn't open the door. Instead he opened a normal-sized one directly across the hall, and Bree could see into a small green room lined with mirrors framed with white lights. Two women were in there. The one standing by a chair that looked as though it belonged in a barber shop was about the size of a sprite. She wore a blue cotton smock, and her flaming red hair was pulled back from her face with a red headband. "Daphne" was stitched on the yoke of the smock. She was carefully touching up the eyelashes of a blond woman in the chair, who glanced at the door.

"No moving, Stacey," Daphne said as she stroked mascara carefully. "I'm almost done."

"Good," Stacey said and lifted her forefinger in greeting to James. "I heard you were still here, James."

"You can't get rid of me. How long are you going to be?"

"Daphne, how long?" she asked.

The tiny woman studied Stacey for a long moment, then stated, "I'm finished with you."

Stacey stood and took off a bib that had covered most of the upper half of her body. She was wearing the same blazer as James, but with a pale blue blouse and a gray wool skirt that hugged her trim hips. "It's all yours, James," she said and left.

Daphne held out the bib to James and smiled. "Ah, a man. Hop on."

Bree stayed by the door, unable to take her eyes off James as he settled in the chair. Since that moment in the office, she'd been unable to look at the man objectively. Now all she seemed aware of was his hands holding the chair arms and the strength of his thighs testing the worn denim of his jeans.

"Hon?" Daphne said with a glance at Bree.

"Yes?" she said, flustered by the bombarding images she was trying to deal with.

"Could you close the door?" She started to tuck the bib in around James's collar. "I don't need that awful light from the hall ruining the flesh tones while I work."

Ten minutes later, Bree and James stepped into studio two, a high-ceilinged space, where banks of heavy lights hung on metal frames and thick cables crisscrossed the cement floor. The walls were hidden by a floor-to-ceiling drape of translucent white that ran on a ceiling track. The air felt as if it wasn't more than sixty degrees.

Bree rubbed her arms, wishing she'd brought her jacket with her, and looked at the set in the middle of the room, a half circle two feet high and tiled in yellow. A U-shaped desk padded with deep red leather was backed by a blank, off-blue screen. Three cameras faced it.

Three men in casual clothes were on the floor, one at the middle camera, one sitting behind the desk in a central chair and another behind him looking at the desk. Each wore a single headphone. "More top light," the last man called out and shifted to look over the sitting man's other shoulder. "And kill the shadows under his chin. Bring up a baby K right there." He pointed at a row of small lights mounted on the platform in front of the desk. He tapped the seated man on the shoulder, then moved toward the cameras. "All right, do sound," he said.

The man at the desk was reciting "Little Miss Muffet" with a completely straight face. He stopped in midsentence where the spider sat down beside Miss Muffet, touched his earpiece, then gave the thumbs-up sign. "Check."

Bree looked behind her to find out who he'd motioned to and saw a booth to the right of the doors. Lights in the booth exposed two men, one giving a thumbs-up sign.

"Are you ready?" James asked as he walked toward the set, carefully avoiding the cables.

The man at the camera turned. "Two minutes, James."

James turned to Bree. "You can go into the control booth or sit over there." He pointed to a canvas chair behind a camera.

"I'll sit in the chair," she said, and made her way over to it.

While she settled, James went on the set and sat behind the desk. He snapped on a tieclip microphone, put in an almost invisible earpiece and attached a tiny power pack to his waistband under his jacket. He tapped it once, then settled in the chair with his papers in front of him.

He looked at the cameraman. "I'm just going to go through the whole thing once. Then we can see if it works."

"All right. When you're ready."

"Who's tossing it to me?" he asked.

The man who'd been behind the desk looked at a clipboard by his feet. "Daryl."

James nodded, straightened his papers, rotated his head as if to loosen tension then squared his shoulders. "All right, and make a note to use the station logo behind me when it's done."

Bree heard the others talking, but she didn't take in any of it. She focused on James completely as the lights got brighter until every detail of him could be seen without shadows. She narrowed her eyes as James took a deep breath, and she could almost feel the cold air rushing into her own lungs.

"Thanks, Daryl," James said to the empty space at his left, then looked into the camera. "Tonight I have something special for you on *Heart of the Matter*. This isn't a story about someone who's been helped, but someone who needs help. Your help." He paused for a second, then said, "Once upon a time there was a little girl with curls and a wonderful smile. Her name was Sweet Little Hannah..."

His voice seeped into Bree, getting deep inside her and making her eyes prick with tears. She realized that all the feelings she thought had died during her marriage had only been hibernating. And now they embarrassed her with their intensity. It had been a year since Dean's death, and a year before that they'd all but stopped making love. Their love life had become sporadic long before that, with Dean not able or not willing to have any intimacy.

Her emotions felt raw and exposed, an uncomfortable sensation. As she listened to James, she knew he wouldn't have any problem making the city care. He was very close to making her care, and it scared her.

An hour later, in his office, James tugged off the tie and blazer. Bree sat behind the desk looking at the sketch of Hannah. "Do me a favor?" he asked. "Push line seven on the phone and ask for a messenger?"

She did as he asked, then put the receiver back in its cradle. "What now?" she asked and glanced at him. He'd kept the shirt on.

"I need to get the pictures to production so the tape can be put together and edited for tonight's program."

She turned over the photo and looked at the back. "You'll need to take it out of the frame, won't you?"

James took the picture. He set the photo on the desk facedown, then reached for a letter opener. Carefully, he pried the thin wooden back away from the frame until the back of the photo and the mat were exposed. He put the tip of the letter opener under the photo and lifted it out of the frame.

James looked at it, then held it out to Bree. "Look at the back."

Bree read out loud, "Charles Landis, Photographer, Hollywood." She glanced at James. "Can it be traced?"

"I don't know." He reached for the phone and pushed three numbers. "Bryan? On the back of a picture of Hannah is a photographer's name—Charles Landis of Hollywood. Will that help?'' He listened for a moment, then hung up and looked at Bree. "He'll check."

Bree sank back in the seat of the Bronco, tiredness permeating her whole being, as persistent as the falling rain outside. Yet tension coiled in her, a tension she couldn't begin to figure out how to ease.

James drove in silence through the parking lot that was bathed in the yellow light from the overhead vapor lamps and sheeting rain. The shimmering glow invaded the car and cast a strangely unreal glow on the man at the wheel.

"It's going to work," James said as they drove onto the street and headed to the freeway.

"I hope it will," Bree murmured, and knew she really did. She wanted Hannah found safe and well, but Bree didn't want it to depend on anything she did.

"I'm going to be honest with you," James said abruptly.

She wasn't aware he'd been anything else after she'd found out who he was. "Pardon me?"

"I need to explain Carson's reactions in his office. He thinks I'm having a midlife crisis."

"A midlife crisis?" she echoed.

"You're too young to get to one of those," James said with a laugh. Then the sound died. "Basically it's when your whole life goes into reevaluation. Renovation, if you like."

She understood that completely. "Why would Carson think that?"

He drove up the freeway ramp and merged into the stream of traffic, surprisingly heavy for eight o'clock on a stormy night. "You have to understand that Carson and I go back a long way, back to Vietnam. We were both there as journalists. War makes bonds between people, unlikely partners. I know it did with us. Even after we came back, we stayed in touch. Carson settled in Houston, got married, got divorced, then moved here during the station's rebuilding. He's into business, into negotiating, programming and worrying about money."

"And you're—"

"Into people, I suppose. I love that one-on-one." He inhaled roughly. "I've been with all the networks at one time or other. About ten years ago, I settled in Chicago and worked at a network affiliate there. That's when I got married. Roots." When he glanced at her, his face was shadowed and unreadable. "Not a good reason to make that big a commitment, but it seemed reasonable for a while."

She knew that roots and expectations had pushed her into Dean's life, and the fact they'd fallen in love had seemed a wonderful bonus. "We all have our reasons for what we do."

"Amen to that," he murmured. "About a year before Carson came to Chicago to persuade me to come out here, I quit the station. I took off and camped for months, needing to be alone—wanting that isolation."

James wanting isolation, to be away from people? That didn't fit, not when she knew how much he seemed to thrive on being with people. "Why?" she asked, turning in the seat until she was resting partly against the seat, partly against the door and she could see him in the shadows.

She watched him smooth his mustache, then take a breath. "Something happened to make me rethink my life. It was winter in Chicago and incredibly cold." He spoke slowly in a low voice, almost as if he were talking to himself. "There was an old man, a retired factory worker. I still remember his name—Leo Jarvis Monroe. He'd outlived his wife of fifty-five years and all his three children. The man was eighty-six, and he lived in a miserable little apartment in what politicians charitably call a low income housing project.

"That winter Leo didn't have enough money to pay his rent and heat his room." James shrugged sharply. "He made his choice and died in a room that was below zero. No one even knew he was gone for over a week. I was sent on a remote shoot when the police found him. Bree, you've never seen injustice until you've witnessed something like that. I couldn't begin to comprehend such a needless loss. But I knew I didn't want to report horrors like that anymore. I walked away from it, away from everything."

He hit the steering wheel softly with the flat of his hand. "As corny as it sounds, I wanted to make a difference. I wanted people to care about each other. Being a reporter didn't cut it. So I took off to think, and everything ended. My marriage, which hadn't been in the best of shape, fell apart. Louise couldn't understand me walking away from a six-figure income. Her values suddenly weren't mine. Hell, they probably hadn't been for a long time."

He shrugged off what must have been a terrible time for him. "Then Carson found me and—" he turned and slanted her a look and a shadowy smile that seemed less than spontaneous "—he made me an offer I couldn't refuse. It's the best move I ever made."

It stunned her that he could care that much and that he'd found a way to make a difference without being destroyed by pain and regret. "And what if it hadn't worked?"

He didn't hesitate. "I would have kept trying." He stared into the rainy night. "I know Carson thinks I'm being overly sentimental about Hannah, that I'm still seeing Leo Jarvis Monroe dead in that awful apartment."

"Are you?" she asked softly.

He raked his fingers through his hair. "Probably, but that doesn't lessen what I want to do for Hannah, or Murray, or William. Can anyone care too much?"

No, but caring couldn't right the wrongs of the world. It couldn't even come close. She knew that better than anyone. "Carson understands, and he agreed to let you do what you wanted to do."

"Finally." He sped up and moved into the fast lane. "Now I have to make it work."

"You will." Bree knew James could never understand why she couldn't take a chance on caring, not when he seemed intent on putting himself on the line all the time.

The rain never let up, and by the time James pulled the Bronco into her driveway, the water ran down the concrete in a river. Bree picked up her purse and camera, then looked at James. "With this rain I doubt I can get shots for a while."

He looked at the stormy night. "A rainy Christmas," he said softly, then turned to her. "When it clears we can head down to take some pictures. Is there someplace I can pull in so you won't get soaked getting to the house?"

"No." She laughed softly. "You know it never rains in southern California. They didn't make any concessions for rain when the house was built in the forties." She pulled on the handle. "I'll make a run for it."

Then she was out in the wind and rain, running up the walkway to the door. But as she stepped onto the stone terrace, she felt her feet shoot out from under her. In slow motion, she soared upward, then fell for what seemed an eternity until she landed with a strangely soft thud on her back in the soaking grass. Her breath rushed out of her lungs, and the rain fell in her eyes, blurring the night.

From nowhere, James was there, bending over her, his body blocking some of the storm. "Bree, are you all right?" he was asking, his hands taking hers when she reached toward him. She felt herself being lifted as easily as if she'd been a tiny child. Then in one swift motion, she was high in James's arms.

"My camera and purse," she gasped, suddenly realizing they were lying somewhere in the shadows.

"I'll take care of them," James murmured.

Instinctively, she turned her face into his chest and circled his neck with her arms. As she held him, he hurried through the rain. At the door, he gently set her on her feet. "I'll be right back," he said and darted into the downpour again.

By the time Bree managed to get her key out of her pocket, James was back with her camera and purse. He took the key from her and pushed it in the lock. The door opened and Bree almost stumbled forward into warm comfort that seemed as welcoming as a soft blanket. She turned as James came in after her and closed the door on the storm.

Her reactions to him seemed only to be increasing in intensity. She couldn't move as she looked at him, at rain glistening on his hair and mustache and darkening the shoulders of his jacket. A smear of grass and dirt streaked the front of the chambray jacket, but before she could say anything about it, James came nearer. Her breath caught when he reached out to her.

He touched her face, brushing at the wet hair clinging to her cheek. "You're soaked," he murmured as his finger trailed heat along her cheek and jaw. "You took quite a spill. Are you all right?"

"Fine. Just wet and..." She couldn't keep talking when her teeth began to chatter.

He shrugged as he unzipped his jacket and took it off. "You need to get out of those wet clothes," he said as he laid his jacket on the nearest box. He looked at her, a smile coming, crooked and stunningly endearing. "You might melt." Then he began to undo the buttons on her jacket.

She stood there like a child, letting him slip the jacket off her shoulders and tug her arms out of it. While he laid it next to his on the packing box, she watched him and felt the cold rain from her hair trickle down her back. He turned to her. "Where do you keep the towels?"

She had to think, her mind unfocused with him this close. It seemed the only thing she could concentrate on was the fact that he was taking care of her. She couldn't remember a man doing that before. "In...in the laundry," she finally said. "I'll get some." She moved past James into a small laundry area. She scooped up a few fresh towels from the linen closet, then brought them to James, who had gone into the kitchen and was rinsing out the coffeepot.

He turned and took the towel she offered him. Draping it around his neck, he motioned to the coffee maker. "I'll get this going."

"Good. I'll be back in a minute," she said and hurried through the house.

"Bree?" James called, and she turned on the first step of the staircase. He was in the arched doorway to the kitchen. "Where's your television?"

She almost said, "Beside my bed," then thought better of it. "It's upstairs, but it doesn't work."

He held on to the ends of the towel around his neck. "It's broken?"

"I can't get a picture on it. Everything's really snowy. Why?"

"I was hoping you'd watch the eleven o'clock broadcast and tell me what you think about it."

"I can bring it down if you want to try to get it to work."

"Bring it down?"

"It's a small set. I can bring it down," she said quickly and hurried up the stairs.

After stripping off her damp clothes, she towel-dried her hair into a tumble of damp ringlets, then slipped on a short white terry-cloth robe over her bra and panties. Barefoot, she went downstairs with the television. James was in the living room sitting on the couch, and the smell of coffee wafted on the air.

"You got the coffee maker going?" she asked as she crossed to the couch to hand James the television.

"I'm very versatile," he said as he stood and took the television from her. "Natural curls?" he asked as he looked at her damp hair.

"The bane of my existence," she murmured and hurried into the kitchen. By the time she came back with two mugs of hot coffee, James was on his haunches in front of the hearth doing something to the television. She settled on the couch, curling her legs under her and resting the mugs on her thighs. "Can you get a picture on it?"

He kept working without turning to her. "It's the cable. Reception in this part of the county isn't very good because of the hills, so it's all wired for cable. You've got the hookup, but I'm having to improvise to make it compatible with your set.''

She sat quietly, watching him work, while she sipped her coffee. The storm buffeted the house, but Bree felt remarkably snug. James finally stood and flipped on the set. The screen was blank for a minute, then it lit up with a recognizable color picture of a cereal commercial.

''That's a perfect picture,'' she said.

He sat by her on the couch, a foot of space separating them, and took the coffee she offered him. ''Small, but adequate.'' He settled back, crossing his legs with one ankle resting on a knee. ''Now you can't say you haven't seen me on the tube.''

She took a sip of coffee, then asked, ''When will you be on?''

He checked his watch. ''Fifteen minutes into the program.'' Then he looked into his mug, cradled between his hands. ''I don't suppose you have a little rum or brandy I can put in this to perk up the caffeine, do you?''

''As a matter of fact, there's an unopened bottle of brandy in the cupboard over the refrigerator. My father sent it to me right after I moved here.''

He stood and headed for the kitchen. ''I'll be back in a few minutes with the medicine. Just what the doctor ordered.''

Bree set her mug on the floor beside the couch, then settled into the cushions and leaned her head back. Just what the doctor ordered? She didn't think so, but it sounded good right now. She closed her eyes and the sound of the rain on the windows seemed steady and sure.

Suddenly, with no warning, no gradual building up to it, the jarring horror of the past was there, tearing at her, going full tilt to the climax. She'd forgotten so completely, she'd been so intent on her reactions to James, that the past had been pushed away. But now it came back, even more stunning than it had been at the construction site when she'd seen William. And before she could stop it, Dean was there, dead, and a scream came from deep inside her.

As James touched the bottle of brandy, he heard a scream. It ripped through him, making his hands jerk so much he almost dropped the bottle on the counter. He sprinted into the living room and saw Bree sitting on the couch, hunched over, her hands in tight fists on her thighs, her hair tumbling forward. And she rocked back and forth, the scream only echoing inside him now.

In a second he was with her, pulling her into his arms and holding her. "Bree, it's okay," he said. He heard her take a deep, shuddering breath as she turned her face into his chest, then she began to sob. His heart lurched, and he tangled his fingers in her damp hair, holding her close as he crooned, "I'm here. It's okay. It's okay."

He shifted, gathering her onto his lap and simply holding her while she cried. Gradually he could feel her settling, her breathing growing slower. Finally her body sagged weakly against him. With a shuddering sigh, she moved a bit to look at him.

"I must have been...been dreaming," she whispered, her face sleek with tears.

"Is it Hannah?" he asked, desperately needing to know.

"No, I...I have dreams, memories..." Her tongue darted out to touch her trembling lips. "I'm sorry."

I'm sorry, he wanted to say, *sorry for whatever tears you apart like this.* "Do you want to talk about it?"

Her clenched hands were pressed on his chest. "No. I...I'm just sorry it happened."

Impulsively he stroked her cheek with the tip of his finger. "If you ever want to talk, I'm here."

She nodded. "Thank you," she breathed.

God, even like this she was beautiful. Her lashes wet with tears, her skin pale, her lips unsteady. And she touched him on every level. He bent over her, intent on kissing away her distress, on giving to her, comforting her, protecting her. But once his lips touched hers and tasted the saltiness of her tears for the second time in one day, he knew he was lost. Lost in her essence, in her very being. He responded to her body, mind and soul.

In an instinct for survival, Bree circled his neck with her arms and held on to him. clinging to his solid reality as to a lifeline.

The horror began to diminish, and it didn't engulf her, not this time. Arms did, warm and strong, and lips that pushed back the shadows and fear. Just like in her dream— but this time it was real.

In a split second, fear and pain were replaced by a hunger that flared to life, a hunger she couldn't begin to define. All she understood was that she needed his touch, his closeness, whatever he offered. She needed it as much as she needed her next breath. Her mouth opened in invitation, and she could feel his heart thundering against her breasts.

She sank her fingers into the thick vitality of his hair and held on for dear life. Pressing closer, she moaned, her needs almost painful, and when James answered her passion with his own, she was lost. When the soft cloth of the robe on her shoulders was replaced by the gentle demands of his touch, she didn't fight it, she arched toward it. She found herself tugging at his shirt, trying to get closer, to feel his skin with her hands. Then she spread her palms on the muscular ridges of his stomach that she'd only touched with her eyes before, then higher until she felt the softness of hair and his heart thundering under her palms. He shuddered at her touch, and his nipple hardened.

Then she realized his hands echoed hers, hot on her skin, searching and finding the swelling of her breasts through the lace of her bra. Then the lace was gone, and sensations exploded in her, fragmenting in the most delicious way until his heat seemed to be hers, his heartbeat coming from her heart.

She'd never experienced such a total loss of control and such a rush of sensations. As his lips trailed along the arching line of her throat and to the soft cleft between her throbbing breasts, she felt raw desire. She'd felt desire before, but never this raging need that blotted out all reason. A desire that threatened to consume her, that made her ache in her soul, that made her need and want things she hadn't remembered existed until today.

It had been so long since she'd had these feelings that she marveled at the fact that James's touch seemed almost a first for her. His mustache tickled and teased as she sank back in the couch cushions with him over her. His mouth tasted her, drawing at her breasts, and she lifted, hungry, eager for his touch, demanding that his lips find her.

She wanted to be swallowed up by him, covered and contained by him and filled by him. Truthfully, she'd never understood the impact sexual intimacy could have on a person. She'd never experienced it with Dean, not really. And she hadn't known that until right now. A man who was almost a stranger to her had shown her a truth that had been either denied or hidden for a very long time.

Every nuance, every feeling she'd experienced in the past two days had been leading to this point, and she didn't deny it. She could love this man with a singlemindedness that was shattering.

Love? The word drew her up short. It cut through her haze of desire. Love. No. Never. And she wouldn't be a user, not the way she'd been used. Coldness seemed to crash over her, and she struggled to be free, to get away, to stop this giving and taking, this committing to a man she should never have allowed to get this close to her. Love? No, she wouldn't let it be that. Not when she knew the pain that could come.

She struggled, pushing at James, and he let her go, sitting back, his breathing as ragged as her own. She pushed into the corner of the couch, awkwardly tugging the robe around her, her fingers clutching the terry cloth together over her breasts. She'd loved Dean, but not the way she knew she could love this man if she let herself. And if the pain she'd received for loving Dean had been almost fatal, she knew she wouldn't survive if the same thing happened with James. She couldn't take the chance.

"Bree?" He said only her name, but she felt her whole being contract. She couldn't even look at him.

She closed her eyes so tightly she could see small explosions of color behind her lids. "I'm sorry. Really sorry," she gasped. "I can't—"

"No, I know you can't." He didn't touch her again, but his voice surrounded her, almost caressing her when he said, "Lady, if you ever think you can, let me be the first to know."

Chapter 12

Bree swallowed hard as she felt James move. "I think I should be going," he said from somewhere above her. "I'll call you tomorrow."

She sensed him hesitate, but she didn't move. She didn't open her eyes. She felt a brushing caress on the top of her head, and when she opened her eyes, she saw him going toward the kitchen. She turned to stare at the television even though all her awareness centered on the sounds of James leaving—his feet on the kitchen tile, the pause, then the door opening and closing. There was a pause, then she heard the Bronco's engine start.

As the sounds faded into the turbulence of the rain and wind, Bree wrapped her arms around her middle and held on as tightly as she could. But it didn't stop a gnawing ache that she knew would only get worse during the night. Gradually, she realized that the news was beginning and she sat very still, holding herself and watching the screen. She recognized what James had meant about getting sick of telling the world about misery and horrors. The world wasn't a particularly nice place. In the international news, Daryl, the red-haired man, reported with grim tones about a ceasefire in the Middle East that had resulted in ten dead and seventeen wounded.

Stacey Mills, the green-eyed blonde Bree had seen in the makeup room, spoke in a clear voice about an American embassy being bombed while the families of the employees were sitting down to a traditional Christmas dinner. Misery and horror. No wonder James didn't want any of it anymore.

The intrusive sound of the doorbell chiming made her jump, and she twisted around to look at the entry. The doorbell? When it chimed again, she scrambled to her feet, almost stumbling over a towel James must have dropped when he left. She hurried to the door. "Who's there?" she called with her hand on the cold knob.

"James."

She hesitated, not certain what to do, then she braced herself and pulled the door open. Just the sight of him with the storm at his back intensified the ache in her middle, and she had to force herself not to press a hand to the spot.

"I came back to give you this." He reached inside his jacket and took out the small box. "I'm going to the station, and I wouldn't want to take a chance of this getting damaged or being mislaid."

"But I don't think—"

"You'll take good care of it, I'm sure." His eyes narrowed and he cocked his head to one side. "Will you keep it for me?" he asked in a rough whisper as he held it out to her.

She hesitated, then reluctantly took the box, still warm from the heat of the car and his touch. "I'll keep it until tomorrow."

"Perfect. Until tomorrow," he echoed, then stepped forward. His warm hand framed her face gently as he stooped to kiss her, a fleeting touch, yet every bit as unnerving as anything that had happened earlier between them. The brush of his mustache, the softness of his lips, then the isolation as he stepped back.

Reaching in his pocket, he took out a card and handed it to her. "My home number. Call me if you need me," he murmured.

Bree held the box and the card against her as she watched James dash through the rain to where he'd parked the Bronco by the gates. As he drove off, she closed the door. She walked slowly to the couch, sank weakly onto the cushions and looked down at the card. *If you need me.* Curling her feet under her, she undid the latch on the box, put the card inside and refastened it, then slowly traced the intricate H on the lid.

She became aware of Daryl speaking on the screen. "For a recap of tonight's top local story—Wayne Concklin, who's being held for questioning in connection with the murder of Detective Andrew Dawson, was at headquarters again today for questioning, then moved to a maximum security area." The pictures that flashed on the screen while Daryl talked were taken at police headquarters.

Then Daryl said, "Threats against his life, although he has not been formally charged, have been coming into headquarters. Chief of police Glenn Hodges explained the situation to our reporter in the field, so we . . ."

The rest of the words were lost on Bree as she watched the commotion she'd witnessed in person at police headquarters. This time she saw it from the perspective of the camera as it backed up and rolled out the doors, and moved outside the building as Concklin was being put in a police van and taken away. As the camera scanned the crowds gathered on the steps, Bree sat up abruptly and leaned closer to the small screen. A man in the back by the doors caught her attention.

Roy Lester stood alone, and his gaze never seemed to leave Concklin. Then, with Concklin in the van, just before the doors were closed, she could have sworn that Lester and Concklin exchanged looks. Roy Lester? She kept watching, waiting for the crowd to be shown again, but the broadcast had returned to the studio.

"And after these words from our sponsors, we'll be back with James Chapman and a very special *Heart of the Matter*."

Bree stared at the screen for a minute, then almost got up to go to the front door, but she realized James was long gone. And that fact sank in deeply, making her feel as alone as she ever had in her life. It didn't help when she touched her tongue to her lips and was certain she could still taste him there—the way she could still almost feel his hands on her.

Her attention was brought back to the screen as the newscaster said, "And now, *Heart of the Matter* with James Chapman."

Then James was on the screen, and even though his image was tiny, the sight made her chest tighten.

"Thanks, Daryl," he said to his left, then looked straight into the camera. Immediately, a bond formed between him and his viewing audience, just as instantly as it had formed between James and her. She could admit that, but not allow it. After this Hannah thing was done with, that would be that.

"Tonight we have something special for you on *Heart of the Matter*. Once upon a time there was a little girl with curls and a wonderful smile..."

As his voice went on, the sepia picture of Hannah materialized slowly over James, then took over until James was gone and the smiling child filled the screen. James kept talking. "In this world, dreams can die in the most unexpected way. I don't know what happened to that little girl, to a child who costarred with some of the biggest names in Hollywood's silent era, but over the years things shifted and altered.

"Hannah is now in her late seventies, a tiny woman with snow white hair, yet still possessing the same vivid smile as the child did."

The picture began to dissolve, the charcoal sketch transposed over it until the sketch finally replaced the photo. The way the technicians did it, the smile stayed in place, but the face altered from the child to the elderly woman.

"Today, Sweet Little Hannah is known as Hannah Vickers. She isn't a star anymore. She's not even remembered by anyone in Hollywood. Instead of ruffled gowns and hair ribbons, she wears an old red coat that comes to her ankles and a floppy picture-brim hat. And her home isn't an estate, it's a single room in a boardinghouse downtown. She doesn't work in front of the cameras, but behind the counter at a small restaurant. On December 13, late in the afternoon, Hannah disappeared."

His voice seemed to flow around Bree, and she held the box on her lap more tightly. Closing her eyes, she felt a painful stab of regret that she wasn't able to take what James offered. She hurt for Hannah, for what could have happened, and she hurt for herself.

When James finished and the newscaster had signed off, Bree slowly stood, set the box on the couch and went into the kitchen. Maybe James was in his office at the station. She wanted to tell him about Lester being at the station and that he'd been at the construction site when William had been found. The man seemed to be everywhere. She dialed the number for Channel Three.

It rang three times before it was picked up by a recording. "Thanks for calling Channel Three, the station with a heart. Our switchboard is open from nine in the morning until seven at night. Please—"

She hung up and almost went in to get the card with James's home number, but she didn't. She didn't want to call and find someone there with him. The idea was like a kick in the stomach to her. No, she didn't want to intrude. And maybe she didn't want to hear his voice.

She spotted the brandy bottle James had left on the counter, and on impulse she picked it up and opened it. Pouring a healthy portion in a glass, she went into the living room, sat on the couch and took a drink. As the heat filtered through her, she sat back and lifted Hannah's box.

December 23

The phone rang, its shrill sound cutting into Bree's dreamless sleep. She struggled to sit up, and it took her a minute to remember she was on the couch and why she'd slept there. The lights were on, the television was going and the box and empty brandy glass had tumbled to the carpet. Careful not to step on them, she got up and went into the kitchen to reach for the phone. "Hello?" she mumbled.

"Bree? James."

She blinked and rubbed her eyes with her knuckles.

"Are you there?" he asked, his voice disgustingly awake and cheerful.

She leaned against the counter and realized that she couldn't remember having dreamed at all. "Yes, I'm here."

"Were you asleep?" he asked.

She almost said, "Of course," but stopped when she glanced at the wall clock and saw it was ten minutes past eleven. She stood upright. "It's after eleven."

"It's almost noon," he countered, and she could hear amusement in his tone.

She rubbed at her eyes with her knuckles. "Where are you?"

"I'm at—" He paused, then came back on the line. "I'm at the liquor store near Bay and Palomar."

Two minutes away. She pushed her tumbled hair off her face. "Why?" was all she could say.

"I need your help."

"My help?"

"I wouldn't ask, but I don't know what else to do. Since last night's broadcast and the first spot, which ran a while ago, there've been a lot of calls to the station. Too many for the switchboard to handle with any ease. Since you'd know more what to listen for and what questions to ask callers, I thought maybe you could help out until they can locate some temporary help to take the calls."

"You want me to answer calls?"

"If you would?"

"What about the pictures I need to take?"

"It's still lousy outside, misty and cold. We can wait until it clears."

Answering calls would fill a lot of time and give her little time to think. "All right." She swallowed. "Give...give me ten minutes, all right?"

"I'll give you fifteen," he said and the line clicked.

Bree put back the receiver, then went upstairs and hurried through a hot shower. She tugged a brush through her curls, leaving them loose around her shoulders, then she dressed in black linen slacks with a white cotton shirt. When the doorbell rang, she was just putting on her shoes—black casual pumps.

The hours of sleep uninterrupted by dreams had left her more refreshed than she could remember being since— She stopped the thought before it could form and hurried down the stairs. Without pausing, she pulled the door open and came face-to-face with James.

Despite the way her emotions seemed to jumble at the sight of him and lingering embarrassment about last night, she felt genuine pleasure at seeing him again. He was wearing a tweed sport coat, darker than the other one, over a V-neck sweater of soft beige along with the usual jeans and sneakers. A cool breeze ruffled his silver-streaked hair, and his crooked smile hit her like a bolt of lightning. She didn't question her response to James, she simply tried to absorb it as best she could.

"Good morning," she said, then corrected herself. "Almost afternoon."

He studied her, his head cocked to one side, his blue eyes narrowed but losing none of their brilliance. The rain behind him was lighter, but still persistently falling from a leaden sky. "You look so—" she could almost see him searching for the right word "—good."

"I feel good," she admitted, a bit shocked by the fact herself.

"No bad dreams?"

That made her falter, but she pushed her thoughts aside as quickly as they came. "No, and it doesn't matter right now." She motioned him inside. "Come on in. I need to get some things, then we can go."

She left James in the living room while she went in the kitchen to get her purse. Then she saw the camera case, with grass still clinging to it. She couldn't understand how she'd forgotten to check and clean it. Actually, she did understand, but she didn't want to think about that now. Later, when she came home, she could clean things up and develop the film.

When she came into the living room with a thigh-length red jacket on, she crossed to James, who was standing at the fireplace by the still running television.

He looked at her as she neared him, and she could see what he'd been doing. The tiny nativity had been taken out of the box and set in perfect order on the bricks by the television. Barely a splash of color against the bricks, the small pieces looked bleak and out of place in this room. Pitiful, just the way Bree suddenly felt.

"Why did you do that?" she asked in a low voice, her good mood beginning to dissolve at an alarming rate. She couldn't risk the nativity scene triggering the memories.

He shrugged. "I thought it should be out of the box."

"But it isn't staying here," she protested, and would have reached for the box if James hadn't stopped her by lightly grasping her hand.

"Why not? It's safe here. And we can let Murray know where it is."

She looked at James and turned her hand in his, trying to free it, but she only succeeded in tangling her fingers with his. "I don't want it here," she said and pulled her hand out of his. "I don't want to be responsible for it."

"I understand," he said softly.

She exhaled but she couldn't stop her hands from clenching any more than she could control her confusion. "No, you don't," she muttered.

"Just leave it here for now. We can take it to Murray later."

"All right, it can stay," she said, but she picked up the box and methodically put the pieces back in their nests. "But I'll feel better if the pieces are in the box." She looked at James as she closed the box and fastened the clasp. "They're safer this way."

"If you say so," he murmured, then stooped and kissed her fleetingly on the lips before he took the box from her to set it on the bricks. "Now," he said as he turned to her, "are you ready to go to the station?"

She glanced at the box, still a bit uneasy about it, but let the matter rest. "Yes."

Hannah sat very still on the narrow bed and stared at the window. She could see the tiny slivers of light through the chinks in the wood that blocked the window. Daylight. But it was still raining, and William hadn't come back.

She nibbled on the candy bar. He'd promised. "I'll be back as soon as I'm finished," he'd told her. But she didn't know how long ago that had been.

She moved on the cot until she had her back against the brick wall. She'd had a watch once, but not a wristwatch. It had been a brooch pinned to her blouse, and it had been engraved. She frowned in the dimness. Who had given it to her? She tried to remember, but it wouldn't come.

She hated that most about getting old. The forgetting. The names and faces that she couldn't quite grasp. Things lost in a haze of the past. But some things never went away. *That face.* She'd never forget it. Or Santa. Poor thing.

She took a bite of the candy bar and found it difficult to swallow. She had never known how quickly she could run until then, until that man had looked at her. Then the people were there, the sidewalks crowded, and she hid in the crowds until she found William.

Why didn't William come back? All he had to do was ask and see if the man was still looking for her. All he had to do was find out what had happened to Santa.

She closed her eyes, but opened them right away when she saw that man in her mind's eye. Some memories would never die. Right then she made a decision. If William wasn't here soon, when it was night, she'd go looking for him. The rain hit the wood on the windows and wind sighed in the alley. Or maybe when the rain stopped, she amended with a shiver.

When James pulled up to the back door of the Cracked Cup Café and stopped the motor, the rain had eased to a light sprinkle. "Let's check in with Murray before we see how William is."

Bree ran through the light rain with James to the door, and when Nate opened it, they ducked inside as quickly as they could. After he closed the door, Nate turned to them and held his hand out to James. "Thought I recognized you. Thanks for what you're doing for Hannah."

James stopped swiping at the moisture on the shoulders of his jacket to shake hands with the big man. "I only hope it will help." He smoothed his hair. "Is Murray here?"

"He's just back from the hospital. I'll get him for you. Come on in and sit. I'll be right back."

Bree sat at the table, opening her jacket and shaking it a bit to try to loosen the clinging drops of moisture. James sat by her and reached to turn on the television. A soap opera was on, and just as Murray came into the kitchen, a station break came on.

"We need your help," a television image of James was saying from the screen. He sat with his hands folded on the desk, his blue eyes looking right into the camera. "Ten days ago an elderly lady named Hannah Vickers disappeared." The sketch of Hannah appeared on the screen, and the three people in the kitchen were very still as they watched the screen. "If you have seen this woman, please contact Channel Three at the number on your screen. The police and Channel Three need your help."

A number began to scroll across the bottom of the screen. "If you have any information about her whereabouts, contact us. She was last seen in the late afternoon in the downtown area near the plaza. She was wearing a bright red coat that's too big for her and a floppy black hat. She's approximately five feet tall, about ninety pounds, and she's seventy-eight years old. Your help in this matter is vital. Trust me."

James switched the set off, then turned to Murray. "Anything yet?"

The thin man shook his head. "Not yet, but I've got hopes. Everyone's been talking about your bit last night and the one spot this morning. Even in the hospital they were talking."

"William?"

"He's hanging on, but the doctors aren't real optimistic." He took off his glasses and began to wipe them on the hem of his gray cotton work shirt while he looked at Bree. "And I want to thank you for the offer of help, ma'am. That's real nice of you."

"I mean it. I want to take care of the bills for William. I'll arrange for it at the hospital."

Murray's eyes looked a little moist as he slipped the glasses back on. He shook his head. "Christmas. Boy, I love it. And I hope—" he shook his head "—I *know* this one's going to be good. At least people are looking for Hannah and asking questions. And not just because she used to be a movie star, either. Not like that other guy."

Roy Lester. Bree had totally forgotten. "James, I saw him yesterday. He was at the site where William was found, when the ambulance was there. Then he was on television last night when they were showing people watching that bald man, Concklin, I think, when they were taking him out of police headquarters.''

James frowned. ''He's popping up all over the place, but I don't see the connection, except for...'' He stopped his words and turned to Murray. He hadn't told Murray about Hannah's room being vandalized. ''We're on our way to the station to answer the calls that are coming in. You keep in touch and let me know what's going on down here. You've got my number at the station.'' He touched Murray on the shoulder. ''We'll find her.''

''Sure,'' Murray said and followed Bree and James to the door. He opened it and looked into the cold rain. ''Lousy weather, isn't it?''

''It's wet,'' James said, then took Bree by the arm and ran for the Bronco.

At the station James set Bree up in an empty office with a phone that had eight different lines. While he worked on more of the fifteen-second spots, she took the calls that came in from the moment the phone was connected. The calls were strange. Some were simply crazy, like the one claiming Hannah had been taken away by a spaceship. Another caller was certain Hannah was a movie star in disguise doing research for a part. Some called out of concern, offering to help but unable to give any information.

Among them a few came in that seemed like possible leads.

''I saw an old lady in the alley just walking. Red coat, black hat, and she was real small,'' one man said. ''Don't know where she went. Must have been two weeks ago over near the mall.''

''I seen her a bit back talking to someone on the street by that new car garage.'' But the caller couldn't remember when it had happened or who the woman had been talking to.

Bree scribbled key words on the pad or simply wrote "Crazy!" from time to time.

"What's the reward?" one caller asked abruptly. When he found out there hadn't been one posted, he hung up.

Then Bree had an idea. A reward. When another caller asked, she told him a five-thousand-dollar reward was available, but only if the call resulted in Hannah being found. "Dead or alive?" the caller asked, and Bree had all she could do to answer evenly, "Found. Period." And hung up.

When James came in just after three, she gratefully took a mug of hot coffee from his hand. But the sandwiches that he set on the desk didn't look appetizing at all. He frowned at them himself. "Sorry. That's the best the commissary can do right now." He motioned to the phone. "Anything?"

She shook her head and sat back in the chair in the sparse office. The sound of rain on the windows was stronger now. The rain was unrelentingly driven against the glass by the wind. "Not really. A lot of crazies out there." She sipped the steaming coffee, then looked at James over the rim of the mug. "I just decided that I'm offering a reward."

He watched her from the other side of the desk and asked simply, "Why?"

"I told you before, I have the money, and that's all some people understand. It may as well do someone some good."

He sat on the desk near Bree. "You're right, and it's a good idea. I'll match whatever you've decided to give. How much?"

She wanted to ask if he could afford it, because she remembered what he'd said about walking away from a six-figure income, but she didn't. "Five thousand dollars."

He shook his head and a low whistle escaped from his lips, but he didn't back out. "All right. Five thousand from me, too."

"I figured you would do something like that."

He studied her intently for a second, then bent and kissed her on the forehead. "I figured you would, too." Then he was heading for the door. "I'll be back in a bit. I want to add the reward to the announcements."

Bree stared after him, then with a shake of her head, she answered the ringing phone. "Channel Three hot line."

"I seen that old lady back a bit."

"When?" she asked.

"I don't remember exactly, but she was watching them workers over near the..."

The calls slowed for about half an hour, then they picked up with a vengeance. The reward really got people excited. The man who had seen the spaceship called back twice. Others called again making sure that if the information they'd given before resulted in Hannah being found, they'd still get the money. And new people called.

"Are you sure about her being little? I saw this big woman, maybe seventy years old, the other day..."

"This old lady, she's the mayor's wife, right?"

"If you leave the ten thousand dollars on Coronado Bridge at the midpoint, I'll call back and tell you..."

"She's an alien. She's the front runner of a new race, a race that starts out old and gets younger."

Bree hung up from the last call and sat back in the chair, not able to stop chuckling. That's how James found her when he came in around five-thirty.

"What's so funny?" he asked.

"How does the idea of Hannah being an alien sound to you?"

He raised one eyebrow. "Interesting. And where does she stay, in her ship hovering over the city?"

"He didn't know. But he wants the money."

"Of course," James said softly and looked at the untouched sandwiches. "Not hungry?"

She shrugged, stretching her arms over her head to ease the cramped muscles in her shoulders and neck. "Not really."

"How long has it been since you've had something good to eat? Something besides candy bars?" He must have seen her surprise that he knew she ate chocolate, because he smiled. "Remember, I've gone through your trash."

She laughed at that. "True. And I don't remember when I've had a real meal."

He reached for her coat, on the back of the chair. "It's time to leave. I arranged for one of the secretaries to come in until seven, when the switchboard closes down. Then there'll be a recorded message to call back at nine in the morning or call the police station. Cal will love that." He held out her coat. "Right now we need some good food and a few hours' rest."

She willingly let James help her with her coat. When she turned to face him, she didn't fight being pulled into his arms. She allowed herself to rest against his strength for a brief moment. Then without a word, he slipped his arm around her shoulders and walked out with her.

The seafood restaurant by the bay was a blur to Bree. She ate her food and thought it was probably good, but she couldn't concentrate on it. By the time they were on their way to her house in the rain, she began to feel depressed. Too much time had passed. The weather was awful. And Hannah was old and frail. Bree didn't know if she could survive herself, out there.

Or maybe Hannah hadn't survived. Maybe all this time… Bree bit her lip hard. It hurt to think of Hannah being dead. God, she could barely think that word. The rain and wind buffeted the Bronco, obscuring the city outside, and Bree felt cold in spite of the car heater.

"James?" she said softly as he drove south.

"Uh-huh?"

She had to ask one thing. "What's going to happen if they find Hannah and she's dead?" The words came out flat and emotionless, with no hint at the raw pain that had prodded them to life.

The car lurched slightly, then steadied. "Why are you asking?"

"I need to know. What happens to Murray, to Nate, to William—if he survives—and, what happens to you?"

He shrugged sharply. "I'll keep on going. Isn't that what's required of the living?"

Yes, and the hardest thing to do. "That's it?"

"What else is there? I'm not going to go running down the middle of the street screaming and crying." His voice was tight, as tight as her chest felt. "I might want to, but I won't." He cast her a slanting look. "How would you deal with it?"

She sank back in the seat and averted her eyes, staring blindly into the rainy night. *I'll hurt, and I didn't want that to happen again, not now, not ever.* "I don't know. I didn't even know Hannah."

"Neither did I," he said softly. "It's not logical, is it?"

"Not at all," she admitted. But when did logic have anything to do with real life? Marrying Dean had been logical, and it had been the hardest three years of her life. Loving James was totally illogical, but... That thought made her draw in a sharp breath, and she pressed a hand to her mouth.

He'd found her at a vulnerable time, and he cared so damned much. That would appeal to anyone, and anyone would love him, but she wasn't *in* love with him. Couldn't be. Never that. Never again. Her hand slowly lowered and curled into a tight ball in her lap. "I want to call the hospital and arrange for William's bills to come to me."

"Wouldn't it be easier to go down there and talk to them?"

"No." She tried to soften her refusal. "I'd rather not. I can give them my credit card number over the phone, can't I?"

He shrugged. "I suppose so. Tell you what. Why don't we stop at my place, and you can call from there? Then if they won't do it, you don't have nearly as far to go to the hospital from there as from your place."

Logical. She nodded. "Fine." And looked out at the rainy night.

James opened the door to his apartment and let Bree go past him into warmth and a room just as skimpy on furnishings as her place. With one big exception—a huge Christmas tree in front of a bank of draped windows on the far side of the room. To the right was a stone fireplace and two overstuffed chairs.

She moved inside, her feet sinking in plush bronze-colored carpeting. While James helped Bree with her jacket, she said, "And you had the nerve to ask me about my house being so bare."

He laughed softly. "I haven't finished moving in, either."

She turned to him as he hung her jacket on a rack by the door. "How long have you lived here?"

"Almost a year," he admitted, and she could have sworn he almost blushed. "But this isn't home. I mean, I'm looking for something else. I just haven't had time."

"Why do you want to move?"

"Carson found this for me when I moved out from Chicago, and I've never really liked it. It's too . . ."

"Yuppy?" she supplied.

"Right," he said and motioned to a phone sitting on the floor halfway between the tree and fireplace. "Help yourself, and I'll get us something to warm our bones."

Bree stepped out of her damp shoes, then crossed and sank down on her knees by the phone. She reached information, got the hospital number and pushed the buttons, then sank back on her heels while it rang. She was connected to billing, and she spoke to a lady there, explaining the situation. After several minutes of discussion, Bree finally got the woman to agree to bill all William's expenses to Bree's credit card. She could go in after the holidays and sign all the forms they needed.

She finally hung up and exhaled. Rotating her head slowly around and around, she could feel the tension in her shoulders and neck. "They'll do it," she said as James sat between her and the Christmas tree. "But I'll have to go in in a few days and sign some forms." She hadn't noticed him near the fireplace, but now a fire blazed, the wood snapping as the flames found the sap in the logs.

"Good." He handed her a snifter of brandy, then leaned over to pull the cord on the drapes. The heavy material parted, exposing sheets of glass sleek with rain and reflecting the multicolored lights of the tree. "The best thing about this apartment is the view. In good weather it's spectacular. Hills, then water and sky. San Diego at its best."

She cradled the brandy in her hands and looked at the brown liquid. Even there the lights shimmered and swirled. "Christmas, Christmas everywhere," she whispered unsteadily.

"Is that so bad?" James asked softly.

"No, I guess not," she whispered, realizing that his presence was a buffer to the past. "I wanted to explain about last night," she began, but couldn't think of the words to do that very thing. All she knew was that loving this man would be so easy, so very easy.

"You don't need to," he murmured as he took the glass out of her hand and set it by the phone next to his. "No words. They only get us all tangled up. Just this."

And as the rain whispered on the window, he reached out to her, and she went to him. A buffer, a blessing with blue eyes and the gentlest voice imaginable. He was like a cool drink on a hot day, as welcome as the peace after the storm. She pressed her forehead to his chest, felt the beat of his heart, and she felt hers beat in unison with his.

If only things had been different. "I . . . I can't give you what you want," she murmured unsteadily.

His hands slowly stroked her back, making no demands but giving a comfort that was so tangible it almost moved her to tears. "And what do you think I want?"

She buried her face in his chest, her words muffled. "Someone to really care, to give herself completely."

"And you can't do that?" he asked. His hands stilled on her.

"No, I can't. I wish . . ." She swallowed hard. "I can't."

He cupped her chin and tipped her face until she was looking into his eyes, eyes so gentle and so filled with awareness that she wanted to cry. "What if I told you I'll settle for what you can give right now?"

"I couldn't let you do that. You deserve the best."

"Let me decide what I deserve," he murmured, and his mouth found hers.

She hesitated for only a moment, then knew she couldn't, no, *wouldn't* deprive herself of this again. He understood where she was coming from, that she wasn't promising anything beyond this, and she needed him. She needed him with a desperation that threatened to consume her. In a way she had never needed a man before. Love? She didn't know, but she did know that no one had touched her like this in her life. No one had made her want to live for the moment and damn tomorrow. No one but James Chapman.

She opened her mouth and went closer, her knees against his, her hips pressed to his, her breasts against his chest. And she held to him while she tasted him and explored his warmth. She wished there weren't any barriers, any clothes to keep her from feeling his skin against hers. She wanted to experience him fully. Once. That might be all she had. Maybe that was all she dared, but she would have him once.

"I need you," she admitted, her voice husky against the side of his neck.

Chapter 13

James framed her face with both his hands, the deep blue of his eyes alive with the fire of desire, his breathing ragged. "Are you sure?"

"All I know is I want you," she admitted.

His thumbs traced slow circles on her cheeks, sending urgent messages deep inside her. "Bree, I've wanted you from the first moment I got in the van with you."

She smiled, but she knew her expression was unsteady. Her insides felt that way, trembling and excited. "I wish I could say the same."

He laughed abruptly, but the sound died when his gaze locked with hers. Then she was against him, each curve and angle of her body melding with his, and she could feel his need for her. Strong. Vital. Urgent.

"God, you're beautiful," he whispered unsteadily. "I want you with me. I want to make love with you."

She simply needed him now. She didn't think past that fact. She wouldn't, not now. Without a word, she offered her lips to him, and he took her in a long, searching kiss that stole her breath. Reality receded, the way the sounds of the storm outside did, obliterated by the racing of her pulse, the thundering of her heart.

She heard his murmurings, not understanding the words, but falling farther and farther into the softness of forgetfulness. She needed him more than she'd ever needed another person in her life. And that need threatened to fragment her, the urgency of it almost frightening.

Together they tumbled backward onto the softness of the carpet, and she was lying with him, wondering at how neatly they fit together. She looked at him next to her, the flickering shadows from the fire playing across his face. And with unsteady fingers, she touched his jaw, then his lips.

She wanted to make this last, not let it be over before it had hardly begun. She'd never known any other way to make love, but James didn't rush. Slowly, his eyes never leaving hers, he began to undo the buttons of her blouse, one by one, until he pushed the cotton aside. His head lowered, his lips touching the hollow of her throat, then moving even lower, roaming to the gentle swelling of her breasts.

She held her breath and closed her eyes, sensations bombarding her with such strength that she could barely absorb them. His fingers slipped the skimpy pieces of lace that covered her breasts down until the fragile material was no longer a barrier to his hands.

Then he was cupping her swelling breasts, and she gasped, arching toward his caress. His lips found her, his tongue trailing a circle around her peaking nipple, and a searing fire shot through her at the speed of lightning. It radiated from the core of her being, "Oh, yes," she moaned, his touch erotically sweet torture. And all the while, she marveled at her own ability to respond, to feel, to delight in his touches.

She felt and experienced as she never had before. She centered on what James could do to her and forgot everything else. She had heard the expression "being pleasured," and she understood it now. She wasn't the one giving and giving while someone else took until there was nothing left.

James gave pure pleasure until she couldn't bear it anymore. It wasn't good enough to be pleasured without giving pleasure. And she found she wanted to give and give to this man, not out of guilt or duty, but out of pure want. And she experienced great delight in touching him, tugging at his sweater to pull it up so she could feel his heat under her palms.

Then James sat up, tugged the soft wool over his head and tossed it away as he looked at her. His gaze met hers, then dropped to her breasts, their dusky peaks puckered and erect. "God, you're beautiful," he breathed raggedly.

So was he. She wasn't sure if she should use the word beautiful for a man, but that's what he was to her. Slowly she raised one hand and tentatively touched his chest. Heat and strength centered under her fingertips, and the contact was as potent as any she'd ever known. The hair brushed her skin, his muscles quivered, then she leaned on one arm and tasted his heat with her lips and tongue.

His low moan of pleasure echoed in her ears, vibrating against her lips, then James abruptly got to his feet. Her isolation stunned her, then he reached for her hand and pulled her up. In one easy motion he held her in his arms, his lips buried in the heat of her neck. And he carried her silently through the apartment into a darkened room.

She could see shadows, a large bed, a window covered by drapes, then James crossed the room and laid her gently on the bed's softness. Quickly, he freed himself of the rest of his clothes, then he neared the window. He reached out and the drapes slid silently back. The storm outside seemed to be a living thing, just as Bree's needs were, and when James turned to her, she was stunned at the sight of him.

Strength and beauty, beyond anything she could begin to describe. There were no other people in the world, just the two of them, and she held out her arms. He came to her and lay with her, helping her out of her slacks and panties, then they were finally together, skin against skin, touching, searching, exploring, trying to know everything possible about each other's bodies.

"Here," James whispered, guiding her hand, helping her to know him, to please him. And she was stunned at the strength of his response to her touch. As stunned as she was by the magic his touch had on her. Then there were words James murmured, lost in the rapid beating of her heart, the ragged attempts to breathe, and Bree simply let herself go. She spiraled upward, rising on sensations, only knowing that she needed to satisfy a hunger that all but possessed her.

His hands pleasured her, drawing her to peaks of sensations then letting her drift only to be taken higher the next time. Then James left her for a moment, reaching to his side, into the nightstand. And he was back with her, the silver packet opened, and he gazed down at her.

"I won't hurt you...in any way," he whispered and took only a moment to keep his promise.

Bree felt her whole being surge. The caring was almost too painful for her to bear, then he was over her, and she reached out to him. She clutched at the firmness of his shoulders, her legs lifted to circle his hips, then she lifted herself to him in invitation.

For a fleeting moment, he looked down at her, the shimmering shadows from the rain-slicked windows washing over him, playing crazy shadows on his face, then he took her in one swift movement that she duplicated with her hips.

The fire grew, consuming and raging, a match for the storm outside the apartment. Then Bree knew in one instant, when it felt as if he touched her soul, that she loved James. Love. But she had no time to dwell on it because the next instant brought an explosion of pure, undiluted pleasure where she soared higher and higher, and at the apex she realized the magnitude of her mistake. She knew that as long as she lived, she'd never be whole again without James.

The ringing telephone cut into the hazy world of pleasure Bree had escaped into, a place where she didn't need to think or act. She simply lay in the crook of James's arm, their legs tangled together with the sheets on the bed as spent fragments of desire refused to disperse. Then the phone rang again and James stirred.

"I'd better get that," he murmured and pressed a kiss on her temple.

"I suppose so," she said, tasting the heat of his skin with her tongue.

He disengaged himself from her, then reached to his left and picked up the phone. Sinking back into the bed, he circled Bree again and held her tightly to him as he spoke into the receiver. "Yeah?"

She felt him tense as he listened, then he let her go and slowly sat up. He pushed away the sheet, then threw his legs over the side of the bed and sat very still, his head bent forward. "Are you sure?" he asked in a low voice. The silence was stretched forever until James said, "I will."

Slowly he put the receiver back, then with a jerky motion ran a hand over his face.

"James?" Bree sat up and tentatively touched his back. She could feel his muscles spasm under her fingertips. "What is it?"

He kept his back to her, and his voice was slightly muffled. "That was Cal. The police found an elderly woman in a red coat by the bay. She's dead." A shudder ran through his body. "Dead."

Bree scrambled to her knees, freeing herself of the sheets, and scrambled over to James. She sank on her heels and her hands clenched into fists on her thighs. "No, no," she whispered, her eyes painfully dry on James in the shadows beside her. "You're wrong. She can't be dead."

"I'm sorry," he murmured, looking toward her, and his hand reached out to touch her knee. "I'm so sorry."

She felt as if someone had driven a fist into her stomach, and it doubled her over until she had to clutch her middle.

Oh, God, she never should have gotten involved. Never, never. Horrible sobs racked her body, over and over again.

Then she was in James's arms, his voice was in her ear, his hands holding her and stroking her, trying to ease the pain. But it didn't help. The pain just came back again and again in burning waves of agony.

"Bree, love, please, don't. Don't. I can't bear to see you like this."

"How could she be dead?" She gulped and weakly struck his bare shoulder with her fist. "How?"

"We talked about this," he murmured as he stroked her hair. "There's nothing more we can do. Nothing. We tried. We did everything humanly possible."

She pushed back and anger tore through her, rage, outrage, and the pain, always the pain. "Merry Christmas to everyone," she spat, then struggled to her feet and pulled free of James. She searched blindly for her clothes, picking up her slacks, holding them to her chest. Then she turned on James standing by the bed. "The season for pain and hurt! Caring doesn't do one damn bit of good."

James was in front of her. "Hey, you aren't to blame for Hannah dying any more than I suspect you were for your husband dying."

She looked at him, her eyes filled with tears that came from rage this time. "You know, you're right. I tried. God, I tried. Over and over again. It pulled the life out of me, it ripped me apart and it didn't do any good. Dean's dead."

He had her by her shoulders and shook her once sharply, her dark curls tumbling around her pale face. "Bree, you aren't God. A heart attack isn't something you wish away or even love away. It happens. I just can't stand the fact you lost someone you loved so much."

"Loved?" she gasped. "Yes, I loved Dean for what seemed all my life, but the night he died I almost hated him. And he knew it."

James stared at Bree, stunned by what she said. "I don't understand."

She felt herself shaking, and the words spilled out before she could stop them. "Dean was an addict. A drug addict!" She tried to take a breath. "And I couldn't help him. I couldn't help him. And he died . . . he died alone . . . and I was . . . was gone." She wiped at her eyes with her fists. "I wanted to leave him. And I did, for three lousy hours. And when I finally had the courage to go back, to try again, he . . . he was dead."

Her pain wasn't for Dean, for a love lost in its prime, but a pain born out of guilt. A guilt she must have carried around with her from the moment she found him dead.

He pulled her tightly against him, and she fought him. Her slacks tumbled to the carpet between them, and she twisted as she screamed, "Let me go! Let me go!"

"No, not now, not like this." He shook her again, anything to get through to her. And she froze. Even in the shadows, he could see the pain in her eyes, the horror there, and it was undoing him. He'd held her, he'd loved her. Yes, loved, he admitted. God, he loved her so much he could almost taste it, and she was going to run and keep running from life because of misplaced guilt. Because she couldn't bear taking a chance on being hurt again.

"Please, James. Please let me go. I have to leave. I should never have come here." She began to shake as if she was very cold. "I should never have agreed to take the pictures. I didn't want to get involved. I can't bear it, I can't."

"Stay, just for a few minutes? Please?" He found himself begging, unable to even think of her walking out the door and away from him.

When she finally nodded weakly, he turned and reached for the blanket. Tugging it off the bed, he draped it around her, then led her to the edge of the bed. He quickly slipped on his jeans, then he crouched in front of her.

He could feel her tension. She sat very still, her hands clasped in her lap, her eyes on her hands.

He cleared his throat, praying he'd say the right thing. He knew everything hung in the balance, and he had to try twice to get words past the tightness in his throat. "Why do you think you're responsible for your husband's addiction?" He had to know. He had to have something to work with if he was going to save her from herself.

She didn't respond at all for a very long time, then abruptly, she started rocking slowly forward and backward. "I could have helped him. I should have been able to," she murmured in a tight whisper.

"I don't understand." He reached out and covered her hands with his. "Tell me what happened."

She shook her head, but when he tightened his grip on her hands and waited, she finally began to talk, and once she started, she spoke rapidly in a breathless voice. And James began to know Dean Gregory, a good man who had been caught in an addiction he was afraid to admit to in case he lost his political career. The man never considered what he was doing to his wife. God, he must have been crazy not to see that Bree could have been better than any drug ever could be.

She shuddered and finished with, "And he tried to stop. He really did, but he couldn't. And I didn't know what to do. I was worn out. I tried so hard for so long. Then he'd start again. And he promised and promised, and he said he loved me, then he'd start all over again. And each time it was worse. Now he's dead, and I'm alive."

He closed his eyes for a minute, then exhaled. What a load of guilt. And how unjust. He stood and looked at Bree, her rigid stance so vulnerable that he had to swallow hard before he could speak. "Did you ever think that you couldn't do a thing for Dean?"

"I was his wife. If I couldn't, who could?"

"Dean. That's who."

"But he couldn't. He didn't have any control. He was sick, and I—" She cut off her words.

"You wanted to give up, didn't you?"

"Yes," she whispered.

"You gave and you gave and it wasn't enough, was it?"

"No."

"Bree, with an addict, you can care for them, you can love them, but you can't take care of them. You can't control their cravings or their needs. Only they can."

She looked up at him. "How would you know?"

"I had a friend in Chicago who had a drug problem. He almost killed himself, then he got help. But it wasn't his family who did it. It wasn't his girlfriend. It was him. He hit bottom, and he knew he either got help or he died." He paused then added, "It was his choice. He lived. Some don't. Some can't." He crouched again and took her hands in his. "Don't take this wrong, but you're making yourself the most important thing in the man's life. You weren't. The drug was."

She tensed, and without warning, she stood. "I have to go," she said as she tugged her hands free of James's hold.

James straightened, but didn't move to clear a path to the door for her. "He had you. That should have been enough," he said. "But drug addicts aren't rational. They're walking chemicals. I suspect Dean wasn't any different."

She blanched and held tightly to the blanket around her. "No, he didn't have me. We…we hadn't slept together more than a few times in that last year. Even before, it wasn't…it wasn't the way I thought it would be. He had problems."

He stood and faced her, but he didn't touch her. "So do we all, Bree, but we don't all turn to drugs. Some of us tough it out and bear all the sharp edges, just the way you have this past year. A year's enough time to grieve, more than enough." He took her by the shoulders. "Can't you let go of the guilt and let go of the pain?"

"I don't know," she whispered.

"Dean made his own choices. You couldn't make them for him. That's a basic principle of life. Responsibility for our own actions.

"All you did is try to love him, to help him, and you couldn't. So you admitted defeat. That's not a sin, lady, that's being human. It hurts like hell to admit failure, but it isn't fatal."

"You..." She couldn't get the words out. How could she tell him how special he was, how unusual, how giving and kind, and how much she was growing to love him? She'd never experienced anything like being with him, never. It was everything she'd thought her marriage would be and hadn't been.

"Listen to me," he said softly, his arms going loosely around her to rest on her shoulders. He leaned closer to her, so close she could feel the heat of his breath on her cold skin. "I'm betting on the fact that there'll come a time when you'll want to take a chance, that you'll want to try again and let yourself trust one person."

"No," she said softly. "It hurts too much when it's over."

"Who says it has to end?" he asked. "And even if it does, the joy could outweigh any pain, couldn't it?"

"I don't—"

"Enough of this," he whispered. "Stay with me tonight. Don't run off into the storm. We can talk. We can sit up all night and talk, if you want."

"And tomorrow?" There was always a tomorrow. She knew that well enough.

"We'll worry about tomorrow when it comes." He kissed her softly on the tip of her nose, then drew back. "I told you before, when you're ready to go farther, I'll be there. If you're never ready, I've got this. I'm not greedy. I just want to be here for you now. No strings. No promises. Just let me be what you need tonight."

His words seduced her, the way his closeness did, blurring her resolve, taking away the raw edges of memories. Would it be so wrong to take what was offered, to stay just a while longer? She didn't have any answer for that either, so she simply nodded. "Tonight."

"Tonight," he echoed as he led her to the bed.

In the shadows of the room, they didn't talk. Bree experienced such a need for closeness, to be held and to hold, that she felt almost frantic with it. She just wanted to stop thinking, to stop worrying about the consequences, and stop the world for one night.

So she took what was offered and lost herself in it as she gave everything she could to James. For one instant she had the incredible urge to thank him for being here, for letting her be here for a while. Then she realized love with this man was impossible and could never be the foundation of her existence.

Love. She accepted that fact. She loved James with a singleness of purpose that staggered her, but she didn't tell him. She kept her secret locked deep inside her. Tomorrow *would* come, and she couldn't afford to forge that last bond with this man.

She turned to him without a word and knew him again as the rain sighed on the windows.

December 24

When Bree woke to silence, James wasn't with her. She turned and saw a room filled with the early light of dawn. She noticed there were only a few pieces of furniture in this room, too—the king-size bed and two nightstands. She sat up, tugging the sheets with her, and felt them skim over her tender breasts.

She remembered the gentle loving and caring, exploring and getting to know each other, experiencing and giving pleasure. And it had been only for the night. Now the light of day had come, and with it the fact that everything was over. This *is* tomorrow, she admitted with sorrow. How could she ever have let herself go like that?

Embarrassment tinged with pain flooded through her. She pushed back until she was sitting against the wall, the sheet held tightly to her breasts. Over. The thought made tears sting her eyes, and right then James walked into the room, dressed in jeans and a plain white short-sleeved shirt open down the front. For a moment she was stunned at the memories that flooded over her of the night past, and she could almost feel his hands on her again and the simple pleasure of ignoring the future. Then she returned to reality with a painful thud and tried to focus on what he was saying.

"I didn't think you were awake."

She pushed at her hair and pressed hard against the headboard. "Morning comes, doesn't it?" she whispered.

"It's almost nine." Polite words that filled spaces. "The rain stopped."

"And?"

He looked at her from the doorway, one shoulder against the jamb, but he didn't come closer. "I need to go and see Murray."

How could she have forgotten about Murray and about Hannah? "I don't know how he'll take this," she murmured. "He was so certain." James had been, too.

"It's going to hurt like hell," James said flatly.

"Yes, it will," she said. Life seemed to hurt like hell most of the time. "I'll go with you, then I'll go home."

He looked surprised at her offer, but simply nodded. "While you get dressed, I'll call the station and see if anything came in on the hot line last night." He hesitated, then spoke softly. "We didn't get to talk last night."

She felt her face flame at the images his words conjured up. "There isn't anything else to say."

"Isn't there?"

She forced herself to look at him, to make eye contact and not flinch. "No, there isn't, James."

When he simply turned and left the room, closing the door behind him, she swallowed hard and exhaled an unsteady breath.

As the Bronco came to a stop at the back door of the Cracked Cup Café an hour later, Bree didn't get out right away. James gripped the steering wheel so tightly his knuckles were white. "This won't be easy," he said softly, the first words either of them had said since leaving James's house. "Do you want to stay out here and wait for me?"

"I'll come in." She turned and tugged the door handle back, then stepped out into the crisp cold of the new day. She avoided the puddles on the cracked cement and went with James to the door where he knocked twice. The door was opened and Nate squinted out at them.

"Morning," he said and stood back to let them pass. "Come on in out of the cold."

They stepped inside, into warmth and unbelievable clutter. Packages of rolls occupied several surfaces, and huge jars of mayonnaise were on the central table by two massive white mixing bowls. Cooked turkeys were lined up on a counter, seven of them tented with aluminum foil. The ache in Bree intensified. She didn't know how James was going to tell these men about Hannah.

Nate closed the door and turned to Bree and James. "Did they give you the message Murray left for you?"

"About Hannah?" James asked flatly.

"No, it's William." The heavy man ran a hand over his beard and shook his head. "He's not doing good. The doctor called early this morning. They had to take him in for some surgery again. Repair work, Murray called it."

"Where's Murray?" James asked.

"At the hospital, waiting. He's real worried. Hell, we all are." He crossed to the table and began to open the nearest mayonnaise jar. "I was hoping you had good news about Hannah. We could use some."

James hesitated, then shook his head. "Sorry." But he didn't tell Nate what they'd found out. Instead, he said, "I'm going to the hospital to see Murray." He looked at Bree. "Do you want to come?"

She shook her head immediately. "No, I...I think I'll go home."

"I can take you—"

She needed distance from all this. "I'll take a taxi. Don't worry about me."

He narrowed his eyes on her. "But I do worry. I worry that when I call, you won't be there."

She shrugged nervously. "I'll be there, but—"

"Good," he said and framed her face with his hands. The contact made Bree freeze, then he lowered his head, his lips brushed her forehead, and she could feel an unsteadiness in the contact. "I'll call as soon as I—" He exhaled, his expression tightening. "I'll let you know what's happening."

She didn't say a thing, but nodded.

Then he was gone, the door closing behind him. She took a deep breath. Running away seemed to be her impulse, yet she knew she couldn't run any more. Now she had to settle her life, to face it and live with her decisions.

"Ma'am?" Nate was saying.

She turned to him. "I'm sorry."

"I was asking if you wanted me to call a taxi for you."

"Yes, please," she said. "I'd appreciate it."

"After all you've done for Hannah and Murray, it's the least I can do," he said and crossed to the phone.

Bree felt her stomach sink, and she went to a chair and sat down. All she'd done? She hadn't been able to help them any more than she'd been able to help anyone—not even herself.

Nate came over to her. "Says they're real busy, but he'll try to have someone here within the hour. While you're waiting, do you want something to eat?"

The thought of food made her feel vaguely nauseated. "No, but some coffee would taste good."

He poured a cup, then brought it over to her. She took it and sipped, hoping the heat would help ease the ache within her.

The phone rang and Nate crossed to it. "Cracked Cup, Nate here. Oh, damn, I clean forgot. Hold on." He turned to Bree. "Ma'am, do you think you could sort of watch things for me for about half an hour? I got to go to pick up some stuff, and I completely forgot about it. I won't be more than half an hour, it's just down the street."

"Watch things?"

"Frank'll take care of the front. Just if you could listen for the phone, that sort of thing, at least until Murray's here. I'd hate to think someone would be calling about Hannah and no one here to answer."

The poor man, Bree thought with a sinking heart, but nodded. "Of course. I'll stay until you're back."

"Thank you," he said, and left by the swinging doors.

Bree stared into her coffee, then switched on the television. A newsbreak was on. Daryl was just finishing an item. "And it seems that Wayne Concklin, the only suspect in the murder of Detective Andrew Dawson, will be released around noon today. And that's it for news on the hour. I'm Daryl Covens for the Channel Three news team."

The screen went blank, then suddenly James was there, head and shoulders, the colors of the set so true that his eyes were the right blue. Then the sketch of Hannah took over, and James began to speak.

Bree reached over and snapped off the set, then stood and went to the telephone. She put in a call to her parents on her credit card, but only spoke for a few minutes to the maid. Both of her parents were out. She left a message that she'd called, that she was fine and that she'd call in a few days. Then she hung up and went back to the table. Gripping her mug with unsteady hands, she almost jumped out of her seat when the phone rang.

Quickly, she got to her feet and crossed to answer it.

"Cracked Cup Café. Can I help you?"

There was silence, then a very small voice almost drowned out by noises in the background. "Murray? I need Murray."

"I'm sorry. He's not here right now, but can I take a message?"

The silence on the line lasted for a long time before the person spoke again. "Please, I need to talk to him."

"He'll be back in a few hours, but I'd be glad to take a message."

She could only hear the noises of some sort of machines in the background, then the person spoke quickly. "Tell... tell him I need him. Hannah needs him."

Chapter 14

Hannah? Are you really Hannah Vickers?" Bree whispered into the receiver.

"Who... who are you?" the tiny voice asked.

Bree couldn't believe it. She felt her heart begin to race, and excitement all but choked her. "My name's Bree. I'm a friend of Murray's. He's been so worried about you, Hannah. He's been looking all over for you." *Keep her talking, just keep her on the line until someone comes.*

"I need him. William never came back. And I can't stay here because the man's here. I know he is."

"Who's there?" she asked, her eyes glued to the door, wishing someone would walk through it.

"The man. He's bad, really bad. William was supposed to talk to him, but William never came back. I thought he walked over to Murray's. Maybe he was working and forgot me. Please, get Murray. I have to ask him. He'll know what to do."

"He's not here. But I want to help. Just tell me what to do."

"You can't. The man..." Her voice trailed off, lost in the background noises, and Bree had the heart-sinking sensation she was going to hang up.

"Hannah, don't hang up. Please, tell me what's going on. Where are you? I'll come and help, I promise."

"He'll hurt you, too," Hannah said in an unsteady whisper. "He will. He's around here. I can hear him."

"Where? Where are you?"

"Down in William's place. Tell Murray to come here and get me. I'll wait there, I promise, but I have to get back. The man will get me. I'm so scared, and the candy's all gone."

"Hannah, please, just tell me where William lives," Bree begged. "Let me help. I'll... I'll get Murray, but he has to know where to find you."

"I have to get down there before the man comes again."

"No, please, don't hang up," she said, but even as the last word was said, the line went dead.

Bree put the receiver back and leaned against the wall. Hannah was alive! God, she'd never been so relieved or so happy. James. He had to know. She pushed the number for the station and asked for him.

"Mr. Chapman isn't in yet. Can I take a message?" the polite female voice asked.

"No, I—" She had an idea. "Is Bryan Lake there?"

"Just a moment. I'll have him paged."

Music played on the line for half a minute, then Bryan answered. "Bryan Lake, here."

"This is Bree... Bree McFarland."

"Oh, sure."

"I need to talk to James."

"Haven't seen him today. I was looking for him, too."

"If you see him before I do, tell him to call me immediately at the Cracked Cup."

"Sure. If you see him first, tell him I've got some information for him."

"What is it?"

"I've got the number for the owner of Graphic Originals."

"Hang on." She crossed to the table and took a pen and paper out of her purse. Back at the phone, she said, "Go ahead. What is it?"

He gave her a name and a number, then he said, "And I might have a call coming in from L.A. about Hannah."

"If you don't get to see James, call here and leave a message if you come up with anything. All right?"

"Sure. Talk to you later," he said and hung up.

Bree looked at the paper in her hand, then dialed the number. An answering machine came on, and she left a message. "My name is Bree McFarland, and I need to talk to you about a specialty job of matchbooks, silver with the letter F on the front. You can call me at—" She gave Murray's number, then hung up.

But she couldn't just sit and wait. She felt nervous, anxious to do something. Hannah was alive. She wasn't dead. It felt good. Then she had an idea. She called the hospital and asked for James or Murray in William's room. The nurse came back on the line. Neither man was there.

Pacing, Bree tried to think. William's place. Hannah was close by. William walked to and from work. But where did he live?

The door opened and Murray stepped in, his face stricken, then James followed, his expression just about as bleak. Without thinking, Bree ran toward James and threw herself into his arms. She needed to feel him holding her and she hugged him so tightly she could feel her arms shaking.

"Hey, what . . ." he gasped.

"You won't believe it," she said, looking up at him. "She's alive. Hannah's alive."

Murray was behind her, and he spoke up. "What are you talking about? James told me . . ."

"No." She twisted to look at Murray. "She's not dead. She called. She called here about fifteen minutes ago."

James had her by her shoulders, demanding her whole attention. "What?"

She told him as quickly as she could, words tumbling over words. And she finished with, "She's alive. I picked up the phone and she was there."

James pulled her back to him, holding her tightly for a long moment. "See, it's magic. Pure and simple."

"Amen," Murray said. "A few minutes ago, I was certain she was dead. Now she's alive."

Bree faltered at that and moved back. James let her go without a fight and she blinked at him. "It was a mistake," she countered. "But how could it have happened?"

"Exactly what I was thinking," he said and went to the telephone. He pushed some numbers. "Detective Browsky, please." Pause. "I know he's on vacation, but could you ring his office, just in case he's in for a while?" He glanced at Bree, about to say something, then spoke into the receiver. "Cal? Yeah, I wanted to ask about the woman they found. Did you get down to see about it?" James listened for a full minute, then spoke. "Damn right. Hannah's alive. She just called the restaurant. She didn't say where she was."

There was a long pause, then James exhaled harshly. "How in the hell could they do that? Yeah, I know. Mistakes can be made." His gaze held Bree's. "It's been upsetting. I'll be in touch." He put back the receiver. "The lady they found was a stroke victim, about sixty and five feet five. She was wearing a maroon jacket, no hat. And she's from El Cajon."

"But why did Cal call you?"

"The call came in while he was in his office last night, and they said they'd found an older woman, dead, with a red coat on. He assumed—" James ran a hand over his face. "It doesn't matter. What matters is that Hannah is alive, somewhere close by and scared to death."

"She was terrified," Bree said as she sank into the chair by the table. "She kept whispering, and there was a noise that almost drowned her out."

"What noise?" James asked as he leaned against the closed door.

"I don't know. A motor of some sort with a lot of air-pressure sounds. I—" She frowned. "I've heard it before, but I can't begin to think what it is."

"Was the call from outside?" James intently. "You know how calls on pay phones sound, that echo and emptiness on the line?"

"Yes, it was."

"You said it came about fifteen minutes ago?"

She looked at the wall clock, shocked to see it had been over half an hour since the call. "No, more like half an hour ago. I was waiting for the cab and the phone rang."

"Where's Nate?" Murray asked.

"He went to pick up something, and he asked me to wait here in case...in case Hannah called. I didn't have the heart to tell him—" She bit her lip. "He's picking up something for the meal, and I answered the phone."

"William's place," Murray repeated with a shake of his head. "Where in the hell is it? It's so cold and wet out there. And the area around here—"

"Close by," Bree said and knew what the sound on the line was. "An air compressor. That's what made the noise when she spoke. A compressor like they use for sandblasting, or air guns for painting."

James came and sat by Bree at the table. "All right. She's around here, within walking distance, and she called from a place that has a pay phone with a compressor near it."

"That could be anywhere. Every street has construction going on."

"It's all we've got."

"Where do you begin?"

James looked at Murray. "Do you have a map of the neighborhood?"

"Yeah. I'll get it." He went through the swinging doors.

As the doors swung shut behind him, a horn sounded outside the back door. James got up and went to open the door. "Your cab," he said as he looked out, then at Bree.

She stood but didn't go to the door. Instead, she looked at James. "Could you ask him to wait?"

He nodded and went out. As he came in and closed the door, Murray stepped into the kitchen. He crossed to spread a map on the tabletop in front of the television. It showed the north bay, an area bordered by the water on the west, the freeway on the east, Balboa Park on the north and the port of San Diego on the south. "It's a pretty big area."

James bent over the map. "I'll call the station for any leads and follow up those that pinpoint Hannah within five blocks of here in any direction." He stood straight. "I'll do it on foot."

"The streets will be packed today, since it's Christmas Eve. The new shops are being heavily promoted, and the mall traffic—" Murray shook his head "—it's going to be terrible out there walking." He looked at James. "I think I should come with you, but if Hannah calls again, I—"

"You need to be here," James conceded.

Bree remembered William. "What was wrong at the hospital?"

"William needed more surgery. He'll be all right, but it's going to be a long haul." He looked worried. "It's going to cost—"

"That doesn't matter," Bree cut in. "I'll take care of it."

Murray smiled. "Things are really looking up, aren't they?"

"Yes, they are," she admitted. At least some things were.

"I need to call the station," James said.

"Oh, the station. I forgot to tell you I talked to Bryan a while ago. He gave me the number for the owner of Graphic Originals. I called and left a message for the man to call here when he could."

James studied Bree. "You're going home?"

"No, I'm going to the station for a while to help on the phones. I couldn't sit still without doing something."

James came closer but didn't touch her. He looked at her. "I'll be calling in, and you can give me any new leads that sound promising. And Bree?"

"Yes?"

"Don't leave the station until I get there, will you?"

She nibbled on her bottom lip. "All right."

"I want you both to know what it means to me to have the two of you in this with me," Murray said. Bree didn't look at him. She couldn't tear her gaze away from James. "It's trite, but true, that a burden shared is a burden lightened. Thank you." Murray headed for the swinging doors. "Merry Christmas and God bless us, every one," he said as he left.

James smiled. "Corny, but true," he said, then turned and headed for the phone.

As he pushed the numbers for the station, Bree quickly picked up her purse and went out to the taxi waiting in the alley.

"God bless us, every one," she muttered as she got into the cab and gave the station's address.

When James stepped in the back door of the restaurant just before three o'clock, Nate looked up from the stove. "Murray headed back to the hospital. William's beginning to come around."

James leaned against the door and took a deep breath. The strain of the day was beginning to get to him with tension in his neck and shoulders. And a constant feeling of dread. Some had to do with Hannah, but a lot of it stemmed from Bree.

If he let himself, he could get all tangled up in memories of last night, but he couldn't allow that right now. He closed his eyes for a minute, then ran a hand over his face.

"I take it you didn't find anything?" Nate asked.

"Nothing. Dead ends every one." James suddenly needed to hear Bree's voice. He needed to hold her even more, but the sound of her voice would be very welcome, the way it had been the other two times he'd called to check in with her. He reached for the phone and dialed the hot line number.

"Channel Three hot line. You don't have to give your name if you don't want to."

He let the sound of Bree's voice wash over him, drinking it in the way a thirsty man would a cool drink of water. Finally he managed one word. "Bree?"

"James? Where are you?"

"At the restaurant." He closed his eyes and leaned his forehead against the coolness of the wall by the phone. "I'm just checking to see if you've heard anything important."

"No, nothing this time, and it's getting late. How about you?"

"Nothing." *Except every hour I'm away from you I begin to see how life will be if you run from me.*

"I'd hoped . . ." She sighed over the line. "I'll be leaving in just a bit."

"What are you going to do?"

"Go home. Have some decent food."

He braced himself. "I mean later, with your life?"

"Get on with it."

The words made a coldness seep into his spirit. "Can you stop by here on your way home?"

"Just a minute," she said without answering him. "James, Bryan just came in with something for you. Here he is."

"James," Bryan said. "A friend of mine came through with some information from L.A. Hannah Vickers really was a child star in the silent movies, under the name Hannah Winston. She's been married three times, the last to Allan Vickers. She walked away from a senior citizen's home in Los Angeles about seven weeks ago."

"She just walked out?"

"That's what they're saying. Hannah's been a resident there for some time, and she said she was taking a vacation. No one bothered to even check and see where she went."

"They sound concerned," James muttered.

"Sure," Bryan said. "My guess is that Hannah must have gotten a ride or—" he stopped, then said "—the train! The Santa Fe comes in just blocks from where you are, doesn't it? She could have taken the train and stepped off here. The end of the line or something like that."

James had no doubt Bryan was right. "She found Murray's and stayed. Good work, Bryan. Put Bree back on the line."

"She stepped out for a minute. She's been at the phones nonstop for quite a while. I think she went to get some coffee."

"Thanks again for everything." He hung up without getting an answer from Bree.

"What's going on?" Nate asked.

James went to the table and sat. He repeated what Bryan had told him, then asked, "When will Murray be back?"

"He didn't say." Someone called to Nate from the front, and he headed through the swinging doors.

James reached over and turned on the television to KHRT and absentmindedly watched a talk show that was in progress. But all he thought about was Bree. He could feel her slipping through his fingers and out of his life. Terrified to care, she was retreating into her shell, and the loss was going to be his.

He ran his fingers through his hair, then rested his head in his hands. He wasn't at all sure he could endure the loss. After less than four days, the lady was a part of him as surely as the next breath he took.

The voice of Daryl caught his attention, and he looked at the screen. "And now our news break at three on three," Daryl was saying into the camera. "The big local story today was the release of Wayne Concklin, the bartender who had been picked up for questioning in the stabbing of Detective Andrew Dawson of the San Diego Police Department. Without sufficient evidence to press for an indictment, Concklin was released at one o'clock after being held for seventy-two hours.''

On the screen was a picture of a bald man on the steps of police headquarters, with his lawyer at his side. "Concklin and his attorney refused any and all statements for our cameras. To repeat, Wayne Concklin, picked up for questioning in the December 13 murder of an officer, was released at noon today. Now, back to our regular programming.''

James flipped off the set, then stood as Nate came into the kitchen. "I'm heading out. I still haven't looked into a report that Hannah's working at a dress shop two streets over. I'll be back in an hour or so.''

Hannah couldn't sit any longer. She'd tried to call Murray, but that nice girl had answered. She couldn't help. Only William could, and he wasn't anywhere. She'd tried to look, but there had been too many people out, even that early in the morning. So she'd have to wait until dark, then go looking again.

She began to slowly pace the small place and she tugged her coat tightly around her. She stopped and pulled the left panel of her coat away from her body and stared at it. A hole. A rip in the fabric by the pocket. She'd felt something catch when she was coming inside, but she didn't realize the coat had torn.

She sank on the bed and fingered the ripped material. Tears gathered in her eyes. She'd promised herself she wouldn't cry. Tears didn't do any good. You had to face life and get on with it. But this was the nicest coat she'd had in a long time, and she'd torn it. Santa's color. That brought her up straight. Santa. The man must have found William.

Roy Lester didn't let James out of his sight. He followed him up the busy street, waiting as James looked inside alleys and at the backs of businesses. Then he went into a small dress shop close to the mall. He wasn't sure what the man was looking for, but he knew James Chapman was his only hope of finding the old lady.

Where could she be hiding? He watched until Chapman headed toward the restaurant, and he fell in step, keeping about twenty feet of space and a good number of people between them. When Chapman turned into the alley to the restaurant, Roy hung back, then headed for his car and pulled it into the end of the alley, partly hiding it behind one of the Dumpsters. He had a perfect view of the back door of the Cracked Cup Café.

James hated to admit it, but he felt defeated. The knowledge that Hannah was still alive had kept him going for hours, but now he felt empty. And worst of all, he didn't know where Bree was.

When he walked into the kitchen, he stopped dead in his tracks. Bree was there, turning toward the door, her face flushed from the heat of the stove. Her hair tumbled freely around her shoulders, and a brown apron was tied at her waist.

Words wouldn't come, so James simply crossed to her and reached out. The hug was a mild version of the contact he wanted from her, but he settled for it. He held her and let the feel of her seep into his soul.

Reluctantly, he let her go and stood back to look at her. "What are you doing here?"

"Helping out. I came down to see what was going on and got recruited." She motioned to a huge kettle of soup she'd been stirring. "I found out I can ladle up soup with the best of them."

"I bet you can," he murmured. "I take it Murray's not back yet?"

The phone rang and Bree called out, "I've got it." She looked at James. "Nate's so busy up front." Then she crossed and picked up the receiver. "Cracked Cup Café. Can I help you?" She listened, then said, "Murray. How's William? Was he able to tell you anything about Hannah?" James watched Bree run her finger back and forth over the plastic slip on the phone that held the number for the restaurant. "Yes, that's a start. Everything's under control here. Nothing, not yet. James is still following up the leads from the station calls. All right. Whenever you get here."

She hung up, then turned to James. "William's going to pull through. He's gradually coming out of the anesthetic, and he's been talking a bit, but nothing that made sense."

James leaned against the table and crossed his arms. "What's he been saying?"

"Strange things. About princesses and make-believe... and about Santa, the way Hannah did."

"Maybe he's living in the past. He took quite a bit of punishment in that fall."

The phone rang, and James saw Bree jump, then wipe her hands on her apron and reach for it. "Cracked Cup. Can I help you? Oh, yes. I did call. I was trying to find out if you remembered doing a special order of matchbooks, silver, sleek, with a single F on them?" She paused for a long moment and began fiddling with a strand of hair, curling it around and around her finger. Then her hand stilled. "Thank you. I appreciate the information."

She put down the receiver but kept staring at the phone. James saw her shoulders move as she inhaled sharply. Then she turned to him, her gaze filled with shock. As she pressed one hand to her middle, she whispered, "I know where Hannah is."

Chapter 15

James stood straight. "You know where she is?"

"She's at the Fenwick Theater."

"How do you—"

She didn't move from the phone, and her voice was low, as if she was thinking out loud. "I got these calls at the station just before I came here. This man said he saw an old woman in red near the theater a few weeks back. The other caller talked about an old lady standing at the back of the theater. And Murray said William was talking about make-believe. That was the man from Graphic Originals." She looked at him with wide eyes. "James, they made those matchbooks for the opening night at the Fenwick. New Year's Eve. They aren't even circulating yet. As far as he knows, they're stored in the basement at the theater."

James was stunned. If Bree was right, Hannah was only two blocks away. "It makes sense," he said, not sure whether to jump and scream or head off at a dead run for the theater.

"Murray should know," Bree said and turned to the phone. She pushed the buttons, but instead of talking, she handed the receiver to James. "You . . . you do it," she said in an unsteady voice.

James took it from her. "Are you sure you don't want to be the one?" he asked softly.

She looked at him from under a sweep of lashes, but shook her head and turned away. Bree McFarland was involved, James realized, so involved she couldn't talk to Murray without crying. And the idea pleased him very much.

When he heard the hospital answer, he asked for William's room, then quickly told Murray what they suspected. He never looked away from Bree as he spoke, watching her take off her apron and put on her jacket. He said, "I'll meet you there," and hung up. By then Bree was at the back door ready to leave.

Running away, he thought with a sinking heart. "You don't want to come and see if you're right?" James asked.

And she surprised him by saying, "I'm ready to go whenever you are."

Roy had made his call, then settled in the car at the end of the alley. With any luck, the boss would get here before Chapman left again. He stared at the back door of the restaurant. Once Chapman found the old lady, they'd have her. One way or another, he'd put an end to this whole deal.

He jerked around at the sound of the passenger door being opened and watched the boss get in the car and slam the door. "You made it."

"I wouldn't miss it," the man said as he lit a cigarette. Exhaling the smoke, he pointed toward the restaurant door. "What's going on?"

Roy looked at the door as it opened. "He's just leaving. You've got perfect timing."

"My lucky day," the man murmured and looked out the window. "I want that old lady dead."

* * *

Last-minute Christmas shoppers blocked the streets and thronged the sidewalks. As the sun began to sink, Christmas music seemed to be everywhere, and Bree felt a real excitement, a surge of anticipation. She was right about Hannah, she knew she was.

For a fleeting moment, Bree had a memory of the good Christmases when she was a child, the carols, the gifts, the family together and her firm belief in Santa Claus. She trembled, pulling her chin down to the warmth of her chest where her jacket parted.

"I've been thinking," James said without looking right or left and never breaking stride.

"About Hannah?"

"No." He walked quickly, his hands in his pockets, his eyes straight ahead.

Bree skipped once to catch up. "What about?"

"Me."

"You?"

He glanced at her but kept moving down the street. "Yes. Actually, I seldom do that, but these past few days I've found myself doing it more and more."

This didn't make any sense to Bree. "What were you thinking about yourself?"

"That I'm a patient man," he stated, and didn't say anything else.

"And?" she prodded as they turned north toward the theater.

"I'm willing to wait however long it takes to have my life be what I want it to be."

That was double-talk to Bree, so she shrugged and kept walking.

After a few steps James spoke again. "I've never been into instant gratification. If something looks good, I'll wait and wait for it."

She stopped in front of a new three-tiered, parking garage next to the theater and touched his arm. He looked at her hand on his jacket sleeve, then at her face. She jerked back and pushed her hands in her pockets. "Are you going to explain what you're talking about?" she finally asked. "Or do you enjoy being cryptic?"

He studied her from under lowered lashes, then finally spoke in a voice so low she found herself leaning toward him to hear the words. "I met you just a few days ago, and until then, I was doing well. My life was fine. Then you were there. And after last night, I know that I'll wait until you decide one way or the other about your life."

A pain started inside her. But now it came from a new source. Not Dean, not the guilt, not the past, but the man in front of her. "Don't wait for me. Don't depend on me, please."

"It's my decision, and I'm the one responsible for it," James said, then began to walk.

Bree didn't move for a minute, then slowly she followed him. When the theater came into sight, with its multitude of lights reflecting off the wet pavement, James stopped and turned to her. "One more thing, Bree."

She bit her lip. "What?"

"Did you really love Dean Gregory?"

The question took her off-balance. She looked at James, the cold breeze ruffling his silvered hair and shadows protecting the expression in his eyes. "Yes, I did."

Without another word, he turned and headed toward the theater. Bree stood where she was for a second, then hurried after James.

By the time she caught up with him, he was at the front door. "It's locked up tight," he said, cupping his hands on the glass of the door to look inside.

She mimicked his action and looked into the lobby. Security lights showed a shadowed expanse done in elegant tapestries and brocades. The sweeping staircase to the second level had been restored with oak and brass, and the glass-and-mirror concession counters were empty.

She kept looking inside, but spoke to James. "Why did you ask me that back there?"

She sensed him moving from the door. "I'd hate to think you were intent on ruining your life for someone you were simply fond of."

The statement hung between them, and Bree stared at the pattern on the carpet in the lobby. "I loved Dean since I was ten years old," she said, not adding, *But not the way I love you.*

James knocked on the wood frame sharply, but no one showed up behind the doors. Bree looked at James, who was glancing up and down the street.

"What now?" she asked.

"Find a phone, call Cal and see if he can get us inside, then wait for Murray to show up."

"That sounds good, but the only telephone I saw was way back at the corner."

"I think you're right. I couldn't find one here today. Let's go."

They went down the marble steps to the damp sidewalk, turned right and walked south, but James stopped near the entrance of the parking garage on the south side of the theater. "How about that?" he said, pointing to a blue and white sign posted near the entrance. "I didn't know they had a telephone in there."

"The garage isn't open yet, so the phones might not be hooked up."

"Maybe not, but it's worth a look," he said as he walked past the empty booth and stepped into the garage.

When Bree went in after him, she saw vast empty spaces barely lit by a few security lights. Then she sniffed. Fresh paint.

"Can you smell that?" she asked James, her voice echoing in the cavernous space.

"Paint." He pointed to a light barely visible in the gloom. "And there's the phone."

They hurried across the concrete flooring to the far corner of the garage. There were three pay phones. James felt in his pocket, then turned to Bree. "Have you got change?"

She searched in her purse, came up with a quarter and handed it to him. While he punched the numbers and asked for the detective, Bree spotted two shapes about ten feet away near a rear exit. She crossed to the closest one and lifted a piece of heavy canvas.

James came up behind her and asked, "What is it?" She let him look at what she saw. "A paint compressor," he said, and as she let the material fall, he reached out to the wall and ran one finger along the gray surface. When he drew back, he held out his finger toward Bree. A faint touch of gray clung to it. "It's barely dry."

She looked at him, the dimness softening the sight of him, making it easier for her to be this close without getting confused. "I think we've found the right place. But Hannah took a chance coming in here. She must have been seen by the painters."

"Her need to contact Murray had to be stronger than her fear of that man she told you about."

"What did Cal say?"

"He left just before I called." James looked toward the exit that led to the alley. "If this is where she's hiding, let's see if we can figure out how she gets inside while we wait for Murray to get here."

Bree went with him to the alley and side-stepped puddles to look at the theater. The building looked almost as imposing from the rear as from the front. A solid brick wall soared three stories into a darkening sky. The theater shared a wall with the parking garage. High windows were grilled with black wrought iron. A cement ramp went up about six feet into a cut-out area marked "Deliveries," and three construction trucks blocked access to the ramp. No one was in sight.

Bree scanned the buildings across the alley. The doors were labeled for a video store, a hardware store, some chi-

ropractic offices and a meat market. All in use, all redone
and guarded with mesh on windows and bars on doors.
There were no hiding spots, no invitingly open doors or
windows.

For a fleeting second, Bree felt distinctly uncomfortable,
as if someone was watching her. But when she turned, the
alley was empty. She walked with James along the back of
the theater, past the construction vans and the delivery
doors. There was nothing to be seen.

A narrow walkway between high brick walls joined the
alley to the street. Nothing could be in there without being
seen. The sound of Christmas music filtered from the street,
and the chill was deepening quickly as night settled.

"Where could she be?" Bree whispered.

James shrugged. "I don't see how she could be in the
theater. Everything's locked up tight." He touched her arm.
"Let's go around to the front and wait for Murray."

They headed toward the garage, but as they came to the
chained opening, James stopped. He hesitated, then went
close to the wall of the theater. When Bree followed him, she
could see that the two walls weren't flush, as she'd assumed. There was about a three-foot gap, but with the
shadows, she couldn't see how far it went. All she could tell
was that it didn't go to the street. Only darkness was ahead,
not the flashing of headlights or Christmas lights from the
street.

"Wait here," James said, then stepped over some debris
that had been piled at the opening and disappeared into the
shadows.

Bree waited, starting at every noise. She turned and
looked in both directions, then thought she saw something
flashing near a Dumpster past the parking area.

"Damn," James muttered, his voice echoing as something crashed.

Bree turned to the shadows. "James, are you all right?
What's going on?"

There was an ominous silence, then he spoke. "Just bumped into something. I wish I'd thought to bring a light."

"I've got a little one on my key ring," Bree called into the darkness as she fumbled in her purse. She pushed aside her wallet and the toy gun, then found her key ring. She clicked the small light on, its beam barely strong enough to penetrate the darkness. but it was enough for her to be able to make out James about twenty feet into what looked like a tunnel.

Carefully, she stepped over the debris and headed toward James. She flashed the small light at her feet onto trash piled along the brick wall and the side of the parking garage, papers, old beer bottles and food packages. But down the middle it was relatively clear.

"Bree, over here," James said.

She moved closer, almost bumped into him, then shone the light past him. A door was inset in the brick wall, wooden, old and without a latch on the outside. James took the light and trailed it around the edges. Halfway up on the right, he stopped. "Ah," he said and reached out, tucking his fingers under the rough wood and tugging.

The door swung back, exposing darkness beyond. James flashed the light in the opening, but all Bree could see was a cracked cement floor. The mustiness of disuse and age mingled with dampness assailed her nostrils. As James played the light over the inside, he stopped and bent over to touch something caught on a nail of the door frame. He drew it back. In the small light, Bree saw a ragged piece of red wool.

She knew where it came from. "She's here," Bree whispered and sensed, more than saw, James nod as he stepped forward into the darkness. All Bree could see was the dull glow of the tiny light bobbing in blackness, then she stepped through the door. She put her hand out, felt James's back and was grateful for the strength under her fingers.

James moved to the left, then he said softly, "A light." With an echoing snap, lights came on, low-watt bulbs under cages set in a curved ceiling about every twenty feet or so along a tunnel that seemed to incline downward.

"Hannah talked about going down to get to William's place," she whispered.

James handed Bree her keys, and when she'd dropped them in her purse, he took her hand in his. She didn't fight his hold, but laced her fingers with his and held on. Then she went with him as he slowly led the way downward. "Come on, but be careful of your step."

They went about thirty feet, rounded a corner, went ten more feet and came to a dead end and a wooden door. James turned the tarnished knob and pushed open the door. He felt inside and another light snapped on, as dull as the others. Over James's shoulder, Bree could see a storeroom of sorts, with boxes and crates heavy with dust piled everywhere.

Then she looked at the floor and saw scuffed footsteps, large ones and tiny ones. She pointed to them, and without speaking, James nodded and moved into the room. Keeping his eyes on the floor, he wound through the piles of crates, past a huge wardrobe box, and the footsteps stopped. At first Bree thought they'd ended at the brick wall, then she saw that they went parallel to it and behind a huge wooden crate about two feet from the wall.

Before she could say anything, James was going behind the crate. Bree hurried after him into an opening all but obliterated by the wooden container. She twisted to her left, then stepped into pitch darkness. "James?" she whispered.

Then a light flashed on, a single bulb, and she saw another room, smaller, square, filled with stacked boxes, but in here there was an order that hadn't existed elsewhere. The boxes were stacked in what seemed to be a screen that blocked the rest of the room from the opening.

Then Bree caught a peculiar odor. She inhaled and realized she could detect something that smelled like chocolate over the musty dampness. Chocolate? She followed James to the end of the boxes, then heard a small, muffled gasp.

She hurried after James and finally saw Hannah. In the gritty shadows of the corner of the room, a tiny person huddled on a cot, pressed against the wall. All but swallowed up by a huge red coat, the frail-looking woman stared at Bree and James, her eyes filled with raw fear.

"Who are you? Are you with that man?" she asked in a thready voice. "Tell him I didn't see anything. William was supposed to tell him that. I never saw it. Never." She gasped breathlessly. "I promise. I never saw Santa die."

Bree moved toward the cot, her hand out. "Hannah?" She sensed James hanging back to let her do the talking and fleetingly marveled at how perceptive he was. "You talked to me on the phone this morning. You called Murray. Remember? I'm Bree McFarland. He sent me to find you. He wants us to help you."

Hannah's eyes darted behind Bree to James. "You...you hurt William, didn't you?"

"No, he didn't," Bree said quickly, "Murray's his friend. Murray sent us. He wants us to take you to him. He'll protect you."

"He...he can't," she gasped, her fist pressed to her mouth, muffling the words. "He can't. The man's bad, so bad. He hurt Santa, and he wants to hurt me. I had to hide, I had to, until I could get to the police. He'll kill me, I know he will, if he finds me."

Bree got closer until she felt the side of the cot press her calves. Slowly she inched closer. "Hannah," she crooned. "Let me help you." She held out her hand and saw the tiny woman draw back as if she had been asked to touch fire. "Please, Hannah, Murray wants you to come to him." She had an idea. "You know what I have?"

The woman shook her head sharply.

"I've got your nativity. It's at my house. I'm keeping it safe for you. And the picture of you and Bill—I've been keeping it for you, too."

Hannah was very still, then slowly sat up. "You have the picture Bill gave me?"

"Yes. The picture he gave his sweet little Hannah."

"Oh, my," Hannah whispered. "Bill. Mama liked him, she really did. He was good..." She inhaled unsteadily. "Not like that man, that horrid man."

Bree had no idea who she was talking about, or if she was lost in some fantasy world, but she kept her hand extended. "You never have to see that man again, Hannah. I promise. We'll take you to Murray."

Hannah seemed to be ready to reach out, then she moved back abruptly. "No, you bring Murray here. I won't leave until he's here."

Bree drew back and spoke to James without turning around. "James, why don't you go and wait for Murray, then bring him down here. I'll stay with Hannah."

James was behind her, and his hand rested lightly on her shoulder. "You're right. You're doing great. I'll be back with Murray as soon as he gets here."

Bree reached to touch his hand. She felt a fleeting kiss on the back of her fingers, then his touch left her and she heard him walk out of the room.

She sank slowly onto the foot of the cot. "Hannah, tell me what happened. Tell me what you're so afraid of."

The tiny woman shook her head. "No, no. The man will kill me. I know he will."

"No, we won't let him," Bree said and looked around the room. A tiny sink was in one corner, boxes were stacked to imitate a table, and candy wrappers littered the floor. Bree reached in the pocket of her jacket and took out a candy bar. She tore it open and offered it to Hannah. "Are you hungry?"

The tiny lady looked at the candy, then moved forward. She took a piece in her mouth and chewed slowly, relishing it. Bree silently watched her until she sank back with a sigh when the last of the chocolate was gone.

"I ate my last candy bar," she said. "Thank you."

The room gave Bree the creeps. As she pushed the empty candy wrapper in her pocket, she asked Hannah, "Can we go outside and wait for Murray?"

"No, not outside."

"What if we just walk to the door and wait there? How would that be?"

"Well . . . I guess so."

Bree stood. "Come on. We'll wait there."

Hannah got up slowly, then tugged at her coat to straighten it. "My hat?" She looked around, then stooped near a crate by the bed and stood up with the floppy hat in her hand. She put it on, covering her snow-white hair, then turned to Bree. "Let's go and wait for Murray."

Bree offered Hannah her arm, and the tiny woman slipped her hand in the crook of her elbow. Slowly they walked out of the room, along the hallway.

"You're so sweet," Hannah said, patting Bree softly on the arm. "Such a lovely girl. I always told William that there are good people in this world. Lots of them. You just have to go looking for them. Can't expect them to drop from the sky right into your lap, can you?"

Bree kept going. "No, you can't," she murmured.

As they approached the door, Bree could see it was open just a crack. She reached for it, but drew back when she heard a strange voice outside.

"All I want is the old lady, you fool," a harsh voice ground out.

Bree felt Hannah's fingers dig into her arm and she looked at her, unnerved by the horror she saw in her eyes. "The . . . the man," she gasped. "That's him. He found me. You . . . you promised, you . . . p-promised."

The man? Bree didn't understand, but instinctively she knew better than to walk out the door and expose herself before she knew what was going on. She touched Hannah's lips with her finger and leaned to whisper by her ear. "Shh, be quiet. I'll look and see who's out there. You stay here and don't make a sound, all right?"

Hannah moved backward, letting go of Bree to tug her coat tightly around her delicate frame. She pressed against the wall and didn't move.

"I know the Vickers woman is somewhere around here, or you wouldn't be here," the voice said.

A man was after Hannah. It wasn't some sort of fantasy. Bree moved closer to the door until she could see out the crack into the alley. In the darkness, she could only make out the shapes of three men. As her eyes adjusted, she realized James was facing a man of medium height with a wiry build. He was wearing what looked like rough work clothes. The other man was larger, heavier and completely bald.

The bald man had his arm around James's neck and was pulling back with so much force that when James spoke, his words were like gasps. "She's not here. Tell me what you want and I'll do what I can."

"Sure," the bald man sneered. "And you probably believe in Santa Claus. Don't be a fool. What's she to you, anyway?"

James exhaled harshly. "What do you want with an old lady?"

"Better you don't know," the other man said, and Bree recognized the voice. Roy Lester. "The old guy got in my way, and he found out the boss and me aren't fooling. This isn't television; this is real life. We want the old lady."

"Take a look in there, Roy," the bald man said, motioning with his head toward the door where Bree was hiding. "I'll keep our friend company." He tightened his hold, making James gasp.

Bree ducked back and reached for Hannah. "Hurry," she whispered. "We have to get out of sight." Hannah understood immediately and moved with remarkable speed down the corridor to the corner. Once around it, she stopped and leaned against the wall.

Bree leaned against the wall by her, barely able to get her breath. She had to do something to help James and stop the men from getting Hannah. "Is there any other way out of here?'' she whispered to the tiny lady. When she saw the shake of her head, she hugged her purse to her middle, felt a bulge in it and knew what her only hope was. She leaned close to Hannah. "Be very quiet, Hannah," she whispered. "Stay here. If you...if you hear anything that scares you, get back in the room and wait for Murray. But be quiet. All right?"

The elderly lady clutched Bree's arm. "Be careful, dear," she said.

"I will," Bree said, then reached in her purse. There was only one thing to do. She took out the gun, touched Hannah on the hand and whispered, "Don't move, don't make a sound, no matter what."

She looked around the corner, saw the corridor was still empty and hurried toward the door. As it began to open, she took an unsteady breath, lifted the gun, held her wrist with her other hand and leveled it at the door. She watched the door open and saw Roy Lester step inside.

He didn't see her at first. He shut the door, then turned and spotted her.

"Don't take another step," she ordered, hating the way her voice shook and the unsteadiness in her hands.

He froze, then he slowly lifted both hands, palms out. "Hey, I don't know what you think you're doing, but take it easy with that gun. I'm not going to hurt you."

If she could keep distance between them, he wouldn't be able to tell it was a toy, she hoped. She motioned with it to the door. "C-call to your friend and tell him to come in here—with James," she said.

She swallowed hard, fear making her feel sick. She was in over her head, and she knew it. She just hoped he didn't. "Do it now," she whispered.

He pulled the door open and called out, "Concklin, come on back here, and bring Chapman with you."

Concklin? Bree knew the name, but couldn't think why. Then she did, and her heart clutched painfully in her chest. The man who'd been held in the policeman's murder. She finally understood. Hannah had seen him do it, had seen him kill Santa, the police detective. And now he wanted to kill his eyewitness—Hannah.

Everything shifted as murder intruded, and she prayed that she could carry this off. She never looked away from Lester, keeping the eye contact, listening for any sounds.

"Roy?" Concklin's voice echoed nearby.

Bree jerked the gun in Lester's direction.

"Come on in and see what I found," Lester called.

Then Bree motioned Lester out of the way of the opening door. She saw James come in first, his arm twisted behind his back by Concklin. Then the bald man was there, turning, looking, seeing her. She raised the gun high enough to make sure Concklin saw it.

Ever since Concklin and Lester had jumped him in the alley, James had been terrified for Bree and Hannah, trying to figure out how to get the men to leave without discovering the two women. He'd never been a fighter, but he realized that he'd do just about anything to protect Bree. If he could just get out in the alley, into enough clear space to do something, anything.

Then Lester called out and James knew he'd found the women. He stepped inside, turned, and Bree was there. He barely stifled a groan when he saw the gun in her hand. Then he realized that neither Lester nor Concklin knew it was a toy. One blessing.

"Let him go," Bree breathed, the catch in her voice wrenching at James's gut. But Concklin eased his hold. "And put your hands up," she finished.

As soon as he was free, James quickly went past Lester to Bree. He got around behind her, close enough to feel her uneven breathing and see the unsteadiness of the gun. "Good work," he breathed, then took the gun and kept it pointed at the two men. "Get over there with your friend," he said to Lester.

The man moved back until he was beside Concklin, and James felt as if he was involved in a stand-off. They had the advantage, but he didn't know what to do except get Bree out to safety. If anything happened to her... He couldn't begin to fathom that. "You two, get up against the wall," he said. "Face the bricks with your feet spread and your hands high." That sounded like a line out of an old movie, but it seemed to work.

Both men did what he said. He spoke to Bree without taking his eyes off them. "Get going. Stay near the wall, and get out of here. Call the cops from the parking garage and wait out there for them."

Bree moved quickly along the wall. Her hand reached out for the door. Then, without warning, Concklin turned and pushed Lester hard, sending him full tilt at James. In a continuation of the move, he grabbed Bree.

By the time James had sidestepped Lester and turned, Concklin had Bree pinned against him, one arm crushing her around her ribs, the other hand holding a wicked-looking knife at her throat. James's heart sank, and a bitter taste filled his mouth. "Drop the gun, Chapman," Concklin said, "and kick it over here."

James had never realized how encompassing love could be, or how much pain one person could endure because of danger to one he loved. What Bree must have suffered with Dean. He understood that clearly now, and it only deepened his love for her.

His love and the horror of what could happen mingled to produce stunning shock. Nothing could happen to her, not ever again. God, hadn't she suffered enough? Slowly, he lowered the gun and let it fall from his fingers to the floor. Then he nudged it with the toe of one Nike toward Concklin.

"Good boy," Concklin growled, the knife pressing at the delicate arch of Bree's throat. "Get the gun, Roy."

Bree was past fear when she felt the knife at her throat, a deceptively seductive sensation. All she knew was that Concklin could kill her with one stroke, surely and swiftly, and the only thing she'd regret more than dying was the fact that she'd chosen not to take a chance and love James.

She closed her eyes tightly for a brief moment. God, she loved him so much she couldn't imagine ever feeling anything this encompassing or this strong again. And she'd been ready to walk away because she was afraid. She opened her eyes and all she saw was James.

If she lived, she'd never be afraid of living again. Surviving wasn't enough, not anymore. She prayed that she'd still be alive when this was over to tell James. In a daze, she saw Lester lunge forward, scoop up the gun, then back up beside Concklin, facing James, the gun leveled at him.

"Now, unless you want your girlfriend to bleed, get the old lady," Concklin said.

"Listen," James said quickly. "Let her go. You've got me. I'll take you to the old lady. Just let her go."

James winced when the knife pressed harder against the delicate skin of Bree's throat. *Don't let him hurt her,* he prayed over and over in his soul. *Let her live and I'll do anything, I'll even let her go without a fight.*

James stood straighter, bracing himself to do whatever he had to do. "Hurt her, and I'll kill both of you."

Chapter 16

Concklin jerked Bree harder against him, and James almost dove at him when he heard her cry out in pain. But he froze when he saw movement behind the two men, the door shifting silently, then a pipe arching through the air to make a thudding contact with the bald man's head.

Concklin seemed to freeze, then with a small whimper he released Bree and crumpled like a rag doll to the floor. The knife clattered on the concrete, Bree stumbled forward into James's arms, and Lester pulled the trigger.

A soft snap sounded in the corridor, and Murray looked up from Concklin sprawled at his feet. His eyes widened on the gun as Lester turned it on him and pulled the trigger over and over again, the weapon making a repeated snapping sound. About to throw the gun, Lester stopped when Murray raised the iron pipe he still held.

"I wouldn't do that if I were you," James said, holding Bree so tightly against him that he doubted she could breathe. "I think Murray would love to use that on you. I know I would."

"No need for that," another voice said from the doorway. Cal stepped into the corridor, his gun drawn. He saw Concklin on the floor, Lester against the wall, Murray with the pipe, James hugging Bree for dear life, and he stopped.

"What are you, a gift from Santa?" James asked, his voice more steady than he felt.

"I got a message at the station from Mr. Landers here, something about you being at the theater looking for Hannah Vickers, and since it was on the way home, I thought I'd take a look. As I came up the alley, I saw this gentleman coming inside with a pipe in his hand—so I followed him."

"Good timing," James said, patting Bree, as much to calm her as to calm himself.

"Murray?" A small voice called from down the corridor.

Murray turned at the sound and stared for a long moment. "Hannah," he gasped. The pipe fell with a clatter near Concklin's head, and Murray took off at a run. James sank against the wall, pulling Bree with him, not willing to let go of her, not just yet.

Cal turned Lester to the wall and handcuffed him. Then he glanced at Concklin, still motionless on the floor, a head wound beginning to seep blood onto the floor. He grabbed Lester by the handcuffs and jerked him around. "I'll take him with me and call for an ambulance," he said to James, then turned and pushed Lester ahead of him out the door.

Then Hannah and Murray came near, the tiny woman looking terrific, walking surely, beaming that smile from the photo and holding Murray's arm. "I'll take you to see William," Murray was saying. "Then you're coming with me to the restaurant. I've got plenty of room upstairs. You can stay there, unless you want to go back to Los Angeles."

"Los Angeles?" Hannah asked, stopping to look at Murray. "No, I think not, Murray." She patted his arm with one tiny, blue-veined hand. "I've lived in enough places and done enough things to realize that I want to be here." She looked at Bree and James. "How can I ever thank you two?"

James held Bree. "Later, we can talk. Maybe you can tell me about your life, and about what happened these last few days, if it's not too painful for you."

Hannah shook her head. "I would be glad to talk to you. Pain isn't all bad, you know. It makes it possible for you to recognize happiness when you find it." She looked as two policemen came through the door with their guns drawn, and her smile died completely. But she didn't shrink from them.

She stood very still, watching silently as the men checked Concklin, then looked at the four people in the tunnel. "You'll all have to give statements. Detective Browsky said to tell you to meet him outside."

"Such an ugly man," Hannah said softly as she stared at Concklin.

Cal walked in right then and looked at Hannah. "Ma'am, I'm Detective Browsky. I understand that you wanted to tell me something."

"Yes, sir," Hannah said. "I do." She motioned to Concklin with one tiny hand. "I saw him kill Santa, just stab him. They were yelling and Santa had a gun on him, then that man ran at him and stabbed him. I ran away into the street, and the crowds were awful, but I saw that man coming after me. William, he helped me get here."

Cal held up his hand. "Tell you what. Why don't I make an appointment for you to come down to headquarters and have a long talk with me?"

Murray patted her hand on his arm. "Are you up to talking to the police later?"

She stood a bit straighter. "Of course," she said. "It's my duty. I would have done it before, but I was so afraid of that awful man. And William said he could talk to him, to make things right. I'm not sure William knew what to do."

"You don't have to be afraid of him anymore," Murray said, then looked at Cal. "I'm taking her to see William, then we'll be at the restaurant." He shook his head as he looked at Bree and James. "Thank God, you two cared enough to come here, to help."

"You started it all," James said softly.

Hannah patted Murray again. "And you were so brave, coming to my rescue. Just like dear Bill did so many years ago. Mama always told me that a real gentleman would do anything for a lady, and you're so heroic . . ."

Her voice faded as she and Murray headed out the door.

Bree didn't want to move from James's hold. In that instant when Concklin could have killed her, her whole life had fallen into place. She'd heard about people facing death and having their lives pass before them. But she'd seen her future, not her past, and it was the first time she'd felt she had a future for a very long time.

She moved just a bit from James, but didn't let go of her hold on him. Cal looked from her to James, then down at the floor where the small gun lay by a puddle of Concklin's blood. He stooped and picked up the gun. "I was going to ask if you had a permit for this," he said, lifting the toy. "But now that I see it clearly, I need to inform you that carrying a toy gun that looks real is against the law." He held it out to James. "Do me a favor—and find the nearest great body of water and toss it in."

James took it and pushed it in his pocket but never took his arm from around Bree's shoulders. "Do you need to take our statements tonight?"

Cal looked at him. "On Christmas Eve? No, I decided that we'll be in touch in a few days. Merry Christmas, you two," he said and turned, then stopped and said, "It's raining outside. Do you need a ride anywhere?"

"Back to the Cracked Cup, if you don't mind?"

"Sure," he said. "Let's go."

James dropped his arm from Bree's shoulder to take her hand. She went silently with him into the dark, rainy night.

The rain fell heavily on the way to Bree's house, and she stared out at the smeared darkness through the windows of the Bronco. She felt drained and weary, but strangely content. It had been so long since she'd understood her life, since she'd felt in control, and it hadn't happened until she loved James.

With nothing tangible to hold to as an explanation, she understood the young woman who had married Dean, the woman who had cared so much for him and tried to save him from himself. And she understood that same woman terrified of failure, of not being able to help and save the man. The woman was gone and wasn't grieved for. She'd done what she had to and she'd lived through the pain.

Pain isn't all bad, you know. It makes it possible for you to recognize happiness when you find it.

Hannah had put everything into perspective. She'd survived seventy-eight years, and she was smiling and still ready to keep living. Bree felt the same way now. She'd been doing okay, but living in a shell of numbness. Now she felt everything, the pain and the joy.

She glanced at a silent James as he drove through the storm. She'd take a chance on there being more joy than pain. He hadn't spoken since they'd left Cal at the restaurant. And she didn't know what he was thinking.

"Bree?" he said, as if he'd read her mind.

She spoke softly through the shadows. "Yes?"

"I promised you I wouldn't ask for anything you couldn't give," James said.

"Yes, you did promise," she echoed.

The car slowed, then she realized they were in her driveway. The rain was falling in sheets.

"I need to go to the station, to do an insert for the eleven o'clock broadcast of *Heart of the Matter*. I think William and Murray should get the reward, don't you?"

She hadn't thought about it, but it made sense. "Yes, you're right. They both deserve it."

"Okay, when I'm done taking care of things, I'm coming back here. It might be after midnight, but I'll be here."

"And?" she asked, her world beginning to settle in the most pleasant way.

He stopped the car and motioned her to get out. "We'll talk later. Make a run for it," he said.

She scrambled out, running for the door, careful not to fall, and when she got to the door, she turned and James was right there, the rain at his back, his hair glistening with moisture.

He braced his hands on the glass of the door on either side of her shoulders. And he looked at her intently. "I'm going to say this once, Sabrina. I love you. I'll love you better than anyone ever has or ever will again. And I'm not perfect, heaven knows, I never even suggested I was. But I promise I'll never deliberately hurt you."

She listened, trying not to absorb the words, yet they seeped into her, building a joy in her that displaced any pain, making the memories begin to fade and blur. "I know you wouldn't hurt me," she whispered.

Without another word, James pulled her to him, his mouth finding hers, the kiss fierce and sure. Tears came, burning her eyes and scalding her cheeks as James stepped away from her.

Before she could do or say anything, he jogged to the car. As he got in, she heard him call over the storm, "I'll be back."

She watched, stunned, as he left, then she turned and went into the house, closing the door. She stood alone in the darkness, rain dripping from her hair, but she didn't move. In the silence, she felt her aloneness, but she didn't have any sense of loneliness. Then tears came in gulping sobs, tears of relief and tears of thankfulness that she'd been given another chance.

December 25

James drove to Bree's house just after midnight, the night beyond the windshield blurred and hidden by the sheeting rain. He'd tried, God knows, he'd tried. And he needed Bree. And he was terrified of going to her house.

He sat in the car for a long time listening to the rain. He'd arranged for a news crew to be at the Cracked Cup first thing in the morning. He'd called Murray and promised to be there tomorrow for the dinner. He'd put together his piece for *Heart of the Matter*, a piece that would follow the lead story of the night, Concklin's arrest for the murder of Detective Andrew Dawson. The special on Hannah would begin with the opening of the Fenwick on New Year's Eve. The mayor's special guest would be Hannah Vickers.

"And all's right with the world," he muttered.

He saw a light flash as Bree's door opened. Even in the storm, he could see her outline in the doorway. The sight hit him like a bolt of lightning. His need for her was overwhelming. And his noble thoughts of being strong enough to let her go seemed stupid now. How could he ever walk away from her?

Flipping up the collar of his jacket, he stepped into the storm and ran for the door. As he got closer, Bree backed up, and as he stepped into the warmth of the house, he faced her, the full impact of the sight hitting him squarely, taking his breath as effectively as a physical blow.

In the light haloing her, he could see her damp hair in ringlets. She'd changed into a soft fleecy robe. Her feet were bare. She motioned him in, then held out a towel. "I thought you'd need this," she said in a husky whisper that ran roughshod over his raw nerves.

He took the soft terry, and she drew back. "Take off your coat and dry off, then come into the living room. I have a fire going. I thought you'd need it. I've never started one before." She turned from him and went into the other room. "I'll be in here."

Quickly stripping off his jacket and toweling his hair, he dropped the jacket and towel on one of the crates, then ran his fingers through his damp hair. In less than a minute, he was walking into the living room.

He stopped in the doorway, trying to take in the picture in front of him. Bree was curled up on the couch. A fire blazed in the hearth. The room was dark except for the glow of the flames. Slowly, he crossed to the couch, and he not only didn't know what to expect from her, he had no idea what to say.

He sank down in the cushions, his knees by Bree's bare feet, and he stared at the fire. Then he saw the nativity laid out to one side of the television on the hearth. He turned to Bree, but she spoke before he could ask.

"I'm taking it to Hannah tomorrow." She glanced at it, then at James. "It looks nice there, doesn't it?"

"Yes, it does," he said.

She looked at him for a long moment, the flickering shadows of the fire playing across her delicate features. Then he could see her breasts rise under her robe as she took a deep breath. "Thank you for coming back," she said softly.

"I told you I would."

"And I'm glad you did. We have a lot of unfinished business."

He felt tension grip him, but he managed to speak evenly. "Yes, we do."

Silently she pushed back her hair with both hands, her eyes shadowed. "You and Hannah were both right, you know."

"Right about what?"

"If you don't go through pain, you can't recognize happiness when it comes along." She took another breath. "I almost didn't. I almost walked away from it ... from you."

He watched her, not daring to believe what he thought he was hearing. "And now?"

"Hannah survived all this time, and she is still willing to go ahead with life, to make breaks, then find new places, new people. She isn't lost in the past."

"Are you lost there?"

"I was...for so long, but not now." Her hands were clenched on her thighs, and her voice dropped so low he had to listen carefully. "You're the first one to know that I'm willing to take a chance on life again. My past is over and done, and I want you to be my future as long as you want to be." She looked at him, her eyes wide. "I love you, James."

Before she could say anything else, he had her in his arms, his face buried in the sweet freshness of her hair. He held her tightly so she couldn't make another escape if she changed her mind. "Oh, God, I was so afraid—"

"So was I," she whispered. "For too long."

He kissed her, tasting her, relishing her, almost bursting from happiness. When he finally drew back and looked at her, he wondered what he would have done if she'd sent him away. Then he blocked that thought. No more what ifs in his life. He wanted reality. He wanted Bree.

"I love you," he whispered hoarsely, then found her lips and tasted her. And she was there for him, everywhere, and all he could do was love her.

And when she slipped her robe off and tossed it to the floor, he took her without hesitating. In the softness of the pillows on the couch, he found that missing piece of himself, that one thing that he had been looking for all his life. He knew her from the silky curve of her shoulder to the delicate hollows at the back of her knees.

Then his hand traced the line of skin from the frantically beating pulse at the base of her neck to her full breasts, circling the nipples as she moaned softly. Then his clothes were gone and her hands knew him, crossing his chest to his stomach, then lower. And he kissed her, leaving no doubt about the power of his need for her.

Then his hands followed the path hers had taken on him, and when she reached up to him and murmured that she loved him more than life itself, he went to her and knew her completely.

Together they found what they'd been looking for, and it culminated in a moment of completeness that bound two souls. And when at last James settled by Bree, satisfied for the moment, yet knowing he could never have enough of her, he held her against him in the cushions. He felt the heat of the fire at his back, the heat of the woman at his front. He tasted the sleek dampness at her temple.

"Do you believe in Christmas magic?" he breathed, his words as unsteady as his heartbeat.

"I didn't," she breathed as the rain beat on the windows. "Not until now. Not until you."

* * * * *

READERS' COMMENTS ON
SILHOUETTE INTIMATE MOMENTS:

"About a month ago a friend loaned me my first Silhouette. I was thoroughly surprised as well as totally addicted. Last week I read a Silhouette Intimate Moments and I was even more pleased. They are the best romance series novels I have ever read. They give much more depth to the plot, characters, and the story is fundamentally realistic. They incorporate tasteful sex scenes, which is a must, especially in the 1980's. I only hope you can publish them fast enough."

S.B.*, Lees Summit, MO

"After noticing the attractive covers on the new line of Silhouette Intimate Moments, I decided to read the inside and discovered that this new line was more in the line of books that I like to read. I do want to say I enjoyed the books because they are so realistic and a lot more truthful than so many romance books today."

J.C., Onekama, MI

"I would like to compliment you on your books. I will continue to purchase all of the Silhouette Intimate Moments. They are your best line of books that I have had the pleasure of reading."

S.M., Billings, MT

*names available on request

JOIN TOP-SELLING AUTHOR
EMILIE RICHARDS
FOR A SPECIAL ANNIVERSARY

Only in September, and only in Silhouette Romance, we'll be bringing you Emilie's twentieth Silhouette novel, *Island Glory* (SR #675).

Island Glory brings back Glory Kalia, who made her first—and very memorable—appearance in *Aloha Always* (SR #520). Now she's here with a story—and a hero—of her own. Thrill to warm tropical nights with Glory and Jared Farrell, a man who doesn't want to give any woman his heart but quickly learns that, with Glory, he has no choice.

Join Silhouette Romance now and experience a taste of *Island Glory*.

RS675-1A

Silhouette Romance®

AWARD OF EXCELLENCE

LONG, TALL TEXANS

Diana Palmer brings you the second Award of Excellence title

SUTTON'S WAY

In Diana Palmer's bestselling Long, Tall Texans trilogy, you had a mesmerizing glimpse of Quinn Sutton—a mean, lean Wyoming wildcat of a man, with a disposition to match.

Now, in September, Quinn's back with a story of his own. Set in the Wyoming wilderness, he learns a few things about women from snowbound beauty Amanda Callaway—and a lot more about love.

He's a Texan at heart . . . who soon has a Wyoming wedding in mind!

The Award of Excellence is given to one specially selected title per month. Spend September discovering *Sutton's Way* #670 . . . only in Silhouette Romance.

RS670-1R